TELLING STORIES

TELLING STORIES

BEVERLEY JONES

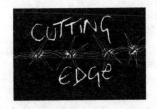

A Cutting Edge Press Paperback

Published in 2012 by Cutting Edge Press

www.CuttingEdgePress.co.uk

Printed and bound by CPI Group (UK) Ltd, Croydon, CR0 4YY

TPB ISBN: 978-1-908122-11-7
E-PUB ISBN: 978-1-908122-19-3

Dedication

With thanks to Kevin Ellis, for his enthusiasm,
his perseverance and his big box of books

In the store

'Do you believe that sins committed in a previous life can come back to haunt you in the next?' asked Cora. We were huddled deep in the soft toy department surrounded by the glassy, unblinking eyes of a hundred mute and furry witnesses, their beady, button eyes staring and relentless. As soft wet snow fell outside, I stared at her too.

Not for the first time I noticed the tears, never far from her eyes these days, were broadcasting a warning of potential embarrassment. She was going to make a scene.

I glanced around to see if anyone had heard. Not the question, but the broken quaver in her voice, one step away from hysteria among the bright-eyed, oblivious children.

I was unsure how to answer, or whether to answer at all. Was I actually expected to? Cora's eyes were almost as glassy and fixed as those of the animal menagerie surrounding us, listening intently, waiting for my words of ultimate wisdom. I always have an answer.

I suspected, by that time, she was taking too much of something. Drugs, I mean, prescription tranquilisers or anti-depressants probably, open to use and abuse. Though it might have been the wine and everything else she'd drunk that afternoon. I was afraid of what she might do if I answered yes, as I was beginning to think it might be true. Maybe we are all paying for our sins all the time. How else could the last year be explained? How else could five people have wound themselves up so tightly in their own web of dependency, the connections sticky with unspecified longing and undefined regret?

What might she do if I said, 'Yes, of course we pay, Cora. There's no getting away from that, even if it takes more than one lifetime.'?

I wondered if she'd shriek like a banshee and, arms bundled with the toys she was clutching for comfort, a desperate, childish, pitiable comfort, dash forward, hurling herself out over the glass and chrome balcony into oblivion.

The last I'd see of my friend would be her top-heavy body sheathed in an over-tight raincoat, gliding out over the shoppers below in a rain of traditional teddy bears. Her stripy scarf would trail into the wind behind her, a fluttering herald of impending impact, her polyester mackintosh inflating into a green, gauzy and all-too-insubstantial parachute.

She would hit the ground with a sickening thump, of course; a small spray of blood soiling other peoples' Saturday coats and clutched dollies, as the head beneath her blue bobble cap exploded like a tangerine dropped by sticky supermarket fingers, wetness on the tiles...

I would screech, 'Oh, Cora, noooo!' clumsy with slow-mo surprise, move into action a second too late, fingers catching just the thread of a hem, a strand of hair. There would be enough witnesses to see that she had brought it on herself. Embraced it – the end. What could I possibly have had to do with it?

Then I would slump into the arms of distressed passers-by, suddenly so sympathetic, but storing up the horror-phrases in their mouths to taste fully later, to season their usually humdrum, predictable lives as horrified families made them cups of tea. That's why, for one scalpel-sharp, incisive moment I almost did say yes. 'Yes Cora, we deserve everything we get.'

I wanted it by then. I wanted it all to be over. And it would mean I wouldn't have to go through with the plan. My plan, such as it was. Weak as it was. Uninspired, dull and unimaginative as it was.

The truth of it hit me like a shot of adrenaline right to the heart. There was the thought at the front of my brain and the knowledge deep inside my chest.

Oh fuck, I have to kill my best friend.

It was four days to Christmas, December 21st – a year, two months and three days after Jenny.

In the snapshot

Cora was plain. There was no denying it. I would not say it to her face, of course. I had lied once or twice when she'd asked if she was pretty. There's nothing wrong with that. I didn't feel bad for lying, or even for thinking it. It was true. She was ordinary, average at best.

But sometimes, when we were painfully young, when we were students, Cora did have a certain exuberance that passed for a temporary prettiness. It was an attractiveness born from the bloom of fresh skin and the unchallenged belief that the world is yours to open up at will, unpeel when ripe, suck out the juice, discarding the husk. And she did have a fantastic figure, let's not forget that.

Neatly formed, with big, surprised brown eyes, pale brown cropped hair, and a magnificent bosom basking in a low-cut top, she could have been Winona Ryder's plainer sister, in a Primark T-shirt and Reebok trainers.

I remember her that night – that seemingly ordinary but oh-so-important night – how she looked almost pretty in the photograph, taken long before the party at Charlie's. Long before the man with the curry, just before the dancing on the pavement, years before anyone died. Back in those nights of cheap wine and long, deep laughter that caught my breath tight in the top of my chest, and held it there, until I felt I was suffocating in a dark and dizzying forgetfulness.

Cora and I had already drunk nearly a bottle of wine before the boys arrived. It was our reward for religiously cleaning the student house, putting up the chains of paper rings and sweeping the magazines and mail under the sofa. Our mothers would have been proud of our housekeeping for once.

It was Cora's 20th birthday and she was wearing that shiny little tangerine coloured party dress in an attempt to upstage me. Nothing Cora wore ever looked quite right. I had done my bit to dissuade her by suggesting that perhaps it was a bit dressy, maybe? A bit tight? A difficult colour to pull off? But it was Cora's middle-class notion of sexy and funky. And she had saved up for a month for this very dress, eating little but tuna on microwaved spuds, bowls of Kellog's Frosties and the odd Kit-Kat for many weeks to afford it.

Somehow we were still too inexperienced to know how to put on make-up properly. But looking back at the photo of that night I think we had never looked so young, so radiant, so all-knowing – so much like friends.

In the six-by-four snap that catches us and holds us right there, Cora is beaming, her arm draped around my shoulder, leaning into me, chest out, shoulders back. I am angled slightly away from the lens, big blue eyes lowered through the blonde bob, looking up into the aperture for whoever was holding the camera. A pose I saw in some magazine, or too much Martini.

The result is devastating in its promise. The best of friends against a wallpaper background of exploding purple flowers and a poster of Tom Cruise in *Cocktail*.

Not sisters, for one girl is tall and blonde and dressed in a loose, flowered, cotton dress, mostly white with red and black, skimming the ankle, buttoned to the breast bone, bare-legged with low-heeled sandals, no jewellery. Almost on trend for the times.

The other is shorter, darker, squeezed into a tube of metallic orange fabric, a dainty gold chain dangling between deliberate cleavage, a heart-shaped ring on one finger. Tights too pale, white court shoes at sober odds with the outfit, heels not quite high enough, managing to make the whole outfit look a bit mumsy.

Look, just off-centre, and a hand clutching a ridiculously large vibrator has sneaked into the bottom of the shot, where it sits glistening moistly. A few feet in men's shoes and the birthday-bought board game version of *Star Trek: The Next Generation* are in the other corner of the frame. I can hear the background guffaw even now.

Stevie was desperately trying to hold the camera still, making sure there was no glare off the poster and we all were in the middle of the frame. Composition is important, proportion, balance. He wouldn't want to spoil it. After all, this would be the archive of our youth, one to show the children. Without the plastic cock, of course. Just-so Stevie.

This image, frozen out of time, is how I remember us now – not the reality but the shot, courtesy of the occasion, a little stage management, some spontaneity.

That night.

The boys arrived at 7.30 sharp, except Mike who was still upstairs in the unreliable shower. He and Cora had probably shared it a few minutes before. I'd heard giggling and whispering, the sliding and sucking of foam and water. They often did that.

Laden with booze, Stevie and Tim parked themselves on the low and lumpy sofa, cans of lager fizzing open.

Stevie, impeccable at 20, pale blue shirt so well-ironed it is obscene against our haphazard and generally crumpled living room, sandy hair already thinning a little, but distinguished. He looked older than his years, was larger than first impressions suggested, and far more ruthless, as it turned out.

Then Tim, loony Tim, tripping over the pile of junk mail in the hall. I have no idea what happened to him. Loud and gangly, he had borrowed trousers from Stevie, which were somehow too long, (though they were both roughly the same height and build), so they pooled clownishly around his ankles.

Tim had brought the vibrator, naturally. But he had put it inside a food mixer box he'd found somewhere in order to make a weak joke. Cora tore the paper eagerly from the sides.

'Something for when you and Mike move in together, eh?' he mocks.

She knows he is on the wind-up: it is what he lives for. The air he breathes and his sole source of sustenance, except for a steady stream of Brains SA, or 'Skull Attack', Cardiff's most patriotic and potent beer. A tirade of 'You live in the bloody 1940s, mate! He can cook his own dinner unless he wants to live with his mother the rest of his life,' might still be required though, just to show that we wouldn't be going in for any of that gender-stereotyping, sexist, doormat, pre-feminist nonsense.

But Cora did cook for Mike then, on his every visit from Swansea, when he could be pried away from 19th century novels, or kicking lumps out of rival football teams. I often watched in awe as she created elaborate pies and stews, toads in holes and plump sponge puddings for him. Sometimes, she'd let me help by passing her the ingredients or beating eggs. She even made bread for Mike once or twice, her efforts evoking the warm and musty memory of after school tea-times, one weekend visit in three for a day and a half. They were old school sweethearts. Long distance love maintained by mail, real, pre-email, letters through the post, and regular reunions ending with dirty dishes.

Then, with a flourish we see the birthday box open, hold our breath, expecting the unexpected – the tasteless, the vulgar. Traditional Tim. Cora's hand dips inside drawing out the stomach-churning, anatomically-correct reproduction of an enormous cock. Horror and disbelief dawn across her face. This was pushing it, even for Tim. We weren't that kind of girl. We'd never seen anything like that then. It was years before Anne Summers opened more than its discrete doors on the high street, before magazines and TV showed such things. Or were we just not looking?

It was the 90s, not the 60s, for God's sake. Yet Cora's eyes grow wider, a shudder of revulsion sweeping outwards like a sound burst. Cora, plunging orange party dress notwithstanding, was the kind of girl who reserved the words 'shit' and 'hell' for special cursing occasions.

For three seconds we all hold our breath. What will she say? Will the occasion warrant a strenuous curse? More than shit or hell, even? Then the expected fury melts into frenzied laughter.

'Oh my God! You pervert,' she gurgles in exaggerated disgust. Then we all erupt into laughter because we know it's alright. This is Mike's cue, standing in the doorway now, swathed from the waist in a threadbare blue towel, skin still steaming, hair unruly as unmown grass, to join the laughter.

'For Fuck's sake, Tim. What is wrong with you mate? That's the last time you come over here for dinner.' Blushes and smiles are blooming on his face, rosy, pink with wet heat.

Dark hair.

Tim reaches forward, grabbing the vibrator, popping it into his mouth in extravagant fellatio before Stevie lands an empty beer can on his head, a clean shot from across the room.

We cheer, wrestling ensues, Stevie allowing Tim to throw him to the floor, then simulating all manner of depravity with his new toy. We girls heckle and gasp, all the time a little shocked yet feeling daring and appreciative and grown-up – we all know our parts. We are a willing audience.

Mike winks at Cora from the door, standing safely clear, can in one hand, opening it before him and rolling his eyes heavenward.

Cora surveys the carnage, smiling indulgently. *My boys*, I see her think. I watch her smile.

Less than an hour later we are on our way to the Student Union and I'm stumbling and clinging to Stevie beneath a crown of soft stars. Mike has livened up with lagers and music and is cartwheeling erratically, along the gutter's edge, singing Blur's *Country House* or *Charmless Man*. Always Blur, never Oasis. And we all join in. Sides were quickly chosen, for that battle at least.

Tim is trailing behind, already wasted.

Then we cross the street. This is the moment. The moment everything started to change, the moment we all changed a little, though of course, we didn't know it then.

Mike is upright and flushed, boogieing deliberately towards Cora and me, a streetlight serenade with imaginary microphone. Grabbing my hand, he beckons me on with a comically suggestive leer, exaggerated mincing steps so there can be no mistake – a performance, a joke, a parody is about to occur. Be sure to set the scene and then steal it. It was his style. I hold my breath, waiting. He takes my hand.

For one brilliant moment I pirouette from his fingertips,

round and round, breathing and gasping, skirt swirling almost indecently, black white red, black white red. We must create our own electromagnetic energy because my hair seems to stand on end and stray chip wrappers are caught whirling in our vortex. I imagine sparks flying out around us and laugh with the sheer joy of movement. The boys whoop. The dark-flooded street fades out. In that one second our fate is decided.

Disorientated with drink, I stumble so he has to catch me, sandal strap twisting, spin failing. The pavement is approaching with great speed, but with a grace that belies six foot two of drunken, gangling enthusiasm, Mike's arm is around my waist, strong and firm. Drawing out of the spiral, we straighten but I am too heavy, the momentum too strong. He loses balance and we tumble, locked together across the bonnet of a nearby sports car, low and sleek and red, breaking our fall, hands still locked above our heads. There is not an inch between our bodies and my breath is caught somewhere below my lungs, much lower.

He is heavy. Our eyes are all we can see. But we feel the eyes upon us.

'Jesus, Mike,' I say at last. 'Are you trying to kill me?'

He says nothing. We rest for one beat only, then in a single fluid movement he pulls me back to my feet, singing. Without stopping, he spins away. Nothing important has happened. No one has noticed anything.

Stevie runs a fussy hand over the bonnet of the car, checking for a dent. Cora shakes her head indulgently, nothing but smiles, as if Mike is a small child.

'He's all arms and legs,' she says slipping her arm through mine, 'God, I love him,' laughing as he trips over the kerb.

And we shuffle onwards and upwards, steps and railings into The Union.

We shimmy to the bar before dancing on and on and on.

In the toilets later I am buzzing with light and rhythm while Cora, perspiration -soaked and flat-haired, leans uncertainly over the sink, as if on the verge of being sick.

'He is such a great guy,' she repeats, 'a great guy.'

She is wearing the gold chain with a fat little heart that he gave her for her birthday. In two days' time it will be their third anniversary.

I know he is taking her for a tasteful, soft-lit romantic meal tomorrow, though she does not know it yet. He has saved his beer money and booked a table, asking me anxiously if she will like it, wanting my approval. I gave it. And God knows she had dropped endless hints about the tasteful little Italian place across town with the candles in glass globes and the imitation frescos and balls of garlic bread. And he is nothing if not attentive and thoughtful.

And not just for birthdays.

I used to hear them sometimes, at night, when they thought I was asleep, through the thin, peeling magnolia coloured walls, when they were trying to be quiet. And in the afternoons when they thought I was watching TV, covers rustling, mattress protesting and Cora gasping *just like that, oh just like that,* almost sobbing on the other side. I would lie there not so much listening as failing not to listen, curious and amused and sometimes lonely. And I'd turn up the TV.

August and Everything After

Who would have thought it had only been two years since Cora and I had met? Our tight little group of optimistic friends was already formed, the parts seemingly inseparable, as if it had never been otherwise. It was surely a lifetime since that first day at Cardiff Uni when I moved into the Senghenydd Court halls of residence, balancing on a sliver of land between the north and southbound railway lines. I was to study English literature, the refuge for people who have no idea who they are or would like to be, but know they have all the time in the world to get around to thinking about it.

That first day was not an easy one, eagerly but nervously anticipated. I had been sickeningly anxious and desperate to like whomever I met, embarrassed by my mother's fussy unpacking and my father's attempts at humour, conscious of their Valleys' clothes, Valleys' accent and colloquialisms, ashamed that they shamed me in the hustle-bustle city.

At first I had been afraid to speak to Cora who seemed very, well, English, and confident, though frumpy in a pair of dungarees and T –shirt. But I needn't have worried about small talk. Once we had shuffled into the flat with the usual breaking cardboard boxes, half-kicking forward the carrier bags of shoes and kitchen utensils, Cora simply said:

'Hi, I'm Cordelia, but my friends call me Cora. I've come from Chester. This is my fern Frankie. I've had him since I was six years old. Isn't he marvellously big? I couldn't possibly have left home without him but I think he'll like it here. Would you like a cup of tea? I've an enormous cake that my mum made. She thinks it's an excellent way to break the ice and I'm inclined to agree with her.'

I thought she sounded as if she'd bounded off the pages of an Enid Blyton school story or a Famous Five adventure. How could I not have loved her instantly? Her voice echoed with the clink of china cups on saucers and head-girl fair-play. I wanted to be part of that world, not the world of lager shandies and gold sovereign rings, twenty-four miles and a world away. Two minutes later Cora was playing the perfect hostess, making everyone coffee from a brand new cafetière, fresh from its cellophane and cutting chunks of gooey chocolate gateau, holding court, courting friendship, sealing her fate.

After that first afternoon we were never at a loss for something to say to each other. We learned quickly, if in a superficial way, about each other's likes and dislikes, and in circumspect slivers about each other's homes and histories. There wasn't a common factor among any of it so we should have had nothing in common. But we were clean slates, so nothing that we thought might have mattered did. What a relief. It was what I had hoped and prayed for.

Instead of relating our well-worn tales we wrote new ones from day one, starting at the kitchen table, with that huge cake, the telling working outwards over the whole city that opened before us, layer by layer, set in concrete and granite and marble and tile, making up memories, hour by hour, day by day. And if we were not quite what we seemed to be, who could say otherwise and who would have cared?

Mike, Cora's boyfriend of nearly one joyous year, was not yet part of the story. He was also studying English at University in Swansea, to be close to her, she said proudly, the badge of his devotion after he'd missed the Cardiff entrance requirement by one grade. Every weekend of that first term she disappeared on the shuttle bus to see him because he played a lot of sport and it was easier that way. Whenever possible, Mike was Cora's whole weekend.

I listened to her talk about him endlessly, tenderly, in those first months-Michael this, Michael that and Michael the other. How honestly in love and grown- up they seemed. Mike sent her a card or a letter almost every day. So while my university-provided pin board held only a few flyers and an odd photo or two, the board in her shoebox room was covered with the brightly-coloured evidence of his undeniable affections. Some of these included quotations from poetry, or little verses of Mike's own. Cora seemed to think this was quite natural and proper.

Each night the phone in the tiled hall beneath would ring at 8pm, singing out above the reverberations of the endlessly opening and closing fire door and clattering feet. Eight times out of ten it was Mike calling for her.

Packages would come to the little mail slots in reception, small, thoughtful gifts and tapes he had compiled himself. Uncoupled, I was touched on her behalf and also more than a little impressed by her certainty that this was how things were done and nothing more than her due. This was love.

Cora had just two photos of Mike in her room. In the silver frame, the two of them were locked in profile, in a passionate kiss – truly ill-advised hair on his part, tufty, teenage, Happy Mondays-ish. The second picture was pinned on the bursting board, *the lovers*, arm-in-arm somewhere green and leafy, hair wavy now, half-blown over his face. For a while he existed for me only in this fragmented world of out-of-focus photographs, a shadowy, wraithlike creature, half-faced, on the fringes of my imagination, provoking just occasional curiosity.

All that mattered to me was that Cora was at my disposal on weeknights and the occasional Saturday when Mike had friends over for boys' parties. We two would camp out in the scratchy-seated cinema on Queen Street, pre-multiplex, pre-reclining armchairs and American ice cream, watching endless trashy movies. Sometimes we would fill a corner of the dancefloor at the Students Union, or lie on each other's beds, introducing the other to our favourite CDs on Sunday afternoons in a litter of tea cups and chocolate biscuits.

Cora was bright and fun and well-mannered, such a relief from the girls I'd known at school a year ago and a million miles away, girls with terrifyingly stiff fringes topping off their poodle perms, swapping hairspray, blue eyeliner and fags in the girls' toilets, dripping gold rings, shrill menace and obscenities. She was all I could have hoped for as a friend and more. I didn't want to share her, not even with her boyfriend. I'd have time enough for boyfriends, a lifetime in fact.

Then, one weekend of the summer term, the inevitable happened. Cora announced Mike was finally coming to Cardiff. She did not say so, but I knew it was because I had been dumped by my second term, six-week, boyfriend, and Cora did not want to leave me to idle around the sun-soaked shopping centre looking at things I could not afford all weekend, drinking wine alone at night.

On the special Saturday that Mike was due, Cardiff languished beneath the weight of another heat-heavy, suffocating afternoon – the norm for that year. The white stone walls of

15

the elegant civic buildings of Cathays Park, the fragmented Victorian semis, windows hung with the tie-dye flags of students in residence, and the functional brick addition of The Union, seemed to breathe the heat back upon us, beneath the unrelenting chimes of the city hall clock and the dry clanking of the trains.

At rush hour the air thickened with the fumes of exhausted cars and buses inching through to the city centre, settling on the back of the tongues making eyes water. Cora and I had spent the morning sweatily cleaning the flat to make it presentable for Mike. Cora's domesticity was daunting in full swing, and we still had the shopping to do before noon. Our pilgrimage to Tesco wasn't so bad through the tatty back streets, past steaming rubbish bins and fat, idle cats dulled by the sun. It wasn't as bad as venturing along the usual rising main route, roaring with traffic, lined with chippies, Indian and Chinese takeaways and something that claimed to be a tanning parlour with blackened windows and a buzzer you had to push for entry. Its oddly placed antique/junk shops were mostly filled with house clearance rubbish that had once meant something to someone but was now worth 50p.Strings of old-lady beads, diamante hat pins and curling paperbacks struggled for prominence in the dusty windows, while the pavements outside were jumbled with wobbly wooden cabinets and school-type chairs. Then over the railway line towards *The George*.

The teeny, shiny new Tesco Metro on the corner was always heaving with students. This was where, once a week, Cora and I would stock up on the luxuries we could afford – proper meat, proper fish, 7p beans and Tesco Value white bread, giant jars of Marmite, family sized packets of penne , Tetley tea-bags. Dolphin-friendly tuna, grapes, broccoli and white wine vinegar for Cora; four-pack chocolate mousses and instant noodles for me. Cora always made sure I had at least one piece of fruit and something green in my basket for the vitamins. I think she was genuinely afraid I would develop scurvy if left to my own devices.

In honour of Mike's arrival, Cora had planned a picnic. The elusive Michael. The real and the imagined, soon to be in collision.

So we bought provisions and treats 'because Mike would like them'. Cora had made a giant pasta salad, but we needed the rare delicacies of white wine vinegar for the dressing, cream, and shiny black pitted olives, for Cora's mother's recipe, of course.

These things seemed exotic and decadent to me then, a girl from high in the coal-deserted Valleys who could hardly conjure the appearance of beans on toast, to be handled reverentially and with infinite care.

They also seemed a little foolish. Who would go to so much trouble over a man? Especially when it was so hot? But Cora was the relationship expert. I deferred to her wisdom.

Cora looked tanned and unusually radiant that day, slim brown legs emerging from her very short shorts below a too-tight T-shirt bearing a transfer of Minnie Mouse. She was wearing a bit of lipstick. She was *making an effort.* She was *doing something with herself.* These were Cora-isms I had come to love because they sounded like the things my grandmother used to say. And I had loved my grandmother very much.

By comparison I was attempting to be sophisticated, floaty and monochrome in a long black sundress and white tennis shoes, slathered in sun cream to keep the familiar burn at bay, hair high in a tight ponytail.

We toiled back with the bags, sweating through the bleached clamour of the Saturday lunchtime. When we panted the last few yards and crossed into our road Mike was leaning against the entrance gate looking uncomfortable, floppy brown hair wilting over his eyes. Mike, made flesh, finally. I knew it was him, despite the bad photographs. Who else could it be?

He was not what I had expected at all. But then how could he be? How could he be that rippling, glowing man-God that Cora lusted after? The man she had impressively first made love to in a B& B's huge four poster bed on the night of her 18th birthday.

Instead of the dapper designer gear I felt sure Mike would be wearing he was clothed in what I would soon recognise as his customary uniform –an oversized T-shirt, which might once have been navy blue, and baggy brown surf shorts. His long pale legs slid out white and gleaming, ending in a pair of trainers so battered and faded that only the doubled-up laces seemed to be holding them together.

Seemingly taller than even her tales had allowed, he was squinting into the sunlight as he raised a hand to acknowledge us, so I could not see his deep blue eyes, a small, contained piece of sky stolen from a far-off country.

At this first sight of him I was relieved. After all, Cora was not even very pretty, not compared to me. He might have a nice way with quotations and rhyme, but it made more sense that someone like this was her life-long love. Someone so... ordinary. I relaxed and smiled as he dashed across the road, grabbing the shopping bags from us, straining a little but refusing my protestations that I could manage. *A gentleman.*

'Oh that's alright,' said Cora, beaming, 'Michael's fine,' as he cheerfully juggled his own heavy rucksack and a fistful of carrier bags.

'You must be Lizzy,' he said, a broad grin breaking through the panting as we tackled the stairs. 'I am sick to death of hearing about you every weekend and no doubt you are sick to death of hearing about me.'

'Don't be rude, Michael,' said Cora curtly, 'Watch those olives,' as he swung the heaviest bag through the flat door. 'You'll only get oil everywhere and I'm not losing my deposit,' she said, pursing her lips.

But in the next second he had thrown his arms around her and planted a giant, slobbery kiss on them, from which she pretended to recoil in disgust. But Cora could not hide her smile. This was the first time I saw their intricate dance of pout and placation, a game I would soon take for granted.

Mike sat down at the kitchen table and started to unpack the bags.

'Cup of tea then?' I offered.

'Oh, yes please,' said Mike eagerly. 'Lovely cuppa tea. Yes please, girl after my own heart.'

'Oh no, here we go,' said Cora efficiently wrestling the food out of the bags and the salads and titbits into her tattered gingham rucksack. 'Ply him with tea and he's anyone's. It's 100 degrees outside, but it's never too hot for tea. He's as bad as you, Lizzy.'

So began our very first performance of the soon-to-be-longstanding ritual at the altar of the teabag. Whenever Mike visited, it was my cue to say 'cup of tea, then?' as soon as possible, once he'd crossed the threshold into the house. Better yet if I could actually call it down into the stairwell as he approached. Cora did not drink tea and would only drink coffee if she made it in her cafetière. I felt this to be an endearing eccentricity, forgivable because she was from over the border and a bit posh.

After the cuppa, which Mike proclaimed to be marvellous, Cora sent him across the street to the Happy Shopper with a handful of small change to buy us lollies.

'What do you think then?' she demanded, the moment he was gone, half-proud, half-nervous. 'Isn't he sexy, just as I told you?'

So I said the only thing I could. 'He's lovely, Cora.'

'No really, don't you think he's got amazing eyes?'

I hadn't noticed, but said yes, thinking her a little silly, but touched by her enthusiasm. How easily pleased she seemed. I was pleased for her, for them both. How sweet.

'I'm glad he's finally come,' said Cora. 'I thought the two of you would never actually meet.'

Soon Mike was shambling back over the doorstep, fumbling with three dripping Orange Maids. He promptly fell over my abandoned trainers, tried to rectify himself and dropped one of the lollies on the grubby carpet where it split in two, the paper packet oozing juice.

He looked so horrified I burst out laughing and then so did he. But Cora was less than pleased. The look on her face said she was not in the least amused at his ridiculous antics. This was how she referred to Mike's often inexplicable clumsiness. *Michael's antics*. He did have a way of entering the room like a gangling force of nature, off-balance and generating a destructive energy that affected things like coats on hooks, mugs full of hot liquid, beakers with pens and pencils in them and, oddly enough, his own stubbing feet.

Cora finished packing the lunch, determined to get to the park before the food became too hot and sweaty and the whole thing was 'utterly spoiled'. She'd planned it to be perfect, naturally. And Cora would prevail.

'You got any jam sandwiches in there?' Mike teased. 'Potted meat ? Pork pies? All we need is to borrow a dog, foil a mugger and we've got our own *Famous Five* plot. 'Five pig out in the park'! Or something a bit more articulate when I can think of it.' So she dug him in the ribs.

Picnicking among the cool trees, all thoughts of the bastard boyfriend that Cora had wanted to banish melted away as the salad and sandwiches disappeared from the plates.

The boyfriend, Jonathan from Part One Ancient History, (or was it Sebastian from European politics?) had not lasted very long. He was nice, and knew a great deal about ancient history (or European politics). But he wasn't much fun. He turned his nose up at Cora, saying she was 'hard work' and never paused for breath.

Cora was outraged at his rejection of me. I should have told him to 'take a hike' weeks ago, she fumed– the Americanism ringing strangely through her soft, plummy, slightly corrupted vowels. The vowels I tried constantly to reproduce.

As the afternoon light went down, we sat screened in the remains of the Bute Park sunken garden, eating and laughing, with Mike occasionally jumping up and turning inelegant cartwheels and wavering back-flips across the springy grass.

'You'll be sick,' Cora said.

She would have quite liked it if he'd been sick, I think. She could have said 'There you see, I warned you,' and held a cool bottle of orange squash to his head and rubbed his tummy with her hand. And he would have let her.

When it was time to return to the flat I knew they would want to have sex and probably go to the pub. So I made my excuses and went off to my room to watch TV, all the time thinking that Mike was great fun but Cora was a bit of a fool to be so obsessed about him. He was not at all like I'd imagined. He was just a nice guy, nothing more, except in that split second when he'd laughed at one of my jokes and I fancied the evening sun might have slipped into the shadow of his smile.

After that he came to stay almost every weekend.

When the new term started in the autumn, and Cora and I moved into a cramped little house in Fanny Street, Mike brought Stevie with him for the weekend to see the nightlife of Cardiff, making our little group complete.

I liked Stevie immediately. He was easy company, if a little dull next to three- ring-circus Mike, who always seemed to be singing something or breaking into a little jig and collapsing into laughter, his eyes crinkling up as if the force of his own joke had taken him by surprise.

I talked to Stevie at tacky, sweaty Charlie's nightclub, our soon-to-be favourite haunt. And the more we chatted the more I thought he was a very nice bloke, gentlemanly, the sort you could trust. It turned out we lived only 20 minutes drive from each other over the hillocks of home, Stevie in the richer parts, where you might play tennis or even golf if you wished. Earnest, polite, good-natured Stevie.

He asked me to dance but did not try to put his hands anywhere I didn't want them. At the end of the night he helped me into my denim jacket and carried my umbrella. Chorusing through the streets we four eventually wound our way on unsteady legs to the house. Cora and I moved instinctively to the kitchen to make mountains of toast.

As we leaned against the draining board, and I was starting to get sleepy, Cora dug me in the ribs and said:

'Well, what about Stevie then?'

Vodka-fuddled, I said something like, 'yeah, he's a good laugh.'

'And?' demanded Cora, barely containing her eagerness, 'What else?'

'He's really polite?' I offered. I was in no mood for one of her quizzes, poking the toaster with a knife to make the burning bread shoot out as Cora perpetually warned me not to do.

'Oooh, for God's sake, Lizzy,' she said, laughing. 'Did he ask you out? We thought he might have, you know. I thought he might when Michael and I made ourselves scarce.'

She grinned. I noticed that she only ever seemed to call Mike 'Michael'. So this was one of her conspiracies. Poor Stevie! He'd been brought in on false pretences, half-promised a new girlfriend. No wonder he had acted like it was a date, buying me drinks and telling me I was 'very lovely' at the bar.

She sighed.

'Oh well, Michael said he didn't think it was a good idea. He said we couldn't thrust people together because it might be embarrassing. But you are our friends and *you*,Lizzy, are so gorgeous. Stevie's on his own and he's *so* nice. Mike loves him to bits, so I thought you'd be good for each other. We could be a real foursome. Still…' she pondered, twisting back and forth on one foot like a little girl, licking peanut butter from a knife, 'You might change your mind. How long is it since you had a, you know…?'

Knowing what I was about to say, and knowing it wouldn't be polite she pre-empted me with a wave of the hand, a dirty little laugh. 'Ok, Ok. I just want everyone to be as happy as me and Michael. You can't blame me for that. More vodka?'

And she was telling the truth. She did want everyone else to be happy.

So we went back to the room where the boys waited, quickly

23

lost in the streaming comfort of the stereo, the mist of alcohol, laughter, stories and promise.

This then, was us, formed and final, finished. Friends.

If there was one problem in those days it was that term time was too short and the vacations far too long. There were too many holidays and reading weeks and Christmas breaks when classes ended, halls had to be vacated and the bubble of my new life and friends would be punctured.

If I wasn't careful I'd end up dividing my time in our terraced home between writing essays in the best room and watching TV with mum and dad. That was when I wasn't working in the newsagent's or petrol station for extra cash, just as Cora and Mike worked silver service in hotels.

Two days of that routine was usually enough to make me grumpy and withdrawn, like an addict going cold turkey. How could it not, when I'd spent months drinking in what it was like to belong somewhere for the first time, with more than just a group of people but with true friends? How could it not have gone to my head, made me drunk and dizzy, guzzling greedily, wanting more?

Imagine it. Imagine how perfect the city of Chester appeared, the first time I visited Cora and Mike during the autumn reading week of our second year. There was Cora, wind-milling her arms on the narrow platform, yelling my name before I'd stepped off the train, throwing her arms around my neck in a strangling hug, as if we'd been apart for months, not just five days.

'What was your journey like? Are you hungry then? I bet you are. We could go and get chips if you want or coffee and cake? I know just the place.' The decision was clearly already made.

'Where's Mike?' I asked, as she steered me towards town.

She'd come straight from the nursery school where she helped out when she could to bolster her CV.

'Mike will be finishing up his shift at the wedding reception soon,' she explained, waving towards the Grosvenor Hotel, in between telling me exactly what she had planned for the visit and how much her mum was dying to meet me.

'You'll like my mum, though I have to warn you she's a bit forthright. She scares Michael half to death, of course.'

Inside Cora's favourite coffee shop she babbled nineteen to the dozen about the school kids and little Liam Parker who had a crush on her, and how she had promised to make 50 fairy cakes for the Christmas Open Day. I was happy to listen.

After tea and cakes we took a tour of estate agents and looked at flats and houses that Cora had set her heart on. She couldn't wait for her and Mike to move in together after graduation.

As the sun sank with winter weariness, twilight softened Chester Old Town, shrouding its tacky, Olde-Worlde facade, the wood and soft-hued yellow stone soaring magically into the ice-blue winter sky. Then there was Mike, bounding out of the gloom to meet us. And we, huddled in our coats, rubbing gloved hands, skipped in and out of the mock Tudor arches, inhaling the scent of hot coffee and sugar-sweet treats, careening round the city walls to look at the slow, glassy river.

The suffocating Dickensian atmosphere was too much for Mike. He insisted on pulling up the collar of his waxed jacket so it stood up straight, wrapping his scarf around his face and bellowing, 'Good day to you, Mr Pickwick,' and other such nonsense, between doffing an imaginary hat and taking invisible pinches of snuff. As Cora and I stared longingly, like Dickensian orphans, into a bun shop, the window steamy with heat and clouded by spray-on snow, Mike vanished. Looking around for him in the throngs of shoppers he reappeared on the bridge that houses the eccentric Victorian-looking clock. Leaning out to us he yelled:

'Boy? I say boy? What day is this?' Cora and I giggled uncontrollably.

'Why, it's Christmas day, sir,' I shouted, ignoring the bemused glances of passers-by.

'Well, then I haven't missed it,' he said, beaming in feigned wonderment. Reaching into his pocket, he extracted a coin and flipped it over the edge with a graceful flourish. In the low, setting November sun it seemed to spiral in slow motion, not so much glinting, as emanating, bright, yellow, cinematic light. I extended a muffled, gloved hand, but, naturally, missed it. Cora and I scrabbled for the precious penny in the gutter, pushing, straining, for the treasure dropped from his hand.

Dinner at Cora's was at eight sharp. Despite Cora's insistence I don't think Phillippa was terribly pleased to meet me. It was still several years before Cora and Mike's wedding. Years before I would help shoe-horn her into her exquisite, red silk, un-mother-of the-bride-ish dress with the corset lacings, and she would hug me warmly with tears in her eyes.

She was older than I expected, taller and more glamorous in a restrained way. Very English too, in the manner that is a complete lifestyle, accent and mien, not just a nationality. Like Cora, she was very well-spoken. She had dark hair drawn back in a neat pony tail. She was quite chic, kind of Lauren Bacall ageing gracefully. French manicure. So Cora must look like her dad. She was exceptionally well-groomed, wearing expensive but low-key black trousers and a black turtle neck, no visible jewellery, only a little make up, neutral, glossy – but enough.

She made us a very tasty dinner: Poached salmon fillets with a secret recipe sauce, petit pois, new potatoes and homemade tart au citron, real coffee and biscotti. She was curt towards Cora and all but interrogated me over the glare of the table candles, in the poky dining room with its air of an overstuffed, upper middle class sitting room shrunk into a smaller space than had been intended.

An expensive carriage clock was ticking off the minutes on the mantelpiece.

'Cora tells me you hail from The Valleys, Elizabeth? Really? You certainly don't sound like it,' said Phillippa, serving the salmon, with Cora shooting me an apologetic glance across the table. 'You are not what one would imagine at all. I mean, if Cora hadn't told me all about you.'

She eyed me up and down with grudging approval, as if I had clearly exceeded the unflattering expectations contained in the phrase *'The Valleys'* and the distasteful inflection with which she said it. I don't think she meant to be rude. 'Cora could certainly take a tip or two from you,' she conceded. 'You all dress like drop-outs now of course. That's standard, wherever you come from. But you have good posture and beautiful skin. I never have been able to get Cora to care in the least about her appearance,' (my turn to return the eye-borne apology in Cora's direction). 'So you want to do something in *the media* after your degree? Well, at least that has possibilities.'

She said this in a way that managed to suggest she thought *'the media'* a vulgar realm, but still made it clear that anything would be better than Cora's wish to be a schoolteacher. She did not mention that she herself had been forced by financial pressures to take up a part-time job as a school secretary at Cora's old private school after the divorce. Perhaps that was different, though, because it was more select, meaning she mixed with a better class of people.

I felt a bit sorry for Cora after that. What a bitter old witch to have as a mother. If Cora had visited me at home my mum would have put on a nice M and S jumper with a colourful pinny over it, made macaroni cheese and cheerfully fussed Cora, asking her about her course, her home, while praising me to the skies in between. It would be a bit embarrassing, but pinny or no, she would have had better manners than Phillippa.

I also realised for the first time that Cora and I had one important thing in common, something that transcended everything–else. Despite her Enid Blyton accent and seeming confidence, I wasn't the only one struggling to escape the shadow of my upbringing. Somehow this made her less impressive, but also more human. And I was relieved not to be the one who needed her so much, in such a one-sided way. She had been searching for me as much as I had been searching for her, before either of us knew it. We were both trying to reinvent ourselves – and we had.

After the visit ended and we returned to Cardiff, where we were new and unbreakable and undamaged again, it was always the weekend. And Stevie was there with Mike, and we were dancing, arm-in-arm along the street, or hands aloft under the streaming lights of a club or pub, and drinking until we were warm and dizzy.

There were any number of nights like this that stretched out for a lifetime, so full of each other, of the sensations of living in our own story, making ourselves up as we went along, redefining, rewriting, in each other's eyes and in our own.

We were convinced we would always be that way, never

pinned down, shifting like lights on the dance floor or the sunshine filtered by the canopy of trees dappling the broken slabs of pavement under our feet. Always to and from something, laden with books and cynicism – coffee on the way to anywhere, drinks on the way to everywhere, iridescent with youth on the way to somewhere. Radiating confidence and optimism, we waited.

When we woke in the night, blurry with sleep, and listened to our neighbours returning home at three in the morning, kicking off shoes and on with the stereo , the bass-line lullaby was a sign that we were living through our youth. The laughter, the pouring of liquid and the sound of breaking glass was how we sounded to others often enough.

With the streetlight sliding between the curtain gaps we listened, cocooned and peaceful. Little could keep us awake, not because our consciences were clear but because we were worn out with life.

And we worked hard, anchored to our desks and tables, buried in books with the sunlight pouring and heaving outside, or with rain, percussive and soothing on the glass season after season. We needed good grades, because degrees cost money and *meant* money.

And we believed at the time that these couldn't be the best days of our lives. After this, life would begin properly, as my parents would say. Decently, appropriately. With proper clothes, proper shoes, proper food, proper hotels, proper holidays, all the things they had lacked. That, they would conclude, was why we were getting a proper education in the first place.

This was what we were like then. Me, Stevie, Mike and Cora. No one else. But there was a life after that. As I shall tell you.

Slight Return

I waved goodbye to University life when Cora's mum's battered Astra left Fanny Street for the last time after graduation, loaded with junk, including that bloody enormous, blue cardboard Erasure castle Cora had begged HMV for when they took down the advertising display. She had dragged it all the way through Cardiff for Mike, though it was twice her size.

We had all caught each other in a long embrace and Cora sniffled quite touchingly. I did not sniffle but felt my throat tighten as we promised to keep in touch and visit often and always call. Mike held me close and his voice sounded choked when he said, 'Come and see us.' I just nodded.

'You're my best friend, Lizzy,' Cora said earnestly and I gave her a hard hug.

Then they were gone and I was left standing in the litter-bowled street with the thump of a neighbour's stereo bass beating the air on the blistering July day.

Thinking about it, we only saw each other four times before their wedding. Four times in four years isn't such a lot is it? Since we were so close and so determined to stay that way? But there were reasons for that. Some of them were practical: we were all busy moving homes and did not have much money. Chester, way up in the alternate border lands of the north, was another

30

country, far enough away for that to seem not so unnatural. And we had to get jobs.

Cora had landed on her feet immediately, as I had expected. She completed her PGCE inside a year and started teaching at a nice little village primary school.

It was different for Mike. He had coasted for almost two years from one admin job to another in his usual pleasant, unhurried way with no real plan about what he was going to do or how he was going to do it. I rather admired this Bohemian attitude of his, the way he resisted sliding into adult life, though Cora was less indulgent and eventually took him in hand.

Through an old friend of her mother's she managed to get him an interview at a PR firm. He'd wanted to work in PR from the start, but linear plans of action weren't Mike's specialty and he had lacked the confidence or the courage to chase applications and bend himself into a suit and tie. So Cora found the advert in the paper, made the call, helped him update his CV. She could only get him a foot in the door, she said. He had to wow them for himself.

And he did of course, because when Mike chose to channel his enthusiasm into a single stream and pin someone in place with it he could convince them that they were the only person in the world who was so like-minded, that they and he alone shared secret truths. That included the Jackson's PR manager who Mike convinced that he would like nothing better than to promote their media clients business for the princely sum of 17 grand a year, plus expenses.

Once he was offered the job Cora and Mike were suddenly a fully-fledged, working, career-type couple, though they couldn't afford to actually live in Chester as they'd planned. Now that she had graduated, Cora's dad had finally insisted the house be sold in the divorce settlement. He was bankrupt and moving back to his family in London and there wasn't any extra money coming from that direction anymore. So they lived in a rented flat near Wrexham.

But somehow Cora still saved like a demon and planned and executed her perfect wedding. Naturally, they asked me to be a bridesmaid.

It was quite an affair. Picture-perfect in fact, despite the fact it was the day we all officially ceased to be merely post-grads, or children, because Mike and Cora had joined the world of permanency and become husband and wife. I see myself in the posed group shots, dressed in lilac silk, smiling, always smiling, with a beautiful posy of cornflowers and white roses. Stevie is at hand, the best man in his immaculate morning suit. Cora is all the things a bride should be, radiant in cream, the blushing bride, Mike the proud groom. The photographs of the day show all of this. The happy ending.

Of course at that time I had never even heard of Jenny. I did not know that the moment we would meet her was already edging closer, and from that moment, everything would be different.

It began to be different from the moment Mike and Cora decided to move back to Cardiff. Mike's firm had opened an office in the newly developed Cardiff Bay area and they offered him a promotion and a bonus if he would re-locate and help head the new department. Since Stevie and I were still in the city, tending up-and-coming careers, it was the natural choice to make. And the obvious argument in favour was that, once we were all back together in one place, there would be no reason not to see each other as often as we wanted, and be just as happy as we had been before.

In September, after a frantic hunt for houses . Cora and Mike moved into a nice little semi in the cheaper end of Roath, where it spills into more student-friendly Cathays. It was near to where we used to live. True, it was some way behind the desirable Victorian villas on the vast, railing-rimmed lake, with its land-locked white lighthouse and wooden tea cabin. It was the part where the houses and gardens are small and boxy, the roofs and windows more modern; the views non-existent, but the litter minimal and the cars well-cared for.

Cora's new name and title was not the only thing that elevated her into the realm of adulthood. The house interior had been tastefully transformed under her touch into a pleasant approximation of magazine-chic suburbia, far superior to my boxy first floor apartment and Stevie's pleasant but masculine flat. I was completely taken aback. It seemed very grown up. *Habitat* in miniature. I felt a prickle of unexpected irritation at the sight of a pair of red enamel pasta tongs.

But I liked the pale lilac walls and the big bay window gulping in the fading light, the gathered gauze providing a feathery privacy. I liked the cool aquamarine kitchen, its vases of lilies and smooth chrome creating the feeling I was floating underwater. I admired the squashy looking king-sized bed, awash with plump pillows, thinking I would like to roll myself up in it and sleep with the soft light filtering on to my face.

This was a tableau of domesticity I had never dreamt of. And for a slice of a second, as I let out a single breath, I envied them the calm, cosy order of it all. The finality.

I imagined taking off my make-up in the tiny but immaculate en-suite bathroom, splashing my face with water that would feel better there than water anywhere else. Tucked under the covers, a few breaths away, Mike might be reading one of his books with his feet poking out from the bottom of the quilt.

About six weeks after the move it was Stevie's birthday – he was the first of us to hit the ripe old age of 28. We had to celebrate. And it was our first real reunion night, a chance to hit the town like we used to – a double excuse.

As soon as we arrived at their house that night Stevie and I could see that Cora had made one of her *special efforts*. She had spread about a dozen candles around the living room. There were coloured lights strung along the mantelpiece. She had bought a bottle of Martini for us and bottled beer for the boys.

She'd been to the new Sainsbury's and, scattered on tables and sideboards, there were bowls of kettle chips and pistachios and little cheese twists, which Mike gobbled by the handful, delightedly proclaiming them 'yuppie food'. There was an M and S party selection on the coffee table. I rolled my eyes at Stevie and he grinned back through a mouthful of sausage.

Brimming with nostalgia, Mike cranked up the volume of the greatest hits of the nineties, volume whatever, on the sleek silver stereo nestled between the tottering racks of CDs.

We ended up in the kitchen, drawn by the wafting invitation of sundried tomato and hot cheese, impatient for Cora's homemade pizzas to cook. She was enjoying being the hostess. We were happy to be served. I was unfailingly cheerful, even though it was all a bit *Nigella* for me and Cora talked a lot about where she'd bought her plush new settee, the difficulty of getting a reasonable mortgage and finding decent flooring, and all manner of things I had no interest in at all.

And soon we found one hundred things to remember and tease each other about, and one or two to forget.

It was one of the rugby international nights. The city had

been clogged all day with fans and it would only get worse. I seldom ventured into town on such days when the streets were crammed with flag-draped boisterous men in tall, allegedly amusing patriotic hats. I fucking hate rugby. Rugby which these days passes for Welsh culture, filling a gaping, yawning void where identity should be.

Passing the roar of the monstrous new Millennium stadium, perched on the river's edge like a poorly parked space ship about to break its moorings and sail off into the sky, I always felt a peevish stab of irritation and disgust. Were it not for those idiots I'd be able to park within two miles of my office and I wouldn't be wading through sick come 7pm.

Bearing in mind the inevitable crowds, we'd booked our taxis for the journey out and the return home well in advance. That year, hailing a cab on St Mary Street on a weekend had become a lottery, a game of skill and chance. Dozens of new clubs and bars were elbowing their way in between the old-fashioned pub fronts, screaming with gaudy lighting and two-for-one offers. By 7pm people would be staggering in the gutters, in the cordoned off streets nearest the stadium exits, hands aloft, swearing at drivers of private cars for refusing to stop. The term 'binge drinking' hadn't yet made the headlines – they were still just drunk arseholes.

We were on our way to Charlie's. I hadn't been there since our student days. There were newer, cooler places to go but for us there had only ever been Charlie's. No one even thought of suggesting somewhere else.

As we tumbled out of our taxi nothing could spoil the mood, not the drunks, not even the middle-aged man on the pavement outside, wearing a battered old waxed jacket, clutching a congealed curry in a cardboard carton, asking for change.

As we made our way inside Cora caught the man-with-the-curry's eye, or at least his attention was drawn to her, awkwardly exiting the taxi in her tight red shirt.

'Spare some change, miss?' he enquired, rather more politely than expected. But he was invisible to her, of course. His voice dissipated into the ether between them so she did not have to hear it. I suppose it was the knowledge of this that suddenly made him furious. He grabbed the car door.

'Don't you hear me, darling?' he demanded, pushing his face into hers. 'Got any change, I said?'

'Go away,' snapped Cora. But Mike was there in a split second.

'Cold tonight, isn't it, mate,' he said breezily. 'Got a bed?'

The Curryman looked so startled to be asked a question about himself that he didn't say anything at all. So Mike said, 'Here's a fiver, get something warm inside you.' He clapped the man on the shoulder and gave him his melting, Mike-smile.

The man clutched the crumpled note for a few seconds and then said, 'Thank you, young man,' in a greatly altered, almost bashful tone. 'You're a real human being.'

Cora grabbed Mike purposefully by the arm and pulled him into the club foyer leaving the Curryman staring at the note.

'Really, Michael. Must you give our cash away to every down-and-out you meet? I mean for God's sake, don't be a mug all your life.' Mike just shrugged and sent me a furtive wink.

The wink said, 'She doesn't get it but we do, don't we? Because we feel the same way. One touch of compassion, one moment of sympathy, costs nothing. He smiled from outside Cora's line of sight and I couldn't help but smile back, the smile growing inside and out as he took our coats and checked them in.

So we bowled through the glass doors into Charlie's and into the way we used to be.

Jenny was already inside, getting closer by the minute.

Charlie's had added new leather booths, a second bar and a bigger dance floor in the intervening years. Mike was just inches away as we danced and I could not help taking snatched, sidelong glances at him, moving angularly and gracelessly but with a sheer enthusiasm that showed anything else could not have suited him half as well. Occasionally he would clasp my hand, spin me round, both of us laughing guilelessly like idiot, hyperactive children. I don't think I had ever been so happy.

He kept looking at me, at least that's how it seemed. And when our eyes met we were aware of being locked into every vibration of the air as our limbs moved in the same element, without touching. I remembered the night of the red-sports car and the tumble across the bonnet.

Eventually, we had to stop dancing to catch our breath. Stevie, pink-faced and flushed, disappeared in the direction of the bar and returned with shots and glasses of misty water. We talked nonsense but it was compelling; each of us with stories, everybody laughing. Remember your birthday? Remember the time loony Tim went into that pet shop? Remember Simon Phelp's Nigerian flatmate who refused to speak to anyone and took showers at four in the morning?

Mike was saying how great it was, the gang back together, repeatedly, his eyes shining like a child with food-colouring fever, and I felt a stab of pain deep in my chest. I realised I could not breathe in the lifetime it took for him to lift a strand of damp hair from my cheek, tucking it behind my ear. Cora slipped her arm through mine and said 'I've missed you.'

I passed Mike his beer and his fingers grazed mine for a second longer than they should have.

Soon another row of drinks was lined up on the bar like little ark animals, two JDs, two vodka and cokes, two bottles of Bacardi Breezer, two pints of Worthington. Not sure how these were divided up, except the Breezers were probably Cora's as she liked the sweet taste and they were still new and quite trendy. The JDs were mine. My vodkas phase had passed now I was a little older, still single. And feeling fine.

The drinks were followed by mouth-tingling Aftershock chasers with their antiseptic kick, the current trend, not because we liked them. The floor space around us began to disappear as the bar began to fill and the band ratcheted up a few notches. Every so often as the jokes and stories flowed I would raise my eyes to survey the pulsing room and the promising faces, catching a few eyes and breaking contact each time. As the drinks worked their way into every nerve and fibre I felt tight, sleek, red-lipped, ready to be looked at.

Now the men who used to level their eyes at Cora's impressive chest were looking over at me, pretending not to, and I pretending they were not. Complicit. To my infinite surprise it had been happening for some years. I could not stop smiling inside at the undisguised attention, my smile breaking outwards with a flick of the head, my toes tapping on the flagstone floor. Cool but suggestive.

Since starting my first job I had folded away the long flowery dresses, faded jeans, and brightly-coloured sweaters that had been all I'd needed at University. I was going through a dark-coloured, close-fitted style of dressing, feminine, I thought, but faintly aggressive; a sleeveless black top with the neck crossing my collarbones with some lace, sleek, black narrow trousers, sharp toed leather boots. A cluster of silver hoops encircled my right wrist. As they jingled towards my glass, and rose to my lips, their charm seemed to work over the immediate circle of men, their eyes drawn upwards to the smooth swallow, the curve of the throat, lingering of pink glossy lips on the glass, catching my smoky-rimmed eyes for a fraction of a second.

Mike notices too. His smile tightens a little.

I realise Cora looks downtrodden. She's aware of this little by-play and it alarms and depresses her. She sees I have changed. She looks much the same as she always did. Her hair's longer but she realises she appears sensible in black jeans and a red silky blouse. She undoes one more button and pushes her hand beneath her hair to fluff up the front.

I feel-guilty and lean forward to shout in her ear 'Come on. Let's dance.' I catch Stevie's hand, grin at Mike. They follow me to the heaving, seething dance floor.

Light pulses and we dance, reservedly at first. I want Cora to enjoy herself. But before long I am finding it hard to play down what is running barefoot through my body. The whisky is kicking in, coursing from chest to head, warm, sharp.

And the beat picks up.

A song from the old days. It's Pulp. It's *Disco 2000*, cheesy, prophetic, glib and nostalgic all at once. We all laugh at its absurdity and brilliance. And Mike is nearby, long-legged in jeans, and the way he looks at me........After all this time. Just as it was, only more real than it ever was in that dark leafy street. It is here and we are moving closer.

I burn inside, loathing myself for it, every minute wanting it. It's harmless fun. Cora won't mind. Seconds out, seconds only. Set the scene. So easy after so long.

And in the next moment he has slid his arm around my

waist, grabbing my right hand, leaning me back so our bodies are pushed up close, into each other's welcoming curves, so easily we fit. An elegant, echoing gesture, like that night in the street, on the bonnet of the red sports car.

He elongates forward, I arch back, so far my hair almost sweeps the floor and blood flushes my face. It is only at that moment I realise I have missed him so much.

Stevie whoops in appreciation. I know how he would like to do this himself. But some of us act and some of us observe. And it might be inappropriate for the personal assistant to a senior member of the newish National Assembly to carry on like that in a tacky club, tipsy and foolish with some high-heeled blonde. He has to be a bit discreet now, doesn't he? From a foot away he feels rather than sees the slide of flesh on flesh, the reaching of nerves through clothing.

Then Mike returns me to my feet and releases me, reaches out for Cora's hand, spinning her round and round so she dizzies and breaks off, relieved, laughing, order restored.

But from that moment on the old order wasn't going to apply anymore.

Suddenly, there was Jenny. Sinewy and unreal, taking shape out of the smoke, hair flaming.

Jenny

Do you believe people can appear out of thin air? Born in a single second, already fully grown? Complete? Fatal? The product of a thousand tiny moments and small decisions embodied in one person, dark and deadly?

I have asked myself these questions a thousand times since that night, if I believe in fate.

Sometimes I think Jenny was sent to us, to re-write the story we had created for ourselves. At other times I think we were just unlucky. But what I know for sure is that when she appeared she caused a subtle shift in our reality. From that moment in Charlie's everything was slightly to the left of where it had been before. Though we didn't realise it right away, the light fell in its usual straight lines but the shadows moved. They expanded outwards across our lives, tracing their fingers along our spines, feathering across the back of our necks, so the soles of our shoes shifted sideways, and with them the direction of our steps.

'Hi,' she beams, opening her arms in an expansive gesture towards us.

Welcome.

Just like that, she appears.

And with only a moment's indecision and vague surprise, we all move aside to let her in.

'You look great,' she says, planting an air kiss on my cheeks, arm around my neck in a pseudo-hug.

I remember how her brilliant red hair in its sleek, salon-smooth bob appeared to pulsate in the reflection from the coloured lighting. She was wearing a black leather skirt, not too short but cut just at the right length to elongate her long, smooth legs in elegant, leather, calf-length boots. The heels were at least four inches high. A snapshot of every wife or girlfriend's nightmare.

I think it was the boots that caught Mike and Stevie's eyes first, though it might have been the black lace vest fitted closely over her pert chest. She was moving her hips slightly to the bass beat of the music and flashed a sort of Julia Roberts smile as if genuinely pleased to see us.

Nobody knew who she was. Or admitted to knowing her.

She looked familiar though, well, sort of. I thought I'd seen her before, somewhere, but she clearly seemed to know Cora and me for she flung her arms around us like an old friend, shouting something like, 'Hi Lizzy, you look fan-*tastic,*' over the relentless pumping din of the giant speakers.

Of course, while she tucked our arms in hers like errant children it seemed impossible to say, 'excuse me, but who exactly are you?'

There, among us, she knew my name, she had her arm around Cora's shoulder. She hailed Stevie with an inclusive wave, yelling 'I'm Jenny,' squeezing herself into the centre of the square we had formed. Suddenly, we couldn't ask her full name, or any of the things we wanted to outright. She was a blank that we couldn't fill, so each of us poured into her what we thought she was, feared she would be, without ever knowing it, this laughing, hugging young woman with great legs and a show-stopping smile.

In the absence of anything else we said multiple 'hi's' and remarked on the crowd, how busy it was, hoping she'd soon get bored and go away, back to her own friends, wherever they were. But she didn't.

She glanced at Mike and Stevie, eyeing them up and down in an appraising and approving way, bestowing a brilliant smile upon each, while the banalities trundled on. We asked her if she liked Charlie's and if she liked the music and came often. And she said 'Lord, no', and told us about a fantastic little funky place, more her scene, in Cannon Street.

It was what I had expected. Anywhere would have seemed more 'her scene' than trying-hard-to-be-trendy Charlie's. Though it burned through my chest to admit it, even then she seemed far too magazine-cover rock-chic for our old place. Though it had gone up in the world a little it was not yet ready for anything as self-possessed, as slick, as unashamedly exuberant as Jenny was that night. Jenny tossing back a Margarita. Jenny sucking the wet lime and licking the salt from the rim of her glass.

To my intense surprise Stevie said he knew the bar she meant. Stevie, who liked the local pub best 'because you can hear yourself think' and wore Burberry shirts. With queasy ease the two struck up one of those 'Isn't the dance floor tiny? Aren't the bathrooms like a spaceship interior?' conversations of the sort that immediately exclude anyone who's never been there.

I couldn't, with any justice, blame him. He was single and she certainly seemed available. But I was immediately, irrationally annoyed. He had committed the cardinal sin, inviting her to stay. Far more disturbing was the way Mike seemed to be hanging on every word that fell from her high-gloss lips. So focused was he that he didn't seem to notice Cora making disapproving eyes in his direction, narrowing, critical, Cora-eyes that she always did so well, mouth pursing a little, a direct stare. It was difficult to hear what they were saying above the band, therefore impossible to contribute. But Jenny didn't seem to notice and the boys didn't seem to mind.

Cora tried to break Mike's concentration by tugging his arm and mouthing that she needed to go to the bar. It was a cue for him to offer to go with her, not to say:

'We'll hang around here for you then, keep our spot, mine's a Stella,' and not a cue to pull up a nearby stool and settle in.

Cora switched her look to me. I knew I was supposed to go with her but I didn't want to. I wanted to bring the conversation and Mike's gaze back to where it should be. Away from Jenny's laughter. Away from Jenny's skirt. Cora grabbed my hand and led me off to the ladies.

'Who is *she?*' she demanded, exasperation emanating from her in an almost palpable, petulant aura. 'Who does she think she is bloody barging in like that? Does she work with you?'

'Jesus, no. I thought you knew her,' I replied as we went downstairs to the underground loos.

They'd had a face-lift since our last visit, and no longer smelled quite so much of vomit. There were no coats hoarded behind the broken cistern. No one was peeing in the hand basins with the archaic taps because there were no basins at all. It had become highly mirrored with dark tiles on the walls and one of those two-tiered birdbath-like communal metal sinks where water squirts out of invisible holes at random.

Stark spotlights gave my face a bleached-out, over-exposed pallor, as I painted on more lip gloss in the mirror.

'I've never seen her before,' continued Cora. 'What a bloody tart, flirting and fawning over Mike like that. Is she one of those twats from his work?'

'Don't know. She looks a bit familiar. Might be from the Jackson partnership. Stevie seems to like her,' I observed, addressing my remarks on safe ground to the door of Cora's cubicle.

'Can't imagine why? She's not his type is she? Too trashy for Stevie.'

She wasn't trashy. But I didn't contradict Cora because I knew what she meant. Stevie was so, well, nice and sensible, almost fraternal. And *she* was, well, overt. The package was well-designed, not slutty, too groomed for that, but subtly suggestive, from the Micromesh tights to the voluminous mascara.

'How do you know?' I countered lightly. 'Maybe Stevie has a secret, dominatrix Miss Whiplash fetish. I mean, he spends his life with politicians.'

I said this not only because the image seemed ridiculous with Stevie in it but also because Jenny's dark eyeliner and leather boots gave her an unforgiving edge, as if, behind the arrow-point precision of that well-aimed smile, she'd like you to be a little afraid of her. And you'd enjoy being afraid. It'd be fun for a while.

Cora didn't laugh though.

'Let's bloody lose her anyway,' she spat. 'Or it'll be small talk and giggling and Stevie's cow eyes all night. Then I'll have to be sick in a bucket.'

I grinned. 'Let's get some Jack's in and dance then. She'll probably have buggered off by the time we get back, on to bigger game.'

Cora emerged from the stall, straightening her blouse, smoothing it over her rounded stomach. 'She's too fat for that skirt anyway,' she added.

Simple as that, Jenny was in the box. The harmless, disarmed box . The too fat, too plain, too stupid, too cheap box, where all women try to put their rivals, whether they fit or not. But Jenny was kicking at the cardboard with all her might: when we returned from the loo she had not buggered off nor even budged an inch. She was still clinging and giggling at the edge of the bar, only her skirt and her laugh were a little higher.

'Ah girls,' she said as if welcoming us to our own party. 'The boys were just saying this is a trip down memory lane for you all, reliving the student life, sort of a reunion?'

The boys. Cora and I both winced at that. The familiarity was one step too far already. How much more could the girl get wrong in less than half an hour? What on earth was she thinking?

'Jenny reckons Spice is great on a Saturday. Maybe we should branch out later,' said Stevie eagerly, 'Try somewhere new?'

Spice – flavoured vodka shots, a great neon wall of a bar, staff like a Gap advert serving with long-limbed casual arrogance, chrome, lots of townies with ironic bare midriffs. But Cora stamped that idea out right away.

'Well, I don't think so. We don't go for that full on dance shit – too monotonous unless you're tanked on speed or E. I'd rather something I can recognise, bump around to.' *Speed?* I groaned internally.

'Speed? E?' said Jenny with amusement. 'The voice of the Brit Pop generation?' and she actually laughed, good-naturedly, easily. This was tantamount to calling Cora old.

'Bit before my time.' Though she was about 24 – at least she could not have been more than five years younger than us – this was *definitely* calling us old. Cora's face turned still darker. 'Me, I just have to get up and dance,' said Jenny.

'Want to then?' asked Stevie.

'Yeah, come on then,' countered Mike. Both were on their feet in seconds and how could we not follow?

The dancing was worse than the sitting and talking and hair smoothing and wet lips on wine glass and the stretching of legs. Much worse.

It wasn't that Mike and Stevie were drooling as such. They were too sensible to be so blatant. But Mike did not touch me, nor sidle over to the beat. He might as well have fucked her then and there, I thought. Something dark needled at my insides and I wanted to cry. I felt a prickly heat under my eyelids and a tightening in my chest. It couldn't be midnight and time for riches to rags already, could it? I still had time to play the princess.

There was little room to move now that the time of night had come when everyone must dance because the drink has started its own rhythm. There were mercifully few rugby fans left, still in their war colours, attempting to grope girls or engage them in drawling conversations that would have been dull four hours ago, but were now downright unintelligible. The place was dangerously full and growing dangerously tense.

Most of the crowd had been drinking since noon, or before, and were bristling with the threat of overreaction, as if at any moment the wrong word might ignite a shower of fists and feet. So we kept being pushed apart and jolted from behind and separated into twos and threes, glass crunching beneath our shoes.

Once, as the surging dancers pushed Mike and Jenny together, I saw her lean in very close and say something in his ear. I have no idea what. I don't know if he did either. It was so loud by then, the beat pulsating, primal, I don't suppose he needed to. But I could've sworn he said, 'Not now.' Innocuous enough in itself, except of course it implied what was unspoken. One word. *Later.*

When a Guinness was accidentally thrown down Cora's front in a brown flash flood we had to stop, admit defeat and retreat to the bar. There were plenty of seats as everyone else was still in the hand to hand, crotch to crotch combat of the dance floor. That was the turning point of the night. The downward dive.

Mike and Jenny seemed to have so much to talk about it was embarrassing. Though we couldn't hear them over the din, I watched their lips move, fast and amused, flexing into little laughs and smiles. Cora was watching too, her temper rising behind a carefully fixed grin, and it was painful, for me, to see that Mike didn't even notice. Cora, dabbing at her sodden clothes, kept trying to turn the conversation around to include us, but the noise made that impossible.

Then Jenny announced she was having a party the following week and was suddenly, magnanimously, extending invitations to us all.

'You must come,' she insisted, yelling the address. 'It'll be great fun.'

'We don't know where that is,' said Cora feebly. 'We don't know the city anymore.'

'Oh, it's easy. Head for the river and then if you see the stadium I'm right opposite it in the third floor flat with the old oak outside.'

As she talked about the party, Stevie listened with rapt attention and Mike kept interjecting, drawing a glowing smile from Jenny each time. Stevie reluctantly excused himself for the loo and I tried desperately not to show that I was miserable and angry. In the end, Cora had exhausted tact, and I was glad when she stepped in to end this nonsense, so I wouldn't have to.

'I think we should go and find Stevie,' she said pointedly, when, twenty minutes later, he had not returned.

But if Mike spotted the hint this time he didn't just ignore it: he torpedoed it with no regard for the shrapnel and debris that would blow back and lacerate him later.

'Well, I'll stay put here then. Just in case he doubles back and you miss him,' he said, giving her hand a little squeeze. 'Do a loop around or we'll all get lost.'

There was no way out of that for Cora. She extracted her hand as if he had just spat on it and had to walk away, leaving Mike and Jenny at the bar. The last thing in the world she had intended to do.

'Let's find Stevie and get rid of her,' she yelled into my ear, striding into the seething throng. 'I want to go home.' She was close to tears now. My sentiments exactly.

But Stevie was not in the corner by the burger bar, at one of the tubular metal tables strewn with greasy cartons. Nor was he curled in a corner with any one of a number of drunken girls, swaying to keep their feet and struggling to hold their drinks. Not Stevie. He was neither entering or leaving the mens' loos nor elbowing his way in at either of the squat bars, fiver in hand. But he *was* back at the bar where we'd started at the end of our loop. Trouble was, he was alone. Mike and Jenny had disappeared.

Stevie looked more than a bit pissed off. He was clearly sulking.

'At last,' he harrumphed. 'Where the hell have you all been?'

'Where's Mike?' demanded Cora.

'Dunno. I was waiting here, thinking you'd be bound to come back for me. Where the hell have that pair gone now?'

With the last trace of goodwill ebbing away, we waited. Our

glasses were dry and there was no point trying to fight our way to the bar for the last quarter of an hour. We had the taxi booked for one thirty.

We waited until they ushered us from the main club. We waited by the cloakroom after Cora had grabbed the coats, and then we had to go out on the freezing street with the drunks and soon to be halves of one night stands. With a cold drizzle starting to fall, my heart was sinking and my feet aching.

In the end there was nothing for it but to go home. To their home. Mike's mobile phone was routing straight to voicemail. We shivered on the corner of the street for almost half an hour until the taxi turned up – late. It was still quite a scrum to get there and shout our names as other people tried to beckon it, making inelegant dives for the door handle. Luckily, Stevie was fast and surprisingly firm. We didn't want to leave Mike, but if we let our taxi go we'd be in the cold and now wet heart of the city until sun-up, for sure.

We dropped Stevie off first and then went on to Cora's. Sitting in the back of the cab with her was like sitting next to a tightly contained tornado. I could feel her spiralling rage, super-charging the atmosphere rippling outwards, almost making my hair stand on end. She didn't speak and after getting no response from my, 'I'm sure he'll be alright, he's probably got waylaid by some idiot,' platitudes I fell silent. I was actually grateful for the cabbie's prattle as we snaked through the shining wet streets with frightening speed.

Soon we were in the hall and I was shaking off my umbrella. The light was blinking on the answer phone. Cora dashed over and stabbed at the button. Mike's voice, distorted by the typical mobile crackle and what sounded like cars rushing by, burst forth.

'Sorry babes must have lost you. If I can't get a cab I'll walk, or worst comes to the worst I'll stay at Gabe's. He's having his post-match party. It's really bucketing down now. My credit's running out. Love you.'

'I'm going to bed,' said Cora flatly. 'Make yourself at home, make toast if you want, I don't want anything. Please put that wet brolly in the stand, it'll mark the wooden floor. See you in the morning.'

I sighed at her hunched and retreating shoulders from the foot of the stairs, carefully popping my umbrella in the long, gun-metal canister that looked a bit like a headless bullet and hanging up my coat on one of the wrought iron school pegs.

I wasn't tired. I padded around the kitchen, guardedly opening cupboards, searching for something to eat, trying to be soundless, eyeing the clock every few minutes. I passed on the organic granola and multigrain crisp-breads and settled for the comfort of toast and peanut butter.

I didn't put on the living room light. I curled up in a squishy armchair and watched TV with the Teletext on so as not to make a noise. I couldn't hear so much as a footfall from above but I kept straining for the sound of feet in the street, a key in the lock. It was only a fifteen minute ride from town and Charlie's had to have ushered the last reluctant few out through the front doors long ago. But then how the hell would Mike have got a taxi? He could walk it, in about half an hour, but maybe closer to a whole one on uneven drunk's feet, in the pouring rain.

I told myself I was primarily concerned for his welfare. It was late; someone could have set on him, taken a swing at him for looking at his bird, for not giving a toss about rugby, for sounding a bit posh.

An hour later, when my eyelids were giving up the battle

against Jack Daniel's last stand, I wearily clambered into bed in the spare room. The house slept silently as my breathing slowed beneath the brand new guest–room bedcovers. I woke twice, thinking I had heard the sound of a car, a taxi, the click of the downstairs door, but with no tread on the stairs, I realised I was mistaken.

Morning after

When I sidled into the bedroom Cora was in floods of tears, slumped over the dressing table, so damp and soggy-looking I guessed she had been there for some time, wallowing in a self-made puddle, marooned amid clumps of sodden, snot-filled tissues.

She was muttering Mike's name over and over. I was taken aback, halted in the doorway, unsure if she'd seen me or wanted to be seen. Cora had always been inclined towards melodrama after a few too many drinks, but now it was a sober 10.00 am. And this was a different Cora. Teacher Cora. Older and possibly wiser with longer hair and more expensive clothes, a house and a car, two cars, a fan-assisted oven and a profusion of muted soft furnishings and coordinated throw-cushions.

She seemed surprised to see me. As if I was the last person in the world she expected or wanted to see. I don't know why because she knew I had stayed over in her peachy, pinky spare room, a wall's width away. For a moment I saw something in her eyes that made me uncomfortable, guilty, made me remember.

A wave of frustration swept across me and I steadied myself against the doorframe. I could see she still genuinely loved Mike, as she had always loved him, in that unconditional way that sometimes made me incoherent with rage, loathing and violence.

53

I wanted to grab her stringy hair, limp from last night's styling spray, yank her head back and scream in her face:

'You stupid bitch. Why aren't you happy?' Or was that later? No matter.

I gave her a moment to blow her nose, trying to think my way back into how we had once been close friends, what I would have said.

'He didn't come home last night,' she mumbled. 'He made up that cock and bull story about staying at Gabe's. I know where he was anyway. Or should I say with whom?'

So he hadn't come back. I'd assumed he would be there by now. That he would have reappeared, as if by magic, while I was sleeping off my hangover. Apologetic and tongue-tied by her wrath, her air of wetness, her helplessness. I waited.

'You don't really think he was with *her*, do you?' I asked as the silence strained out to breaking point.

'Where else could he be all fucking night?'

The expletive was released with precise venom, ricocheting around the room, before her eyes became beseeching, drowned in tears again. She was begging me not to tell her what she suspected. I knew what she meant right away. It was the silent elephant in my head too.

'What? Where do you mean?' I asked gently, offering her a bit of crumpled tissue from my pocket.

'With her! With that stupid fucking slut, all tits and nails and 'oh, Mike you are so fucking funny darling'.

This was worse, tits and slut too. I had to tread carefully now. I tried to remember the old steps. Let her get it all out and then administer a short dose of common sense and reassurance.

'You mean *that Jenny*?' I said, feigning confusion.

54

'Of course I mean *that Jenny*. Who else would I mean but *that Jenny*, who else would fuck my husband?'

I hesitated, trying to think of something helpful to say. But I was out of practice.

'I mean, I know what Michael's like,' she continued. 'It's all just games with him, the dancing, the flirting, but not to her.'

She was shrill now, small and verging on hysterical so I sat down on the bed, ready to be reassuring from a safe distance. But she was on her feet instantly, pacing the floor, leaving a little wake of shredded loo roll. I felt confused and oddly inadequate, dishonest. Somehow, so little had changed, though a lot of time had passed. And I wasn't sure how it had drained out each day, swirling each one of us round and round until my feet had touched the ground here. Next to Cora, old and new.

I looked at her in her Calvin Klein, lilac silk dressing gown. The colour didn't suit her. It gave her sallow face an almost blue cast, as if she were slowly and silently suffocating. On the bedside dressing table was a neatly filed rank of expensive face creams I felt I wanted to try out, poke my fingers in and smear about. Their exotic French names, shiny and gilded, whispered promises of youth and beauty from the lacquered tubs and tubes.

The bed quilt was rumpled but everything else in the room seemed pristine, very different from my own bedroom in my little flat that attracted all the debris of the day, receipts sheafed into the cubby holes between the photo frames and perfume bottles, pennies and buttons in the ring tray, shoes appearing by osmosis from the wardrobe and under the gaps in the doors, in secret trysts with socks and pairs of tights.

In Cora's bedroom there wasn't a shoe or a bra or an odd crumpled sock in sight. That morning it was Cora that looked crumpled and all the Calvin Klein in the world wasn't going to change that. She looked very young at that moment.

At a loss to say anything useful I sat next to her and offered her Kleenex, my hand on her arm in mute, dumb comfort. At least five times in five minutes she told me she loved him. You see, she had given him everything for years, everything, and he had let her down for one fucking floozy, one tarty bitch. Her heartbreak was etched across her face.

He was the first and only man she had ever slept with, she said again, the only man she'd ever loved. She had used the same words years ago, before I even met him. She had never stopped reminding me. Where the hell are you, Mike? Wherever you are, it looks bad.

Then both of us froze as we heard the front door rattle, swing open and gently bump shut. There was a moment's silence from the hall. A sound of shuffling and keys being discarded. Then a heavy foot on the stair.

'It's Mike,' gasped Cora redundantly, as it couldn't really be anyone else.

'Give him a chance to explain,' I pleaded, pressing her arm, excusing myself. 'It's probably not what you think. He wouldn't do that to you.' I sidled hurriedly out of the door as Mike reached the other side, unkempt, but boyishly handsome in last night's clothes.

He beamed, seemingly upbeat. 'Morning babes. Big night eh? The princess up yet?'

The princess simply said:

'Come in here. I need to talk to you now.'

Her voice, low and reasonable, fooled neither of us. And the rather rumpled charming prince obeyed.

Moments later, I could hear Cora screaming through the

wall, though I would have been able to hear her anywhere in the house, or anywhere in the street, for that matter.

Over and over again she asked, 'Why, why did you do it? Why did you do it?' Something mumbled ... 'you couldn't leave her alone could you' ..... 'you promised, you *promised*.' Silence from Mike's end for a minute or so, then Cora's voice, rising higher and higher, 'I don't believe you. Why should I believe you? Why did I ever believe you?'

'I phoned to explain.....there was no signal.... I slept late...,' punctuated by her staccato questions, then weeping.

I desperately wanted to hear his explanation. To know what had happened. Could he really have gone off with that Jenny? Surely not? I wanted to hear him make everything okay. But he wasn't my husband.

I shoved my belongings into my rucksack, threw on my coat and left, closing the door as softly as possible behind me. Their conversation looked as if it would go on for some time anyway. I imagined Cora stamping a foot, putting her hands over her ears as she chanted, the angry mantra reverberating down the stairs, through the hall. *'You liar, you liar, you liar.'*

Could he talk his way through this one? Just like the old times when she was angry with him? Be patient and coaxing and weave a story that would eventually, with little tiny butterfly kisses on her forehead and stroking of her hair, convince her that she was mistaken, nothing had happened and he was still her Mike and he loved her? I'd scribbled a note for Cora on a scrap of paper and left it on the hall table: Call me soon. Love Lizzy. I added a kiss like a good friend, knowing I would have to wait for my answers.

Tea and sympathy

The desire to find out what had happened between Mike and
Cora continued to itch away at me all that day and into Sunday,
through its predictable cycle of food shopping, trip to the gym
and my bi-monthly saunter to Stevie's for tea.

Stevie just made it worse. He was supremely unconcerned
that Mike hadn't come home after Charlie's. He'd called Mike
to see where he'd got to. He'd said he'd got separated and stayed
at Gabe's and that was all. In the way that only men can be,
he was satisfied with the path of least explanation.

By Monday, with no answer to my phone calls and messages
for Cora, that itch was burrowing into the bone and I had to
find a way to scratch.

I phoned her at school during her morning break because
I knew she'd have to speak to me if I called the secretary's office
– if only to promise to call back. She said unconvincingly that
she was OK, it was all probably a misunderstanding. Mike was
feeling poorly and had taken the day off work.

I was glad of this because, to be honest, it was Mike I really
wanted to speak to. And it was much easier to nip over to Roath
than to trek out to his sterile, goldfish bowl office in the Bay.

Jackson's PR was one of the new high-rises starting to soar
from the ashes of Cardiff's Victorian dilapidation, behind

hoardings with promises of designer retail space and loft living *coming soon*! The city was going not outwards but upwards then. Prime real estate springing skyward in the heart of the traffic-choked city, office complexes and multi-storey car parks replacing the whistling, gap-toothed warehouses; shiny sailing boats, theme pubs and multi-screen cinemas displacing rather than replacing the prostitutes and pimps that used to cling to the dockland streets like the scum that used to cling to the fetid water, empty of the coal barges for so long. Parking was a nightmare!

After two rings on the doorbell Mike came to the door, hair ruffled, in his pyjamas. Not the pyjamas you see in idiotic toothpaste adverts but a pair of loose jersey track pants and a T shirt, rumpled from bed.

'Are you alright?' I asked, smiling in spite of myself, warmth in the pit of my stomach. 'Cora said you were sick?'

'And you've rushed around to nurse me? Excellent! Where's the nurse's uniform? Where are my grapes?' he beamed. I offered up a packet of Wagon Wheels I'd grabbed at the garage. His favourite. 'Even better. Tea then? You'd better come in or people will think we are having an affair, you know.'

I grinned and followed him in. The house was orderly except for the dismantled newspaper, tea cups and a crumbed plate, that had obviously made up Mike's morning and represented one of the localised oases of clutter in which he was most at home. I leaned on the new breakfast bar as he went through the tea ritual, the fast-boil kettle speeding up the process considerably.

'You're not ill then?' I asked , tracing the toe of my new black leather boot across the polished tiles. 'Lazy git.'

'Nope not ill, as such. Just knackered really.'

'Well, I'm not surprised.' I paused a beat. 'Did you have a tiring day yesterday?'

He sighed into the fridge, picking up the milk, his dressing gown cord catching in the door so he had to reopen it and free himself, before he poured it on the swirling storm of tea. He sighed again.

'Cora went nuts on me, if that's what you mean.' He stirred in his sugars energetically, making some tea splash on to the counter and drip down the doors before fastidiously wiping it up and handing me a mug. 'I know, I know. I deserved it. It was pretty stupid of me. To get so plastered and get separated. Started walking but I was soaked to the skin. I ended up at Gabe's.'

'I heard. What happened?'

'Oh, I lost you all in the club. I spent ages traipsing round the dance floor trying to find you all, but I was very pissed. Guess I'm just not used to drinking like that anymore. Bit of a lightweight now. I must have missed you. Then I bumped into a mate from work and we had a pint. By that time they were chucking out. It was like a circus outside.'

'What happened to that girl?'

'Oh, her. She went off at the end.'

'Why didn't you get a taxi?'

'At that time of night? On *International* night? On the night of the great horse fetishists fair?' (This was one of his regular *Blackadder* references, one of the many TV and literary asides that Cora never got but would usually send us into a ping-pong of companionable ripostes and smiles. Not today, however.)

'Not for love nor money,' he continued. 'And I even offered one driver a shag but he turned me down. That wouldn't have happened five years ago. Cute bum like mine.'

I was perched on the armchair where I'd carried out my

night time vigil. I didn't smile. He was spread across the sofa. He caught my eye. I looked away. After a moment I asked, 'So how did you end up at Gabe's?'

'Walked there. It was on the way. The lights were still on and it was pissing down. You know Gabe – sad party man – open house. I just crashed. He didn't mind. He had mates down to watch the match. Doubt he even noticed me.'

'And you couldn't find a phone? We were worried.'

The "we" caused amusement to flicker briefly across his face.

'Gabe doesn't have one. It's all mobiles now isn't it? Privacy for all those 0800 sex numbers. Did you wait up for me?' he said, half-smiling. I drank some of the tea. Who the fuck doesn't have a phone?

'You and Cora have made it up then? Everything's OK?'

'You know Cora.'

'She was really upset. She thought…' I paused. I didn't want to throw anything into the mix that wasn't there already. But Mike supplied the rest.

'She thought I was shagging that Jenny. Yeah, she said. A dozen times. Where does she get these ideas? I don't know why she's so jealous all of a sudden. Why would I do something like that? With her, of all people.'

'Well you can understand how she might be suspicious,' I countered mildly, though when he said it aloud his denial sounded plausible, reasonable.

'Yes, she might I suppose,' he said looking directly at me. 'You don't think I was shagging that Jenny girl do you?' He looked hurt.

I glanced out of the window to the blustery, leaf-strewn street. 'How would I know?' I said eventually. He was still looking at me. I could feel the pressure of his gaze as I kept mine focused on the road and the approaching bin men. After a while he switched on the TV.

'Well I wasn't. Chance would've been a fine thing. The state I was in.'

He was trying to make light, to bluff everything away. I knew the expression on his face well enough, now that he was the one looking away.

'You seemed to know what you were doing earlier. We couldn't drag you away from her all bloody night.' I had snapped, suddenly and without warning. My voice sounded like a whip crack over the mumble of the TV. His head shot round and our eyes collided. It was too late to pretend I was disinterested, that I wasn't judging him. The most obvious question still had to be asked. I'd been working up to it.

'Who the fuck was she anyway?' I demanded, surprised at the force of my anger.

'I don't know really,' he replied after a moment's pause. He was considering what to say, I could tell. 'Think she might've been someone I met once through work, one of those conference things. I don't really remember. It seemed like you and Cora knew her though. Thought you might know her from Jackson's or one of the press agencies.'

'No, I *don't* know her,' I retorted incredulously. 'You mean she's not a colleague of yours?'

'No, I can't think…That's weird.'

'Weird?' I couldn't think of anything else to say. I was puzzled and annoyed, and suddenly half wanted to cry. (I was making a habit of that and I wasn't used to it.)

'She ruined the night for us, didn't she?' said Mike ruefully, seeing I was upset. 'It was supposed to be just us four – all back together.' I swallowed, insides clenching to weather the challenge. I couldn't speak. I had no right to make demands.

'So you were at Gabe's the whole time? You walked there in the pissing rain?'

'Yep. Thank God there's always an open invitation. You know Gabe. The eternal student.' There was hint of defiance in his eyes. He was tiring of this. A warning note sounded in the lower register of his voice.

'Where's your jacket?' I asked. I couldn't swear it but I thought he looked startled.

'What?'

'Where's your leather jacket, the one you were wearing on Saturday?'

'I wasn't wearing it was I? Oh! I was. It's about somewhere.'

'You weren't wearing it when you got here on Sunday morning.'

'It must be at Gabe's then. I'll have to call round and pick it up.'

He stared with renewed interest at the TV. 'Thanks for coming round, Lizzy.'

He bit open the Wagon Wheel packet and then into the wheel. 'But you know I'm not stupid enough to go mucking around behind your backs like that.'

He would say no more on the matter now. He had closed me down, returning his gaze to the TV. So we munched our biscuits in silence and watched a makeover.

I wondered what had passed between him and Cora on Sunday. I didn't know whether to believe him. It seemed plausible enough. But it was also implausible, depending on your point of view. A simple drunken mix-up − a glaringly suspicious lie. There was evidence for both.

I didn't know what Cora believed because she refused to talk about it at first. Flat refused. So the Jenny subject seemed to die down. It was something between them. It seemed she would, of course, forgive him.

But it didn't really die, it just dipped under the surface, waiting, like Jenny herself, her fingers beckoning. We had borrowed a little time – soon Jenny would demand its repayment.

Supper

With the panoramically enhanced view of hindsight, I can see now how a new dynamic entered Cora and Mike's relationship a few weeks after the night at Charlie's, subtly, at first. It was not that unusual for Cora and Mike to bicker in front of Stevie and me . Mike in his enthusiastic, often boisterous way, was always making a mistake or doing something to trigger Cora's disapproval, though it was never anything very serious.

Usually she projected her displeasure with raised eyebrows and 'looks' and the pointed pronunciation of his name in a firm tone. This technique reminded me of how adults discipline children, or maybe a young dog, in a half-cajoling, half-threatening voice, that promises worse to come if bad behaviour continues or does not improve. She had used it long before she actually became a teacher. She was a natural. At first I had not found it particularly annoying.

Mike always took it in his stride. But in the weeks after the encounter with Jenny, Cora seemed to find more to take issue with. It was difficult to pinpoint exactly what the subject of it was except that it was uncomfortable to witness. One Thursday night, two weeks after my Wagon Wheel breakfast meeting with Mike, Stevie and I went round for dinner. We were avoiding all talk of you-know-what.

We were treated to one of Cora's mountainous Bologneses and a towering stack of garlic bread topped with sprigs of fresh basil. It was during this meal that Cora's new approach revealed itself. It started with veiled comments about the wine Mike had bought, too cheap for her tastes, about his proposed promotion, how he was always one who aimed to please, then moved on to jibes about the incorrect way he held his knife. It was nothing monumental, but there was unmistakable tension in the room.

They had both been over-solicitous when Stevie and I arrived, the way couples tend to be when they've had a row right before you knock at the door but are determined not to show it by being anything other than perfectly good-natured and excessively charming.

Mike was playing tactically by being soothing and attentive, and I must say, I admired his commitment. He was dedicated. Nobody mentioned Charlie's or Jenny and on one level the conversation revolved around the dining table from work to the cinema to the perils of parking in the city centre. All safe territory.

But their body language had changed. Usually they were to be found twined around each other on the settee, snuggling at the kitchen sink, wiping imaginary smudges of dirt from each other's brows in an absent-minded yet oddly reverential way. That night Cora was seated at one end of the glass rectangular dinner table, Mike at the other, a crackle of tension evident in her upright back and elongated neck, in the stubborn set of her mouth when speaking to him.

Mike seemed more gangling than usual, struggling to sit up in the ramrod-backed, silvered Ikea chairs, with nowhere to rest his arms. I could see his feet kicking at each other through the edges of table top to my left as he courteously passed me bread and wine, his unruly hair, in need of a trim, haloing his face in the candlelight.

Cora's food was so good that at least it gave us a neutral subject to discuss, and her a chance to be gracious. She genuinely loved to cook, or more accurately, to feed people, to watch them eat what she had prepared with enjoyment on both sides. She was not very adventurous, but had lately branched out from old perennial favourites like toad-in-the-hole to casserole-style confections with wine and tarragon, sun dried tomatoes and rosemary. She had been the first to start watching bloody Jamie Oliver. She had all his books.

Mike always eagerly anticipated the treats she prepared, hovering around the kitchen like a child, begging for a taste until she had to feign annoyance and chase him out from beneath her feet. Then he would eat with lip-smacking relish, with extra helpings of everything. By the time the second bottle of wine was opened Mike had almost overdone the compliments to the pasta, but I thought she was beginning to soften.

Unfortunately, that was when Mike, and his lack of cutlery skills combined with three large glasses of wine, got so excitable mid-anecdote that he had to fling up his hands for emphasis, sending a globule of scarlet, sun-dried tomato sauce streaking through the air from his fork. It landed like a clot of blood on my pale blue woollen jumper.

'Oh for heaven's sake, Michael!' shouted Cora, slamming down her own glass. The fragile veneer of truce shattered at once, though Ikea's finest held firm. 'What is wrong with you?'

Mike was dashing towards me, waving a serviette, dabbing at my chest.

'Don't touch her,' shrieked Cora. 'Don't touch her with that,' she amended. 'The dye in the paper will fade the wool. You'll ruin it. Leave it alone. Come with me, Lizzy and I'll sponge it for you before the stain gets in.'

Ignoring my protestations she steered me firmly upstairs, guided me into the bedroom, pulling off my jumper with so much channelled aggression I felt like a five- year-old being hurried into my school clothes, with parental tempers fraying. I didn't have the energy to resist.

After a minimum of rummaging in her wardrobe she selected a pristine white cotton T-shirt for me, cursing Mike's clumsiness.

'Are you OK?' I demanded, trying to snatch the top from her before she could roll it back and force it over my head. 'Are you and Mike OK? What's going on?'

For someone who makes a living through words I'm not really very good at emotional advice.

'What?' she stopped short, seeming to deflate before my eyes. She looked weary. 'Of course. Of course we are OK. You know how it is sometimes. Married stuff. I'm just still so mad with him about two weeks ago. Honestly, sometimes I don't know why I put up with him.' She slumped against the dressing table, pushing her hand through her hair, releasing a wry half-laugh. 'Am I nuts? I must look like a nut. I'm just so furious.'

'Well, I don't blame you,' I conceded. 'It was a stupid, thoughtless thing to do. You can't let him off too lightly.'

'Quite'. For a moment she looked as if she was about to say something more, but she must have thought better of it, saying instead: 'You change. I'd better check the pudding and get this in to soak.' Without allowing me to say any more she dashed downstairs.

I pulled on the t-shirt which, despite my flatter chest, was too tight in the shoulders and with some difficulty, the wine making me flush with effort, stripped it off, cursing under my breath. I was in my sock feet, shoes long since removed. As I rummaged in the cupboard for a less restrictive top, something sharp dug into the sole of my foot.

Swearing, I stumbled backwards, losing my balance as my legs caught the seat of a chair with Cora's old college teddy on it, and the small cabinet beside it, sending the contents slithering to the floor. Cursing again I lifted my stabbed foot, inspecting the damage under the sock. A tiny bead of blood appeared before my fingers.

Rubbing the expensive carpet I caught a glint of something silvery. I realised it was an earring half-stuck in the deep shag pile by the cabinet leg. I picked it up and looked about for a place to deposit it. It was very like one I had bought Cora one Christmas. On the dressing table there was a small china trinket box so I popped it in there with others like it. That's when I saw Cora's wedding ring was inside.

I hadn't noticed that she wasn't wearing it. This seemed ominous and I didn't want her to know I'd seen it. I began to gather up the other nick-knacks.

The photo frame had popped its picture, a wedding shot of Mike and Cora. Not the official picture-perfect photo, just a snapshot from later in the night, both of them a bit boozy, Mike clutching her, inclined towards the camera in an impromptu kiss. But beneath it was a picture of us all. Cora's birthday. The edges trimmed down, her in that God-awful tangerine dress, Mike holding a lager in the doorway. It struck me that it hadn't been removed, just superseded and I felt a sudden surge of regret, a sobering suspicion that we were all just pretending to be these people – people who still knew and cared about each other.

I pulled on a looser T-shirt and headed downstairs. The wedding ring was not a good sign. I paused at the top step to rub the sole of my foot, spotting another dab of blood on my fingertip, afraid it would come off on the cool, cream carpet. Cora was clattering in the kitchen and by the living room door I heard Mike's hushed voice speaking to Stevie.

'For god's sake, don't let anything else slip,' he was saying. 'Don't tell her that. I've got to stick to the same story. We both have. Or she won't believe it.'

That was it. I smelled a secret, a secret of Mike's, and at once any pretence that my curiosity, rolled up into a ball and twined round with a long thread of discretion, had anything but unravelled was gone.

I felt the tug where it connected to the place right under my hammering heart, travelling on through my arm to the first finger of my right hand clutching the top of the banister – the hand that usually held my pen – the fingers first to hit the keys and start the sentence. Its target had to be Stevie.

Stevie

Secrets and Stevie don't mix well. He's one of those rare people who are basically honest and can't stomach deceit. Sometimes I find it hard to believe, but these people do exist and Stevie is one of them.

If he has to handle intrigues and untruths they sit lumpily in the pit of his stomach, threatening regurgitation against his will. He wasn't really suited to be around politicians. So after not too much effort on my part, it was Stevie who revealed that Jenny had worked in Mike's PR firm in Wrexham, had worked there for more than a year.

I'd gone around two days later to whinge to him about that dinner party, tell him how worried I was about Mike and Cora, subtly weasel around for information. After what I'd overheard on the landing I had to find what, if anything, he knew, and how, exactly, the story had to be kept straight.

Stevie offered me a thrown-together dinner after my ten am till seven shift. He made pasta with shrimps and olives and a sort of pesto dressing with fresh shavings of parmesan. There was even a bruschetta, a bottle of nice white and a tablecloth –linen with white and green squares. He's good at things like that. The details. Likes things to be just so – so much so, in fact, that I'd wondered for a while if he was gay. Then I realised he was just thoughtful.

I used to tell him that he would make someone a fantastic girlfriend. I meant it kindly. And he would sigh and look sheepish and say 'Yes, but when, Lizzy? And who?' Then his eyes would fall, he'd release a little stoic sigh and become very interested in his cutlery or whatever he was holding.

When I observed Stevie, eating his excellent meal and drinking his good wine, as we had many times before, laughing and talking and telling tales, I saw all the things about him that my mother would adore. The boyish face, the fair hair soft as a baby's, the rare but remarkable smile, the good manners. They were all things that I too adored. He was imbued with a courtliness, a gentleness that was a touch out of time, like an Edwardian duke forced to dress down in jeans and a Cardiff City football shirt.

A cravat and a pin would have suited him. I could imagine him with a cane in one hand and a copy of *The Times* in the other. He did actually read *The Times, Time Magazine* and *The Spectator*. This had seemed eccentric to the point of extremism at university, but was impressive now. And when drunk enough or lonely enough, or bored enough, I would look across at him and wonder how it would be if I kissed him, how he would feel, how he would taste. Curiosity, I suppose.

I loved his flat with its grown up furniture and boy-things, the neat, compact stereo, glamorous and black with a faint sheen of the expensive. I loved going there because it was so unlike my own flat. Cramped, half-finished, rented. I traced a finger across his bookshelves, smiling indulgently at the subject matter – *Philosophy for Beginners, The Concept of the Superman, The Russian Revolution, The Odyssey*. And just in case you thought he might be unbearable, every Terry Pratchett book ever written and a copy of *Bravo 2 Zero*.

So there I was, enjoying the pasta and drinking more wine

than I should have. After a bit of time we both said how awful it had been at the dinner with Mike and Cora.

'Who the fuck was she, anyway?' I demanded, pushing another prawn into my mouth. 'That Jenny?' This was the second time I had asked this during the evening. 'I mean who goes up to a group of people she barely knows and starts chatting like an old mate? It's weird. Do you think someone put her up to it?'

'Maybe,' said Stevie, for the second time shielding himself from the question by taking a swallow of wine. He was lying.

'I heard what you said. The other night. About 'keeping the story straight'. You two have such big mouths. What is it that Cora isn't supposed to know?'

Stevie sighed, as if he'd expected this and decided it was best to concede defeat. He set down his knife and fork, calmly and deliberately. I waited. You couldn't ambush Stevie, he had to be handled with a certain circumspection.

'Can't we leave it alone, Lizzy? You know Mike asked me not to say anything.'

I just looked at him with my practised, expressionless face, neither reproachful nor approving and said nothing. I use it regularly in my job. It encourages people to speak, because they are expected to. They need to fill the gap, the gap between me and them and the silence that spans it because that is human nature. Fill in the blanks, the spaces, the gaps, fill them with words, even if it means saying something you don't want to.

After about six seconds he sighed again. 'Mike did know her, a bit, nothing serious, like. He said he met her at some PR do in Chester. She put him on to a few contracts. Nothing more. I think she came over to see him once or twice at the office. Got a bit of a thing for him. Been a bit over-keen, won't take no for an answer. Got the impression that might have had something to do with their move back here. Nip it in the bud, you know. Mike didn't say a great deal. Then she moved down here not long ago for a promotion with a different department.

Stupid bugger didn't want to hurt her feelings and cut her dead, straight off. Didn't exactly invite her that night but told her we'd be out at Charlie's. You know how he is. I think she was a bit lonely. He didn't want to tell Cora he'd told her where we'd be, or say he'd had some girl chasing after him back up in Wrexham who'd now turned up. She'd have gone into one of her sulks, read all sorts of things into it. Well, you can see why she might not have been pleased. I didn't know myself until after you came back from the loos. Quite liked her myself, actually. Bloody typical, isn't it?' He made a 'humph' sound which said he was used to it. 'The ones I want are always looking elsewhere.'

When he could see I had chosen to ignore this remark he picked up his cutlery and resumed eating.

Now that Stevie had said it, an image jolted into the front of my brain, a latent memory. It had been about two weeks before that night at Charlie's. Half-dozing in the Costa Coffee near the railway station, I was nursing my mocha with cream, upstairs among the feverish click-clack typing of internet users, watching people down below on foot and in cars jumping the traffic lights, darting and accelerating. I was willing myself and every muscle in my body to find the energy to return to the newsroom and get through the rest of the day.

Just as I was mentally rehearsing my excuse for taking a long lunch, a grimy double-decker bus rounded the corner from Mary Street towards the Central Station. On the top deck, alongside a few cosy-looking couples steadfastly ignoring a generic shaven-headed weirdo in a hooded khaki anorak, was Mike and a woman.

I was sure it was Mike, even though I only really saw the profile of his face and the kick of his hair around the back of his neck, against the light of the windows on the other side. His face was turned half away. But I would know him anywhere.

What startled me was that there was a girl opposite him, also in profile, twisted towards the aisle. She was wearing a colourful, stripy woolly hat with what looked like spiky bits of hair poking out of the bottom, leaning in towards him as if she knew him well, intimately. I could not see below the window line but it seemed only right that her hand would be on his knee there. More than a colleague perhaps?

His arm was stretched out along the length of the window, fingers drumming soundlessly on the frame. I got the impression she was speaking, though I couldn't see her mouth properly, and he was listening. It lasted maybe eight seconds, then the lights were green and as my head snapped around a fraction slower than my mind the bus pulled around the corner and away.

Then, the very next day I'd gone to a media briefing at a dull medical conference at the Park Thistle Hotel, rooting about for stories, and, thinking about it, Jenny had been one of the girls handing out the plastic ID badges, hadn't she? She'd looked different from the Jenny we'd seen at the club, unremarkable, like one hundred other graduates. I vaguely recalled an ill-fitting, cheap grey suit, hair scraped back in a take-me-seriously city pony tail. Could that have been her? Renquist PR – that would fit. They were part of Jacksons. That would explain why I thought I'd half-recognised her at Charlie's, I'd just had no context to put her in.

So he'd wanted to keep her away from Cora that night so she wouldn't say something out of line. Could it be that simple? That innocent? Good old Stevie. He had made me feel so much better. That's all there was to it. Some stupid girl with a crush, pushing herself forward.

'But don't tell,' Stevie insisted. 'He told me to keep to the same story.'

Typical Mike. So he'd been like a human limpet in the club because he didn't want Jenny to let it slip that they knew each other from Wrexham. Not because he was smitten with her. Quite the reverse. She must have recognised us and decided to come over. Maybe Mike had a picture of Cora and another of all of us at the office. That explained the greetings. Simple elimination. No doubt he'd talk about us at work occasionally too.

I felt relieved. For a few seconds. 'The stupid idiot,' I laughed. 'Why didn't he just introduce her and tell Cora? That would have seemed a lot less suspicious than hanging on her every word.'

'Well maybe, I dunno. Not if Cora's been suspicious already and this girl's a bit of a handful.'

Then I remembered something else. 'But he was out all bloody night Stevie. He wasn't by his bloody self.'

'He was at Gabe's,' he said. 'Anyway, why should you care so much?'

'Cora's my friend,' I retorted quickly.

'Yes, she's mine too. Well, that's all I know, Sherlock,' he said. And refused to be drawn further.

There was something in his face that said he was holding back, or at least didn't quite believe this story either, but how could he be anything but loyal to Mike? Then I didn't feel so good again. That's the trouble with questions: the more you ask the more you end up with.

Gabriel

I shouldn't have gone to Gabe's. I realise that. I shouldn't have started to dig. I should've gone home and forgotten about it. I should have said to myself, 'Leave it alone, Liz. This is none of your business.'

I suppose I could excuse myself by saying that it's part of my job to chase the answers, find the facts and get them straight, iron them smooth, as seamless as possible – leaving myself just a little leeway for artistic colour. But it wasn't that. By the time I left Stevie's, convinced he was holding something back, I just wanted to know where Mike had really been so badly I could taste it, like blood in my mouth.

Gabe, forever the 18-year-old. Gabe, who would be forty and still dress and act like he was in a teenage rock band. Mild-mannered photocopier salesman making a dispiriting mint of money by day, but by night, intrepid air-guitar player, spending a packet on beers and trips round the country to rock festivals – an early mid-life crisis at not quite 30. I rang the doorbell wondering if he would still be sporting that terrible curly mullet. I was relieved to see it had been replaced by a passable spiky crop.

His flat, though, was in an atrocious state. That is the one thing I did not miss about shared student houses. Neither of his three flatmates were students any more, of course, but they had that air of domestic incompetence, of being away from home and their mums for the first time, so all their clothes were only half-ironed and their hair a bit too long. A junior banking assistant, a factory administrator and Gabe. Three bedrooms off a single hallway, kitchen at one end, a shadowy realm of perilously stacked plates and cold mugs of coffee and don't even think about what might be in the fridge.

Just inside the front door was a large living room with two enormous sofas draped in faded throw rugs, adrift on a sea of *Loaded, NME, FHM* and car enthusiast magazines. A large wilting palm was sharing its pot with a one- armed action man, bravely toting a rifle.

Gabe, unfailingly polite as ever, had been embarrassed and flattered to see me on the doorstep. He invited me in without hesitation but hovered near the threshold. We weren't really friends any more, but if spotted across the pub he might come over for a drink before I decided I had to be somewhere else and made a quick getaway. He was still in mild-mannered mode, shirt and trousers, from the office, though he'd removed his tie and shoes.

He must have been baffled to see me as I had never in my life called on him alone, not even when we were at university and he'd lived in a similar flat above the Thai takeaway. I had merely passed across his field of vision now and again with Mike and Cora, on the way to better places, better friends.

'Did Mike leave his jacket here?' I knew I was getting to the point rather too hastily but I was trying to ignore the faint whiff of damp sports kit that was emanating from somewhere nearby.

'When?' he asked, confused, wary and bashful all at once. He reminded me of the shy teenage cousin I had never had but could imagine in detail. I don't think he'd ever had a proper girlfriend. He still had the hole in his left earlobe where he'd once worn a little crucifix dropper. But that would certainly not have been U Copy salesman regulation wear.

'Two weeks ago, you know, international night, when he crashed with you?' I gave him a bright, brisk smile.

'No, he didn't. I mean he didn't leave his jacket here. I don't think he did.' Gabe gazed around as if he expected to see a jacket materialise in front of him.

'But he did crash with you after the rugby?'

'Yep, of course, yep. He was in the spare room.'

'Well, could you check for his jacket? I mean, to save him coming back for it later? Since I was passing.'

'Passing? Through here?'

'Yeah. Work.' That's usually a sufficient explanation.

'Sure,' he said, glancing around, as if wondering where among the shambles a jacket might live unnoticed. 'Come right in. Sit down for a mo?' I was still hovering half in, half out of the living room door.

'Ummm. Can't really stop.'

'I'll check if he threw it in the small bedroom or something. Hang on.'

I stood patiently but he was back in half a minute. The jacket wasn't there. Anywhere.

'Oh well, another one eaten by the club cloakroom no doubt,' I mused. 'Must've been some party here, then.'

'It's nice to see you again, Lizzy.'

'What time did Mike arrive then?' He looked blank.

'Dunno really. I was pretty wrecked that night actually. You know how it is. Always glad to see Mike though. Good bloke, Mike. Always got time for Mike. He got me some free gig tickets for the stadium a while back, through his PR thing. I never even had to ask him. Over a hundred quids worth just 'cos he knew I wanted to go. A top bloke.'

'Oh, yeah. Top. So Stevie stayed over too then? Said it was one of your best bashes,' I continued, knowing this wasn't part of the story. I ask questions for a living so there are very few I feel to be too nosy.

'Oh yes. I think so. Like I said, I was pretty out of it. Guess they crashed in the back together.'

'What time did they leave?'

'Dunno, Lizzy. I was asleep until about midday. You know how it is. Still rock'n'roll – though more roll than rock these days eh?' he said, patting his thickening waistline. 'Not you, obviously. You look really good, Liz. I just boiled the kettle. Do you want a cuppa or something?'

Thinking the 'something' was likely to be botulism, and being unable to extract anything more of use, I declined politely and left him hanging, still faintly baffled, over the twisted wooden banister, watching me leave.

'Good to see you again, Lizzy. Come for a coffee some time if you're passing again.'

'Thanks, Gabe,' I called as I raised a hand at him from the foot of the stairs.

Tug, tug. Bits were unravelling.

Cora

'I can't bear it,' she said again. 'I can't bear it. The thought of him having sex with someone else, with anyone else, let alone her. It cuts through me like a knife every minute of the day. It's made me crazy. I'm crazy, not like myself. I just don't know what to say to him now, what to do. I don't know who he is anymore. Who *I* am.'

Cora was in monologue mode. I let her run on. I wasn't really supposed to answer these questions. I knew that. I wasn't sure what had brought this on. I thought everything had sidled back to normal.

It had been a month since what was initially referred to as their big-bust up, but later became known only as 'That Night,' said in hushed and nervous tones. Calling it anything else became superfluous, since each of us knew exactly which night we meant. There was only really one night now.

I had endured one more silent treatment-veering-towards-hysteria dinner with Mike and Cora before, slowly, the air had warmed again, breathing became easier and it seemed all was forgiven. I suspect Mike was feeling he had got off lightly and I noticed he was paying extra little frivolous attentions to Cora whenever we were all together.

So when Cora launched into her tirade about Mike's

phantom infidelity while we were at Bar Europa having lunch, I felt my heart deflate a little. Technically, *I* was having lunch, tucking into a char-grilled chicken melt with a generous blob of sweet onion chutney. Cora was simply breaking the lumps of tuna in her salad niçoise into ever smaller flakes, spearing the seeds from the tomato slices and knocking back her second large glass of house white with great determination.

I still didn't know any more about 'that Jenny' and I was getting impatient that Cora was continuing to stew about her.

I heaved an inaudible sigh and tried to be reassuring. 'Cora, not this again? You don't really think he slept with that Jenny do you? Come on now.' I kept my voice calm and measured, hoping it would rub off on her. 'I mean, you do trust him and he's not stupid enough to risk everything for a one-night stand with some tart. Be realistic. You know how useless Mike can be. It was just one of his typical cloth-head balls-ups. You don't really believe this, Cora. I know you don't.' So snap out of it for fuck's sake, I added in my head. 'Don't you think you should slow down a bit?' I suggested, gesturing to the almost empty wine glass with a lettuce-loaded fork.

But she was gazing out on to the high street, to the shoppers bundled and bagged against the sharp wind slicing down Queen Street. Though it was lunchtime it seemed dark enough to be evening in that hinterland of late November, as the braids of Christmas lights go up, chasing back the winter gloom. Bar Europa was cosy despite the outsize glass windows replacing one wall, filled with comfy leather sofas. The wooden floor and wood-panelled bar seemed to glow beneath the low wall lights, the day's newspapers soaking up the heat and breath of the diners, the white-aproned staff moving efficiently through the minefield of feet and loaded carrier bags. It would soon be Christmas. I wanted to feel festive.

In the old days Cora and I had always done something special for Christmas. Decorating the tree and the house had been something of a ritual. In our second Uni year Cora made a full Christmas dinner, eaten under a sprinkling of fairy lights, their tacky, lovely gleam reflecting from the tinsel and baubles dangling over the dining table.

The lights had been bought on the cheap from the Hyper Value in town, all we could really afford. The veg were cheaper still, from the outdoor market, served to us loudly by the blustering stall-keepers, maintaining an endless patter in-between blowing on their raw cold hands and swishing the food into plastic bags. But Cora had worked miracles with a turkey roll and even the £1.99 white bubbly we drank took on a more refined air, served at her table.

One late December morning I walked into the living room to find an oddly silent Cora standing guiltily next to the Christmas tree. It took me a few seconds to notice her hamster cheeks and the distinct absence of the six chocolate reindeer we had strung on the branches minutes before. Brown juice trickled out of the corner of her mouth as she burst out laughing.

With this happier, sillier Cora in mind I realised I was actually looking forward to Christmas, to decorating and gift buying. But Cora was only interested in one topic of conversation. She was spoiling the festive mood. I wondered when I had started to become so impatient with her.

'We've been together ten years. Ten years,' she mused for the second time in as many minutes, breaking my reverie in half. I sighed audibly this time and in defeat ordered another large glass of house red from the nearest waitress.

'You don't know what it's like, Lizzy,' she picked up. 'You can't know what it's like. We've grown up together. Been everything to each other. I know he's lying. I always know. I can always tell he's keeping something from me. He must think I'm stupid. You don't know how that can make you feel, what it can make you do.'

'Then why don't you ask him outright, Cora? I mean, you do have a right to know.'

'Why should I have to?' she countered, her gaze sliding back to me. 'Why should I need to ask? If I trust him? But I have and he says nothing happened.'

'Well, then you either believe him or you take a break – see how you feel about each other.' Shock tactic! I knew it would work.

'Leave him?' She looked astonished. 'Leave him? He's my husband. I could never leave him. I'd do anything for him, give him anything.'

Out of the blue I thought, *maybe that's the trouble, maybe he knows it.* But instead, I told her, 'And he'd do anything for you, Cora. So get a grip.'

'Did he say anything to you?' she asked warily.

'Like what?'

'About it. I know he thinks the world of you, Lizzy. Did he confide in you?'

'Cora, if I knew anything I would tell you,' I said, making my eyes very big and the rest of my face very steady. It was a foolproof expression, telegraphing the hurt I should have felt at my best friend doubting me. 'Why would I lie to you about something like that? I don't think there's anything to tell.'

That much was true. After my trip to Gabe's, my ferreting had yielded nothing more.

'You. The two of you,' Cora stuttered, leaning in confidentially and looking away across the heaving room as if she expected to see Mike peering out from behind one of the embossed menus in surveillance mode.

'I bet he tells you lots of things. I'm paranoid. I'm jealous. He would tell you, Lizzy.' I looked as aghast as I could.

'He has never said anything of the sort,' I said mustering up my best disgusted face. Though he had, on occasion, lamented to me about her when they'd had rows or disagreements.

'What else does he tell you?' she demanded.

'Cora,' I cut in sternly, unwilling to play any more on such treacherous ground. This was going to get us nowhere. 'I don't believe he slept with that Jenny. I think you need to give him another chance. It was a stupid mix-up. Put it behind you. Please? You've got so much together, so much to save. Don't throw it away because of doubt and all this nonsense. I know he loves you to death.'

She grinned wryly. 'Yes. I suppose he does.' She was placated

'Good. I replied. Now please eat something or I'll have to carry you home.'

It wasn't that difficult to put Jenny out of our minds, with Christmas bearing down upon us. We had such a great time at the winter fair a week later that I was sure everything was as it should be again, and would be forever.

We had bundled up ridiculously warm and I was grateful for the little pink woolly hat Cora had bought me, because she couldn't resist a bargain and, perhaps as a guilty sop to the ruined lunch. We had huddled around the outdoor heaters in the courtyard of coffee stalls and hotdog sellers, drinking steaming sweet cappuccinos from paper cups, muffled in woolly hands, taking the piss out of Stevie's rather shorn, new, spiky hair cut, pretending he was developing a beer belly.

I was enjoying the severity of the cold, its cleanness, its ability to sweep away any invisible ills clinging to us, knotted together against the theatre-like backdrop of the white dome and carved pillars of the illuminated façade of City Hall. Its fluted spires and crenulations rippled like a carved ice palace in the glancing fairground lights, against the black back-scenery of the December sky. Cora was in good spirits, in the same woolly hat but in dark green, and an enormous faux Russian revolution greatcoat that swamped her to the tips of her toes. She looked bright-eyed and relaxed for once and Mike was making an extra fuss of her, tipping me the odd smile that could have thawed the glassy sheet of the ice rink and sent the skaters plunging into the ornamental pond beneath.

Stevie was beaming and bought everyone chocolate muffins. I wanted to skate but not alone. And as neither Stevie nor Cora could, Mike obliged. It was far too crowded to do much more than slide along with the throng and in that anonymous mass it was good to feel his hand in mine. Though I could not feel his skin, I thought I felt the pulse of his blood. Flushed faces spun in and out as we wobbled and weaved in circles, while Cora watched and Stevie whooped from the sideline until we were breathless.

What could have been better, except the hours afterwards, sitting in the bread-scented Italian restaurant gobbling pizza, our fingers glistening with grease, getting drunk together? Sod Jenny, she couldn't interfere with this, spoil this, I thought.

Christmas slid in and on – each of us slipping back to our family homes for dinner on the big day and filling the time with the usual round of office parties. Mercifully, I missed mine as I was working the late shift on the designated night. I worked most of the holidays, or what students had started to call *the vacation* with no sense of irony, including Boxing Day and New Year's Eve until 9pm and New Year's day until 11pm.

Exhausted, I spent the last gasp of New Year's Eve with my mate Luce from journo training, who'd happened to fetch up for a spell on the short lived *Welsh Mirror*, in her house in Canton, drunk on red wine.

Then it was January. Jenny was back. And she was dead.

After

As I sat on the hard, wooden bench outside the opening of the inquest into Jenny's death I felt a blankness I had never yet known, gripped by an inability to think, to move in any one direction. How is it possible to be so full of words you dare not speak one? They were rattling about inside my ribcage, trapped below my voice box, my conscience throwing stones. I was afraid someone might speak to me, in case they noticed the blankness in my face or somehow heard the brittle bombardment within, even above the sound of the rain drumming on the roof .

I was steeling myself to move when the good-looking policeman with the cropped dark hair I'd noticed in the courtroom appeared a few feet away. He was carrying his hat. After putting it on and straightening his tunic, he spotted me perched near the door in the draught sweeping up the cement steps from the deserted road. The drunks and car tax dodgers had sloped away long since. It was nearly lunchtime.

He looked uncomfortable and I looked at the floor. I had no intention of catching his eye. But I saw his feet when, after a moment's hesitation, he stopped in front of me and I had to raise my head from my hands to meet his gaze.

'I'm sorry,' he said. The first, last and worst platitude spoken by people who don't know what else to say, when fear of other peoples' grief has robbed them of their sincerity, their originality. I had approached families in the same position often enough, always sympathetic, enquiring, understanding, but never 'sorry' nor saying it. It would have been one step too far. But somehow, when he said it, it seemed more truthful than when I had heard it before.

He smiled weakly, plucking his hat from his head adding, 'I saw you in there. Such a shame,' with kind eyes. 'Were you a friend?'

'Not really,' I answered. 'I'm a journalist.'

Jenny's body had been found in the river three months after she had been reported missing. She was discovered, as such unfortunate individuals usually are, by an elderly man walking a terrier along the riverbank early one morning. She was tangled up in a fallen tree that had also caught all sorts of rubbish like plastic bags and, of course, a shopping trolley, her body bobbing in the swollen winter water.

The old man, who didn't want to be identified but was actually Thom Thomas, don't forget the 'h', aged 82, of Welby Road, Canton, who lived alone and had one daughter, wasn't even sure it was a body at first. But Princey had known. Barked and barked, he did. Mr Thomas, sprightly and pragmatic for his age, had found a long stick on the water's edge and leaned out as far as he dared on the slippery, shoe- sliding banking to give Jenny a couple of curious prods.

Though 82 you know, and prone to a bit of arthritis, Mr Thomas's investigation was energetic enough to make her hand bob up and down in the water a few times as if she were waving at him. That's what he said in the quote. Naturally, Mr Thomas had whipped out his mobile phone then and there – this was, after all, the 21st century – and called the police, waiting with Princey until the uniforms arrived.

She was in a terrible state of course, in the water for all that time, blackened and bruised by the fast flowing current, bloated and discoloured. He wasn't sick. He'd seen worse back in the war, you know. But he admitted he had felt pretty close to becoming suddenly reacquainted with his high fibre Bran Flakes and the orange juice his daughter-in-law force-feeds him to combat his cholesterol.

I didn't put any of that in the paper, obviously, the stuff about her being bloated and discoloured I mean, or his breakfast. It would have been too lurid for the readers. We weren't that kind of newspaper.

Jenny was fully clothed, even to her leather jacket, wearing her watch and a gold bracelet embedded deep in the sagging flesh and one gold earring in the shape of a star that the deft, chilly fingers of the current had failed to unhook from an almost unrecognisable ear. Only her red hair , scarlet, pulsed with the eddies of the water. I mean, I imagine it did. I got the details on the quiet from the coroner's clerk. I didn't see her. Her body.

I hadn't realised it was Jenny when the press appeal for information came through. It was a Sunday. I'd pulled the weekend shift and it had been a slow news day, the newsroom air and the skeleton staff sluggish and muted. Slow news day. That's what journalists say when there's nothing of interest but a few petty muggings, suicides and non-fatal car pile ups clogging the news wires. Time dozed by and the phones were silent. So much for the cut and thrust of the newsroom. No chance of ITN or Newsnight head-hunting me at this rate.

Deadline was hours away and I was twiddling my thumbs at my desk, under the frown-inducing fluorescent strip, drinking another cup of plastic-tinged coffee from the machine, leafing through *The Mirror* to find a story to lift, meaning steal/ make relevant/ 'Welshify', thinking about what I would like for lunch.

Just when I thought I might make it through a whole morning in peace, the dreaded Owain, senior-editor, burst through the newsroom doors, head clamped to a mobile phone, black coffee swilling in a paper cup clawed in one hand, police press bulletin in the other, charging towards me in a haze of expletives. Owain, and that's Ow-wine not O*wen*, did not wear red twangy braces, but he should have. He had everything else befitting a slightly pathetic throwback to his heyday in the 1980s – the slick-bordering-on-greasy hair, the slightly florid colour suggesting blood pressure on the boil, a dark pinstriped suit, impeccably cut and an un-impeccable paunch, hanging over the top of an Italian leather belt.

He had died in 1987, been embalmed and loosed upon us for eternity, vulgar with self-importance, reeking of Kouros. The word 'swaggering', or 'buffoon', might have been invented for Owain. Mostly, the reporters just referred to him as *that prick*.

Seeing him I instinctively ducked behind my monitor, pretending to be searching for an invisible but vital something near the empty wastepaper basket while he yelled something about possibly having to *'Stop the Press'* into his mobile phone. Yes, in addition to his *Wall Street* fixation, Owain had also watched one too many of those American films about frantic yet endearing newspaper hacks and was living the dream. There was only one problem. We were in Wales. And he couldn't write for shit. And he probably couldn't even spell shit. Ow-wine would have to say shite.

Most of the reporters hated him, partly for being wealthy and well-spoken, and partly because he only got his job because his daddy was a prominent West Walian councillor and then an MP. Everyone knew this, and he knew they knew, which was the only real cloud on his *Hold the Front Page* horizon. Still, he could talk the talk, even if he couldn't write the sentence. And he liked to talk. A lot.

'Then get the fucking photographer there now,' he yelled with obvious relish, punctuated with an explosion of saliva.

Since it was a mobile, and a little one at that, he couldn't slam the phone down but he ostentatiously flicked the handset closed as he took it from his head, hovering over my desk waiting for me to sit up.

'Lizzy, just the girl,' he boomed, planting himself aggressively on the desk corner, crotch aired between his spread legs. In his delusional, spittle-lubed, high- decibel world we had a sort of *His Girl Friday* dynamic going on. In his world my indifference, contempt and occasional open rudeness was merely banter fired by the obviously sublimated sexual tension. As I said, he was a real arsehole. I was waiting for the day he laid a hand on me or made a pass in the pub: then I'd crucify him.

'You look pretty damn radiant today, Lizzy,' he bellowed, though he was less than three feet away, grinning. 'Very nice blouse. This is ideal for you: from those wankers at the police press office. Some young girl found in the river. Basic bollocks but it's so dead these days we need something to pep the front few pages up. Bet there's a good human interest story there if nothing else. Pensioner found her. Some old twat walking a corgi as usual but if he's fairly compos I bet he'll give all the gory details to you, blue-eyes.'

I sighed audibly. He ignored me. 'And get on to your pet Sergeant thingy at Central station and get a name if you can. Course there'll be no formal ID yet but we can move on the family as soon as, yes? Get a cute picture, yes? If she's pretty we can lead with it on page three. If she's a dog we'll run without. If it's a sex thing, kinky and suspicious, we'll lead on the front, yes? You're good at this. People will tell you anything. Get me a nice juicy splash, kid.'

I stared at him with undisguised disgust, as much for the number of clichés he'd crammed into those by-the-book instructions as the lack of sentiment they expressed. Plucking the paper from his chubby hand, scanning it, looking as bored as possible, I asked.

'Which bit of town?' I hated to let Owain think I was even vaguely intrigued by anything he thought was a hot story. It undermined his judgement.

'Down from the stadium somewhere – find out.'

'How old's the old geezer?'

'About 100.'

'How old's the girl?'

'20s. That's all they said.'

'Rape?'

'Dunno.'

'Reported missing when?'

'Dunno?'

'Great story, Owain.'

'Well get on the phone and find out. Chop, chop – want it in by 2pm, that's what I pay you for.'

'You don't pay me half enough you tosser,' I mumbled under my breath, then flashed my most brilliant smile, as he turned to harangue someone else.

I got on the phone and did the ring-around thing, coppers, ambulance, local councillor, local colour, spoke to Mr Thomas and Princey, then wrote the story. There was no formal ID and no name released, so for three weeks I went about my job as usual without being any the wiser, without ever realising that my life as I knew it was beginning to be over.

Jenny did not become very newsworthy until she was named. Initially there was no media fuss. This wasn't surprising. There'd been an original appeal about a missing girl called Jenny Morgan before Christmas but few papers had run it. People go missing every day. They usually turn up of their own accord.

This Jenny, it seemed, was nothing special, no one significant. She had not been in Cardiff long enough to have friends to miss her or gossip about her, speak to journalists, make pleas or speculate. She'd only left Wrexham a few months before.

There was no lurid content to her disappearance to catch the journalists' eye and bump the story up the page. There were no heated rows with boyfriends to loosen neighbours' tongues, no flat left in a state of turmoil, no rummaged-through drawers or drug paraphernalia on display, no suspicious callers or wistful love letters. No debts. No, at first, she was not very newsworthy at all. Later, when I checked the archives, I could see Owain had buried that first story as a paragraph on page four, among all the silly-season festive nonsense.

Partly, I suspect, because some of Jenny's clothes and jewellery seemed to be missing, and she was believed to have friends in the Bristol area that she might have visited, or mentioned she might visit, (so the police press release said) no one seemed immediately concerned. But she was not with friends – she was dead alright, and had been for quite some time.

You had to question police efficiency, I thought to myself, opening the appeal and formal ID three weeks after she was found – seeing the photo for the first time. There *she* was. *That Jenny.* She was the girl in the river. I realised what the dates on the release meant at once. The last night she had been seen alive. It was the night of Charlie's. *That night.*

Suddenly she wasn't just an anonymous body any more. She was *the deceased* Jennifer Morgan. *The* Jenny. *Our* Jenny.

Now the story had human interest angles and grief-ravaged loved ones to quote. Lots of reporters wanted it. But because I'd done the story on her unidentified body being found, Owain insisted I had to write the follow-ups, with as much heart-string tugging as I could muster.

With a deafening cacophony of questions tolling in my head it was time to do my duty – the usual ring-around – bleed my police contacts and, of course, death-knock the nearest and dearest for a tribute and sob story.

I have never been so glad that the family in question were not local. At first I just picked up the phone, made sure I was speaking to the right Mrs Morgan, offered banal commiserations and then asked the customary detailed and intrusive questions.

But my stomach and brain were churning with the implications, none of them about the story that I had to write. I knew at once that we, me, Cora, Stevie and Mike had probably been some of the last people to see her alive. And, if I didn't believe Mike's version of events, someone close to me might have been the very last. He wasn't with us at the end of the night, was he?

The police were now making a concerted appeal for information and perhaps we, I mean, me, Mike, Cora and Stevie, had some. But did we want anyone to know that? What would happen next? I had to talk to Mike.

I couldn't wait for my six-o-clock escape to come. Ripping through the last stack of press releases with indecent speed I was away from the office on the dot of five, waving my hand in salute at *that prick* as way down the office he opened his mouth to protest, waving a sheaf of papers accusingly.

I phoned Mike from my mobile, hidden in an alcove on the icy, echoing stairwell by the print room, where the whirring machines would mask my voice.

'We need to talk,' I said. 'Jenny. Jenny Morgan, she's dead.' There was silence on the line.

'Are you sure? Are you sure it's her?'

'Meet me from work.'

'What about Cora?'

'Don't say anything – until we've talked. It won't make the news until 10.30 anyway, if at all today. Just come. Say you have to stay on for a bit at work. Come to the pub straightaway.' I hung up before he could say anything else.

Later it occurred to me he had not asked 'Jenny who?' or seemed in the least bit surprised. I had not said 'that Jenny from work' or 'that girl from the club.' We knew who we were talking about. She had never really left us.

I met Mike in the Prince of Wales around the corner. It was early and near-empty. We hid away upstairs. I felt secretive and cautious, though we were just two friends having an after-work drink. The converted music hall-cum-theatre with its vaulted ceiling and little curtained boxes had been rescued from demolition by the Wetherspoons behemoth and turned into one of their soulless, two-for-the-price-of-one pubs, the first of its kind in Cardiff. Usually, it amused my cynical side but that day I just wished it had a juke box to drown out our voices.

'You're sure,' repeated Mike, seated across from me in his office clothes. His face fell as he saw my nod.

'Well that's a shame.' He was being deliberately – or purposefully – vague. Was he waiting for me to spell it out?

'Shame has nothing to do with it. Do you realise what this means?' I wanted him to acknowledge it, say the words. *This is trouble, Lizzy.*

'But they don't think there was anything funny about it, do they?' he responded after another long silence. 'Looks like she fell in the river, doesn't it? There's nothing much more to it, surely? Maybe we should tell the police what we know. I mean, when we saw her.'

Mentally I gaped, imagining my mouth falling open, my eyes widening to saucer size. I took a glug of wine. 'What *do* you know Mike? What do you think is worth telling them?'

'Nothing. Only that we saw her in the club for a bit then left her about 12pm.'

'Did you go to her flat, Mike?' He was startled by the directness of this, the air of demand in the question.

'No, of course not. I told you that at the time.'

'I know what you told me, but did you go to her flat? This isn't a game now. Was that Gabe thing a pile of crap, Mike? Because if it was I have to know now. No more bullshit. Was it?'

'No, I didn't go home with her.' His big imploring eyes irritated me. I wasn't about to back down. Whatever else he had to say this was it, my chance to really probe, to find out the truth using my so-called profession as leverage, an excuse to pose the questions I hadn't dared to ask before. And I had the added edge of a good reason for doing so. I launched the attack.

'Good. Then the coppers won't find anything of yours in her flat then? Hairs, fibres, fingerprints, anything else? Anything to implicate you? ' I spoke flatly, without emphasis and sat back, waiting for the response.

I was playing a slightly wild card. I wasn't sure what stage the investigation had reached or if they would be treating Jenny's death as suspicious, but Mike was clueless about all that, about procedure. The police had been very careful with the wording of the press releases so far, very neutral. All they had said was they were trying to trace her movements, she was believed to have taken a taxi to town the night of the big match, around 9pm. They were 'keeping an open mind' etc.

But that could change in the time it took to hit six keyboard keys. I didn't want to say the word *murder* in front of Mike – the word that was inevitably, even hopefully, jostling around the newsroom, coalescing into the best kind of advance headlines for the editors and subeditors with pages to fill.

It might not have been murder, probably wasn't anything of the sort, with the details so sketchy, but I wasn't about to say so to Mike. I was employing a little dramatic flourish, helped considerably by the slow drip of TV police dramas into public consciousness, to get him on the wrong foot, make his imagination leap ahead.

I could see that behind his eyes he was already concocting the worst case scenario; a picture of men in head-to-foot white uniforms scouring Jenny's flat with tweezers, evidence bags at the ready. The microscopes were being dusted off, the finger-print powder dusted on to every surface. If there was ever a time to find out the truth about 'That Night' it was now, while I had the perfect excuse.

He bit his thumbnail and sat back. Tick-tock, tick-tock, truth or lies? To give him an extra nudge I said, 'She was wearing a leather jacket when they dragged her from the river. It was yours, wasn't it?' I was guessing. The coroner's officer had said fully clothed, leather jacket, off the record. But Mike had lost his jacket That Night, the jacket that was not at Gabe's, and had not appeared anywhere else either.

'Oh fuck,' was his response.

'Tell me,' I said softly.

Now I didn't want to hear what he had to say. He shifted rigidly in his chair, took a swig of his pint, coughed. I sat immobile. Knowing when not to speak is just as important for a journalist as asking the right question.

'I did go to the flat with her,' he said. I closed my eyes. 'No, no it wasn't like that,' he insisted. His hand shot out across the table, grabbing mine around the base of my glass. 'We'd lost you. She couldn't get a cab. She was drunk, I mean really legless. I couldn't leave her in the middle of the city with all those drunks and idiots around could I? I'd lost you all anyway.' Mike the gentleman.

'I walked her back to her flat. It wasn't far. You know, just over the river. She asked me if I wanted a cup of tea.' He looked away for a second. 'I know, I know,' he said after a moment. 'Why do you think I couldn't tell you or Cora? Nothing happened. She wanted me to stay sure, I admit it, she came on strong but I said 'no way'. I just got out of there.'

'But you didn't go to Gabe's?'

'No. I wouldn't bloody stay there, you'd need anthrax jabs to risk it. I went to Stevie's. About two-ish.'

'Why the fuck didn't you say so?'

'I didn't want to get Stevie involved. You know how Cora is. She'd interrogate him. He might let something slip. How likely was she to see Gabe? And I'd already told her that's where I'd probably go when I left a message.'

'Oh, for God's sake.' I pulled my hand away. 'I know you already knew her, Mike. You knew her much better than you told me. She's from your firm in Wrexham for fuck's sake. A coincidence? What the hell has been going on? Here? There? Is this an affair? Is that why you came down here?'

'Oh God, no. Stevie told you, didn't he? I *did* know her in Wrexham a bit. We met at one of those PR buffet things. Yes, she was keen on me but there was nothing to it. She asked me for a drink once so I went along.'

I snorted. 'What the hell for?'

'I was flattered, I suppose. Networking and so on. It was just nice and friendly. But she got a bit over-keen after that. I'd told her about me and Cora from the start. She knew I was married. I saw her once or twice at a couple of dinner things. That was it, honestly. Then she came down into one of the Cardiff branches a few months ago, after we did. At first she kept making excuses to come round to the office, errands and other bollocks. Then she asked me if I wanted to go for lunch. I only said yes because I thought it might get her off my back for a bit.

We went to Canton, somewhere out of the way, good job because she was coming on really strong. Then she turned up that night, made a bee-line for you and Cora. She'd started to go on about how she wanted to meet you both. Especially you, being a journalist... and I suppose I was always saying this and that about you.'

I remembered how she'd hailed me, 'Hi *Lizzy*!', then hugged me, her arms around my neck, as if we were old friends.

'She wanted to be a journalist or a writer too,' explained Mike. 'She didn't like PR much. I think she was a bit lonely down here in the city, wanted to meet people, fancied meeting a real live journalist. I didn't know what to say.'

This all sounded too much like a statement to me, a rehearsed one. Police and journalists learn early on that most people, when telling lies, or constructing alibis, make the lies too detailed, too convincing, too neat. And Mike sounded well-prepared. As if he'd known he might need to explain.

'You obviously weren't fighting her off with a stick or anything,' I snapped back, not even trying to hide my disbelief. 'Why didn't you just tell us?'

'Because Cora had started to get paranoid about girls from work. I think Jenny called the house once or twice up there before the move and Cora answered. They were hang-ups, silent calls, but I think it might have been her. I had told Cora I was having lunch with one of the blokes from work that day I met Jenny for lunch. It just seemed easier. That night in Charlie's I thought she was going to start saying things, give Cora the wrong idea. I just wanted to keep her occupied, keep her happy. Cora can get really jealous for nothing. Jenny said if I walked her home she'd let me off. Let me off what I don't know. I couldn't just dump her there at that time of night could I? She was a troublemaker, that's all, just couldn't take no for an answer.'

'And you couldn't refuse? This is bullshit. You've had months to think up an excuse and this is the best you can do? How stupid do you think I am? I've been on the other side of this routine, you know.'

I got up to leave but Mike reached out and grabbed my wrist again, with a sudden, unexpected violence. His eyes had hardened. He looked more furious than I had ever seen him. 'It's not like that. Look, I shouldn't have humoured her from the start. I know that. She was just young and eager and yeah, I liked the fact that she seemed interested in what I had to say, asked for my advice. I should have put an end to it but I didn't. That was a stupid fucking mistake. My mistake. Sit down please.'

He was still clutching my wrist. People were glancing over. I sat down, oddly pleased and mollified by his ferocity. But I wasn't ready to let it go.

'You bet it was your mistake,' I said coolly. 'Now who knows who'll end up paying for it? Didn't you wonder why she stopped bothering you all of a sudden? Why she disappeared in the last few months?'

'I just thought she'd got the hint. I was pretty firm that night. Lost my temper a bit, to make the point.' He looked down at his hand on my wrist and released it.

'Lost your temper a bit? How much exactly?'

'No, Lizzy, nothing much, just gave her a little shake. Told her it had to stop. I'd had enough. There's nothing more to it than that. No need to make it more complicated. There's no reason for anyone else to know is there? I mean no one saw us with Jenny. There's no link to me. She was in a different office in Rhiwbina. I didn't do anything. I bet they don't know anything, or they'd have said.'

I didn't necessarily agree with this but I didn't say anything. 'You don't have to tell anyone do you?' he continued, sensing uncertainty in my silence. 'I mean you don't have to declare any sort of interest in this because you're working on it, say that you knew her?'

That hadn't actually occurred to me. Ethics could, in theory, prohibit me from writing a story if I was closely involved in it, if I had a conflict of interests. But then I wasn't involved, not really. And at least if I was covering the story I could keep up to date with what was going on. I'd have to be careful, but it could be an advantage.

'I'm not a fucking doctor or a lawyer,' I pointed out. 'It's nobody's business but ours. For now.'

'Alright, then. It's no big deal. We don't have to tell the police do we? I'm sure they'll find out where she was dropped off and what happened to her. It's not as if I can tell them anything useful. If I come forward I'll have to tell them I went to her flat, and Cora will find out. I'll never be able to convince her it was innocent. All hell will break loose. I'm not sure Cora and I can take all that, and for what? Can we just let it go? I don't know what happened to the poor girl but it's nothing to do with us. Don't make this into something it isn't, Lizzy. We are not one of your stories.'

I knew he was waiting for me to sanction this hand-washing away of all contact with Jenny. The easy approach was to sit and wait and stay silent, hoping it would all go quiet. I knew better and I should have said something then. But I also knew he was right about Cora.

'Don't say anything to the police yet,' I said eventually. 'Let's see how it goes.'

'Yes. Why make Cora fuss and worry? It's not very likely she'll even see the newspapers. She hardly ever watches the news these days anyway. It'll all blow over soon, I expect.'

'I'm writing the story, Mike. How can I say I didn't think she'd be interested? That I didn't make the connection or think it worth mentioning?'

'If she finds out, say you didn't want to worry her. You always look out for her, Lizzy. She'll understand.'

Curryman

It was the man with the curry. I recognised him after a few moments searching my mental face-files. There are reams of them stacked and racked, ready for reference. I'm usually good with faces. I have to be. Trouble is, in my line of work you speak to a dozen people a week, interview them, see them at press conferences, in the court room, at launches and events; faces on the street, in press pictures, in the dock, leaving the security vans in custody, handcuffed, half-cloaked in a coat or jumper. Sort the fraudsters from the paedophiles and don't mix up murderers with victims.

You are only interested in them at that moment because they are your story. They are the means to get your job done quickly, one more in a stream of names and faces you then reduce to words and pictures, their images archived, mentally, once the story's yesterday's news. But they remember you with a unique intensity, as you are exceptional in their existence, the person who listens and sympathises, badgers or cajoles, insists or suggests, for better or worse.

Terrible, then, is the moment you find yourself confronted by one of these faces, completely at a loss to remember anything about them. That morning, the picture interface inside my head was jumbled with mental notes from the first half of a court case involving a bus driver who'd run over a kid outside a school. I saw the man's face, began to process it, thought the word 'curry', then the word 'Mike'. He was staring at me. He was processing, too, but completed his check first and rose from the bench to walk towards me. Two seconds later it clicked behind my eyes – a flash, a snapshot. *Him.*

I was in court again for the usual Friday sessions. It was three months since Jenny's body had been identified and the meeting with Mike, and there was the Curryman, sitting in reception. Cleaner and more sober, but the man with the curry nonetheless. The man from outside Charlie's, the one who had accosted Cora as she left the cab that night. *That* Night.

As he walked towards me I instinctively altered my path into the ladies' loos, swinging my bag busily, not rushing but in an efficient hurry. It was just a gut reaction, a move away from potential trouble. I smiled calmly at the court number one usher who always helps me out with tricky address details and spelling of foreign names. Jan, with the peroxide ended hair and 'Caardiff' accent. 'Back again, lurve?' she said with a grin and a look of mock exasperation. 'We'll have to get you your own season seat at this rate. They does it for the rugby.'

I grin because Jan is nice enough and at least has no illusions about the grandeur of her profession. 'Been in with the bus guy have you, lurve? Shame about that kiddy. Loadsa scumbugs today as well, you know the usual, shoplifting, dole fraud, but not a lot else your lot would be interested in like.'

She was right. My lot would want sex, murder or violence. A combination of the three would be best or my day in court would only be worth a filler paragraph. Ordinary peoples' shame would not make even that much unless you were a bus driver who'd flattened a kid, meriting a promotion to page two or three.

I didn't want to talk to the Curryman. There'd been some coverage of Jenny's death by then, you see, by our newspaper competitors and one or two quick bulletins on the local TV news.

Jenny's Post Mortem was inconclusive, though I had been told off the record that the cause of death was very likely drowning. There were no obvious signs of violence except bruising to her thigh and her face probably caused when she went into the river, wherever that had been.

There was only so much media interest because it had been a quiet, tragedy-free spring and the photograph her mother had given the police was very glamorous, quite sexy really, sharp-cut shiny red hair, head coquettishly turned to the camera. It looked like she was at a party, though of course we'd cropped out the friend she was draped over for the sake of sensitivity.

After I'd taken as long as feasibly possible to smooth my hair in its neat clip at the nape of my neck and reapplied my uniform colour of understated pink lipstick, I assumed the Curryman would have gone. I didn't think he could really have anything to say to me. Perhaps he hadn't recognised me. I mean, that look could just have been a typical man's look. You know the kind. The stare, not of specific recognition, but of impersonal appraisal that men turn on any even vaguely pretty woman. I contended with that every day without ducking into loos.

So when I strode out of the loos I did not expect the Curryman to be hovering by the row of nicotine-dulled orange plastic chairs near the notice board. He had a definite look of lurk about him. He was not just waiting there by accident.

'I know you,' he said, as I hesitated. It was said reasonably, neutrally, but there was no uncertainty about it. It was a conversation opener, not a passing comment.

And he clearly did not intend to let me get away with a casual but hasty, 'Well, I'm here a lot.'

'Well, I'm not,' he shot back, waiting for a more definite response. He was wearing an ill-fitting suit that had seen better days and probably better owners. The grey shirt was cinched around the too-big collar with a blue and red plaid tie beneath a chin that would just about pass as clean-shaven. He'd made an attempt to tame his unruly curls with some sort of hair gel but it hadn't worked. He reeked of cheap aftershave that reminded me of using the bathroom as a child after my dad had taken a shower, Old Spice fumes watering my eyes. He was obviously up before the Magistrate for something.

I see a lot of people like him. People who have that air of the displaced, of desperation. They've made an effort for the occasion, for the clemency of the court, but they know the borrowed clothes, the ties drawn from the back of sock drawers or borrowed from dads, are years out of date. They know the attempt at neatness emphasises the helplessness that clings to them like the imprint of track suit jackets and faded anoraks they have left at home, just this once.

The people who pass judgement upon them know nothing about their lives, their loves, their humiliations. So they must stand meek as they feel, or as defiant as they can, with the weary and impatient instruments of justice gabbling away amongst themselves. I know because I came from among them once. They could be anyone because they are no one. But this *was* the Curryman.

'Saw you at the club, didn't I' he said, not asking a question. 'With your snooty friend?'

'I'm sorry, I think you must have mistaken me for someone else.' I tried to shuffle past him through the heavy double door, pleading business. The waiting area was empty but ushers and a security guard were idling nearby and there was still the clattering of washing-up and a pall of cigarette smoke coming from the coffee shop. But he blocked my way.

'Remember the tall chap too. Nice he was. Real gent. Gave me a fiver.' I blanked. I didn't know what to say. What I *wanted* to say was, 'Fuck off mate, fuck off, you pathetic piece of shit. What makes you think I have the slightest interest in anything you have to say? Life is too short and too busy to waste another three seconds of speech on you.'

But I said nothing, trying not to antagonise him more than was necessary. He saw I was startled, though, and smiled a little. At that moment I could feel fingers of slow panic begin to climb up through the tiled floor, winding around my ankles. Not wanting to give myself away further and needing to say something I said 'What club?' Pathetic. He smiled knowingly, almost pityingly, it seemed.

'Saw the girl with the red hair too. The dead one, from the paper. Good picture of her. You write that story in the paper?'

'Yes, I did,' I said, grabbing the door handle as movement returned to my legs and set them working. But he caught my handbag strap as it dangled over my shoulder, fingering it in a ruminative fashion, arresting my escape attempt.

'Thought it was you. Such a pretty face isn't easy to forget is it? I saw you here on my first appearance. They got me for drunk and disorderly again that night. Bit of bad luck that, eh? Bad night for a lot of people really. Might get stitched up if I get the Stipe this time. Bitch. But maybe you could do something about that like? As you write for the paper? Don't fancy forking out another fine or going inside.'

It didn't seem like a threat exactly. How could it? It seemed more like an opportunist enquiry. But it wasn't. I knew that even as I turned on my high-voltage smile.

'I'm afraid I just report on the courts, that's all I do,' I said apologetically. 'Just a reporter.'

'Well never mind,' he said, releasing the strap. 'I'm sure you have other uses.'

I fled. I kept my head up and my pace to a brisk, upright trot, but was still fleeing, back into the courtroom, where the bus driver was trying not to cry in the dock as he explained how he'd hit the brake, but it was too late and the kid was under his wheels. I sidled into the press seats, not hearing a word of what came after that. I knew I had not seen the last of the Curryman. I knew he would be back – I wondered what uses he would find for me.

Inside information

Two hours later I sat at my desk, so numbed by inertia that even the prospect of making a cup of tea was an event requiring a vast expenditure of energy. Every last bit of willpower I owned seemed to have seeped out of me, congealing in a sticky pool beneath my chair, thick as toffee, trapping me in my seat. The phone was only an arm's reach away, but looked vastly distant, perhaps only an hallucination, and I prayed that it wouldn't ring. Please don't ring. Everything was fragmenting. Everyone was sliding out of their familiar and allotted place. I needed to draw everything back in, to where we were all supposed to be.

I experienced these bouts of blankness every few months anyway, but with everything that had happened lately the urge to hibernate was overwhelming. I just wanted to be the hell out of there, away from the city, from the gloom and deprivation, the ringing phones, the deadlines and the dead, Jenny, the Curryman and all the other dark eddies sucking at my feet, lapping higher and higher the harder I tried to kick up and away.

As the day lengthened into evening I found I was longing, more than anything, to be back in those university halls of residence with the old Cora, curled up on her bed as the old me, broke but resourceful, watching films on her video player, eating Smarties.

Or in one of those perfectly vivid, Technicolor moments we all shared, the like of which I have never experienced since. When I belonged somewhere. With someone. When I didn't have to try so hard, every damn minute of every damn day. Where my voice and words had been my own for the first time. Where everyone knew exactly who they were and what that meant.

Like that late September day, at the start of our second year. That so perfect, so joyous-reserved-for-lottery-winners day, when we wound our way towards Worms' Head on the Gower coast. The day we went for our first road-trip to the seaside. Mike and Cora, Stevie and I, in Stevie's little white fiesta with the big radio cassette player, singing. Oasis, Elvis, Calon Lan (to take the piss), Del Amitri, Crowded House, Tom Jones, tone deaf, too high, hysterical with the spirit of adventure.

Stevie's car had sailed down the fast roads, sky above us painfully blue. It was warm inside, though you could see the first fresh fingers of a-more autumnal breeze brushing over the steel and stone stubbornness of our country's second city. The best bit came after Swansea's cement sea-front, the relief of the road over the old common, complete with cobwebby ponies grazing. Slow, fast, slow, fast, rolling in the back seat to the rhythm of the swaying country lanes. Stevie was wilfully obeying the speed limit and we were cursing him for it as the end of summer sunshine violently splashed the colours of late roses and gorse on the verges and into the fields.

Along the road, into the green tunnels and over pitted stone bridges, we took a slide back in time to dragon days, fancying the emblem of Wales might still be found stalking behind each tree, clawed feet crushing the old season flowers, releasing the smell of harvest time. With each left-right motion of the car Mike and I, sitting in the back, swing gently apart and then together, thighs brushing, right, forearms, left. I can smell his aftershave, the longer curls at the back of his head tickle the back of my neck. I know he knows this. He does not move.

I can see Cora's face in the rear view mirror. She's in front because otherwise she gets carsick, accompanying Supergrass as they sing 'We're alright', shoulders jiggling, doing a little hand jive, captured on our own private music video.

Stevie concentrates on the road where it winds, humming under his breath. An overwhelming sense of affection washes into my throat, strong and metallic. We were like this once. Always. And I love them.

We stand on the cliffs where the wind is gusting, causing the white, scything waters to surge on to the break with a knee-trembling boom.

'I love it here, at the edge of the sea,' I say, inhaling the sharp, seaweedy air.

'It's not really the sea that you love, Lizzy,' says Mike beside me, flinging out his arms theatrically and lifting his face to beg dregs of heat from the sun.

The sea is just a vast, featureless surface.' He grabs my hand and holds it aloft as I copy his stance of embracing the day. 'No, what you love, what *we* love, is the drama of where that sea meets the land. Look at that – feel that. You're not meant for a bland ideal of desert island waves kissing the shores, that romantic shit – you live in the sound and the fury, the destruction, the chaos, the immovable object meeting the unstoppable force, the stubborn cliffs and the determined breakers, the passion, the elemental struggle.'

'God, you're feeling very metaphorical today,' I mock, though my heart roars and my lungs surge with spray, 'Or should that be metaphysical?'

'Both, potentially,' he grins, swallowing the wide world with his smile. 'Either way, it's true, isn't it? Bit pretentious maybe, but true.

We have lingered in the chambers of the sea…?' he begins, leaving a question mark at the end. It is a test, a challenge. He is waiting for me to finish the line.

'By sea-girls wreathed with seaweed red and brown. 'Til human voices wake us and we drown.'

He grins with undisguised delight. A little frisson of union shivers up my spine as I see his approval. I have passed the test and completed the quote. We are of one mind for one moment. Then the connection breaks.

'I want ice cream,' puts in Stevie, from the path a few feet back from the edge.

'I want to go down on the beach,' shouts Cora. 'What are you two doing out there? You'll fall!'

'Coming, my little albatross,' shouts Mike. And we trip down to the beach along the broken path. Worms' Head rises to our left, littered with sheep and day trippers, bending in submission to the sea.'

When the wind washes the coast it is suddenly so cold that, though I am wearing gloves and a scarf, I shudder, face burning, breath deserting me. But this does not for one moment stop us shedding shoes and socks when we reach the sandy beach. The tide is in but starting to retreat. A strip of wet sand opens before us, slick and hard, so we run like fools between the shells and driftwood, around the ribs of an old fishing boat picked clean by the sea.

We strafe and swoop across the sand making exaggerated

fighter plane noises, crash-diving towards each other with flat-footed glee, breaking off at the last minute, soaring round until we cannot breathe.

Cora and I head straight for the sea, my longer legs overtaking her shorter ones near the shoreline where the waves are rushing in. Ignoring the now-genuine pain in my raw and protesting feet, we splash on and in, calf deep. For a moment all is salt, sunshine and low grey sea, our bursts of breath and nothing else.

Exhausted, we laugh and slump against one another for support, hobbling on numbed stumps to dry land.

Mike sprints towards Cora, catching her up in his arms, spinning her around in a graceful circle, his eyes fixed on mine, over her shoulder where she cannot see. 'You two are out of your minds. You'll get pneumonia.' he says. *You are both mine*, he does not say, except through the little sadness in his eyes. But Cora beams back at me for the both of them, in an endless smile. And it's alright.

Eight years later I was sitting at my newsroom desk, unsure how those four people on a cliff-top had become part of the story I was now writing about Jenny. I swigged down the last of my cooling coffee, opened my pad to my page of notes and tried to make a concerted effort to pull myself into the present and become a cool, collected journalist again, writing a cool detached story about just another dead girl.

Then the phone rang. It was a part-time filing bloke I knew at Police Central with a bit of a tip-off: CID had gone to Mike's office and asked some questions, relating to a new development in the investigation. He didn't know any more. But the young policeman who had spoken to me at Jenny's inquest did, as I learned the next day, when I bumped into him at the magistrates' court. He was unusually forthcoming for a copper. That made me a bit nervous. Normally they're reticent to say the least. And nowhere near as handsome.

It wasn't difficult to spot me sitting in the stale coffee shop, by the bacon sandwich and cup of tea for £1.99 special offer board. It was my usual seat, because it was the only one where, before the smoking ban, you could open the steamed-up sash window, let out some of the acrid cigarette air and inhale a gust of slightly fresher city air.

'How are you?' he asked, as if he genuinely wanted to know. 'The not-friend-but-journalist, right?'

Absorbed in checking and correcting my notes, I hadn't seen him come in. He was holding a tray with a limp bacon sandwich and a mug of tea on it, and what looked like a jumbo Kit Kat hiding discreetly beneath a paper napkin.

I smiled quickly. 'Busy actually. Lots on today.' Hoping he would get the point I returned to my notes. But I was rather taken with the striking blue of his eyes, a little like Mike's, perhaps, but no, Mike's were a deeper shade.

He hesitated for a moment and then sat down opposite me, wrestling slightly with the plastic chair, which gamely resisted his intrusion on my behalf.

'Big case?' He was not serious. He smiled half-playfully to show it.

'Oh yes, absolutely,' I replied with mock gravitas. 'And you too, no doubt?'

'You're still covering that girl in the river story then? I've seen your pieces.'

'I don't put those stupid headlines on you know,' I blurted. It's the usual defensive comment. People tend not to realise that what appears in the paper often bears little resemblance to what the by-lined journalist wrote, and we don't determine the presentation of the bloody pages. We leave that to fuckwit designers with a flair for cliché.

'Yes, I know,' he laughed. 'Yours have been pretty faithful though. Not too lurid. Fair play.'

Fair play? Well that's all right then. As long as you approve, my life is not worthless. I sat back, realising he wasn't going to leave any time soon and I would have to work him a bit. 'You've been visiting her office, I heard.'

'Who told you that?' his eyes narrowed. He didn't really expect me to answer, so I didn't. He toyed with his collar, one finger inside running back and forth. He was very attractive in an earnest way. Neat, shiny dark hair, the firm shoulders beneath his tunic suggesting hidden strength. Yes, quite handsome.

'Well, yes. It's no secret,' he said after a moment. 'I shouldn't really be telling you this, but we think she may have been having a fling with someone she worked with.'

I kept my eyes steady and level, with great effort stopped my fingers clamping around my tea cup, stopped my brain churning images of Mike's office, and the inevitable *suspicions* this young, cute officer would leap to if he knew what I knew.

'Oh, really? That's not uncommon is it?' I said, best bored voice on.

'No, not really.' I could feel an invisible spotlight centred on my face, its glare and brightness bleaching the room into white-out. I swallowed deep inside but didn't show it.

'Any luck?' I offered. Disinterested voice now.

'Off the record?'

(No such thing.) 'Of course.'

Pause, glance round, lean in. 'No. No one's saying anything.' Grin. My move.

Return grin, relax, show appreciation of weak joke, stroke ego. 'So how did you get the idea? Inspired policeman's hunch?'

'Well,' he shifted a bit in the seat, releasing air from the padding in an undignified burp. He glanced about as if the empty café might be sheltering hidden eavesdroppers somewhere. 'I shouldn't really be saying this.'

'You just said that,' I replied with a smile that I hoped was coaxing, encouraging and just a little bit coy. (Trust me, see my big blue eyes, trust me with your secrets, your job, your life.)

He grinned. 'You can't print this. There was a diary. In her room with entries about a bloke she was seeing. She didn't mention his name though, just referred to him as 'him'. "Spoke to him today, had coffee with him, passed him in the hallway, met for lunch."

A diary. Oh my God. Smile, you fool. I said, 'Usual office romance though. That won't be much help will it?'

'Well, you can't print this yet, but she said she was going to see *him* that night. The night she went missing, going out for a drink with *him* and some friends she knew were going to be there, in a club in town somewhere.'

My eyes must have widened a little because he looked slightly smug, pleased, and said, 'Ah yes, so you see, if they did meet up then this mystery boyfriend could be the very person we want to talk to.' He regarded me keenly. 'Don't you think?'

I had no idea why he was telling me this. Was he stupid? Did he really trust me? I wondered if he was baiting me and watching for my reaction. But my instincts said not. Oh God, of course, he was flirting, trying to impress me. That was it.

Sensing the appraisal behind my silence the smugness faded. He looked worried.

'You know you really CAN'T repeat any of that right? I'll get in shit-loads of trouble. I'm only doing some shifts with the CID in preparation for my sergeant's exam.'

'Print what?' I smile again to reassure him, before it really cracks away, on my game now that he's on the back foot. I rise, toss my head and say 'Good luck with it.' Turn for a last glance and add, 'See you around no doubt, officer.'

It has the air of an invitation hovering within it, as I intended. He could be useful. He wants to say something else but doesn't. As I walk away he watches. I know this without needing to look back. But underneath my poise and careless half-dismissal what he has said twines itself around my insides, threatening to choke me.

It was the day after this encounter that I began to think I was being followed by a police car. Paranoia feeds on itself of course, feeds on the idea that someone somewhere may know more than you'd like. Because you know more than you should. Once the switch is flicked, the energy is self-perpetuating.

It happened after court. Naturally, there are loads of panda cars at the court and I didn't pay any attention as I walked to the pool car a few streets away. I had intended to go round to Cora's. I knew Mike would be there. I'd spoken to Cora the night before about some trivial thing or other, arranging a duty dinner with her that week, though I could not have felt less like it at the time. She had told me Mike would be working from home for a day or two while the office was being repainted or rewired or something.

I wanted to tell him what the police officer had told me.

Not on the phone. Ask him if they'd questioned him at all. There was no real purpose to it except that I wanted him to worry and be uncomfortable and to feel guilty. It seemed more likely than ever now that there had been something going on between Mike and Jenny. He had either lied outright or played down her fascination. Look where his (unproven) fucking around had got him and so on. There was also the real chance that the police would make a connection.

I was parked in a depressing Victorian red brick terrace , each house perched right on the broken pavement, facing off with an identical partner opposite and chip papers and curry cartons playing idly in the gutter. It was one of those days when, even without the diary business hanging over me, I would wonder even more keenly why it was that I didn't do something useful with my life.

It was April and alarmingly hot for so early in the year. The heat wave had caught the whole city off guard in our winter-heavy suits and woolly coats and even prompted a page three lead in the paper. My hands were clammy with perspiration and I dropped my car keys not once but twice as I wrestled with the sticking door lock, the air around turning a frigid blue with violent curses, the heat of the day clinging to my slick skin.

The police car drove by as I straightened up, got in and coaxed the engine of the paper's pool car to start with further profanity. Struggling against the lack of power steering, I fought to extricate myself from the space left by some twat in a big flashy jag who had parked right up my bumper. I contemplated landing a kick on the driver's door, watching that smooth, buffed maroon skin bruise.

It startled me sometimes, this urge I had to lash out at random objects. It seemed to be my regular fall-back response to a world intent on racking me out to the extent of my patience. That morning I'd lobbed an empty coke can at next door's collie because it wouldn't stop barking. But when it came to the Jag I wasn't sure how far the CCTV reached around the court house, so I kept my feet in check.

As I approached the junction I saw the police car was stationary, not seeming to be waiting for the traffic to pass, just...waiting. As I stopped at the traffic lights a few minutes later it was still there, about two cars back. My only thought was that I would now have to religiously obey the speed limit, so I manoeuvred into the nearby garage to get a pint of milk.

It was only when I managed to pull out a few minutes later, after much edging and gesturing and beeping, that I realised the police car had pulled into a lay-by, up ahead on the right.

Sure enough, as I drove past at a law-abiding pace it pulled back into the traffic and followed. At least I was pretty sure it was following. I wondered briefly if my brake lights were out or something. Hardly anything else worked on the bloody pool car. Not only was the tank always empty (the last user was supposed to leave it at least half-full) but the windscreen wipers shrieked in all but the most torrential downpour, the gearbox rattled and throbbed and you had to pull the handbrake up about three feet to get it to catch. I cursed the car in vivid, imaginative terms, just controlling the all-too familiar urge to rain blows on the dashboard and pull off the steering wheel.

But the police car's lights did not suddenly cycle to pull me over. It just followed, a few cars back. Steadily.

I started to panic, slowly and edgily at first and then with increasing speed. It was pretty stupid. I hadn't done anything wrong. But the coffees I'd drunk to keep me awake in court were making my heart race and my head followed suit. What if somehow, someone at Mike's office had told them about Mike knowing Jenny in Wrexham? Had seen them together? Gossip alone might be enough to suggest to the police that they were not seeing the whole picture.

'Oh yes, well she was very fond of Mike you know, yes they had lunch together. No they weren't an item, well, I don't think so, but then you never know do you?'

What if they'd somehow found out that Mike and I were friends, or suspected we were friends, seen my dedicated interest in the case? I'd been to his office once or twice in the past. As I mentioned, people tend to remember me. What if they were following me right now to see if I went to see him? What if that cosy cafe chat with the PC yesterday was a plant, a test, a trick to send me running to him? See if it prompted anything? What if they thought Mike and I were having an affair?

I almost laughed at that, suddenly sick with nerves. Stupid bitch! I gave myself a solid invisible slap in the face and then another. Of course that was nonsense. It was a coincidence. I had to stop thinking like a journalist. Not everything had a tabloid angle. I certainly did not.

You probably shouldn't go to Mike's, though, said a voice in my head. So far there was nothing to link me to him, and nothing to link us to Charlie's. I wanted to keep it that way. So instead, controlling my breathing as best as I could, I mirrored, indicated and manoeuvred, with textbook precision, into the outer lane and headed back to the office. About 100 yards from the building the police car swept past.

Good Copy

I think it's only fair to say at this point that Jenny's death was good for my career. For months a big watery question mark hung over the circumstances of her demise and the surrounding mystery made for very good copy. Plenty of room for speculation. The police questioned and poked around and gathered up statements and stalled on doctor's results. And paid visits and said little and didn't seem to be getting any closer to an answer.

While they did this I was earning myself a reputation as a dogged and committed reporter. I could hardly believe it. This was something new. In the past I had remained distanced from my stories, even the good ones, the bloody ones, the dark and twisted ones, the ones that sell.

'That prick' liked to bang on about the importance of 'taking ownership' of a story, following it through, fighting for new angles and ever more unsubstantiated rumours to spread. But truth be told, half the time I couldn't be bothered. After only six months on the daily it seemed that dredging through crime and strife was more an exercise in creating news than uncovering it.

The daily bread of the weekly papers, where everyone starts out as a trainee, were not 'sexy' stories as 'that prick' would say. They were not the sort of stuff that would have BBC Foreign service banging on your door offering you jobs. But they were solid community issues, like the new bypass that would either drive shoppers from the town and local family retailers into the ground or attract developers in droves, or the struggles of pressure groups campaigning for the replacement of the drainage systems, so old and decrepit that they burst forth with faeces and sewer water every February with distasteful predictability.

At the time this was fine with me. I realised quickly that I did not want to be Kate Adie standing in a flak jacket, bullying frightened locals to talk to me from whatever war zone was fashionable in the name of bringing the news to the public. That can be done without looking picturesque and haggard in a dust-shrouded street, revealing nothing new, just spinning the same old bones until everyone is confused, a bit dizzy and under the impression they've been let in on a secret, just one they don't quite understand.

Deep down I fancied a bit of magazine work, or travel journalism, or current affairs, or perhaps the best of all, a bit of TV work, presenting or researching, something vague and glamorous with lots of holidays. Not a nine-to-five, nothing that required too much effort.

Instead, the daily newsroom staples of sex crimes and assaults, sudden deaths and child abuse, coupled with the inane surveys and features, were becoming more and more unbearable and pointless every day I clocked on.

Not to say that there hadn't been perks to liven up the tedium. In my first six months, I went to see three free performances of the Welsh National Opera on review tickets, French and Saunders at St David's Hall, and the Counting Crows and Catatonia at the Cardiff International Arena – from good seats, with warm interval wine and peanuts in the press room – money for old rope.

Mike thought this was fantastic. He was overly, overtly impressed because this was the kind of thing we liked to do anyway. I took him along to the opera a couple of times. Cora would have been bored if she had tagged along with me.

I also enjoyed two free stays at two five-star hotels, one spa package, a long weekend in Brussels and two nights in a gorgeous little coaching inn on Dartmoor.

Then there were the semi-celebrity interviews which I adored because they were so twee. I fondly remember sitting in Cardiff Homeworld drinking coffee with Lawrence Llewellyn Bowen discussing curtain tassels, asking Bargain Hunt king David Dickinson if he minded the 'Orange Lovejoy' jibes, and causing Uri Geller to lose his temper by refusing to speak about his new show planned for the Swansea pavilion, quizzing him about his mate Michael Jackson instead.

There was some fun to be had – and I had it.

But once the Jenny thing took off I dropped the external distractions and developed a new methodical approach to crime, making it pay, for me, making sure I knew exactly what was going on at any given minute of the day or night.

My zeal became noticeable in the office. I phoned the police daily to check on the status of Jenny's post-mortem, the questioning and fingerprinting. I wandered round the area and spoke to the locals, systematically badgered them for gossip under the guise of sympathy and concern. So if there was anything new, anything to link Mike, or that night at Charlie's to Jenny, I'd be the first to find out.

That prick was impressed. He would say things like, 'glad to see you're getting your teeth into this one' and 'keep up the good work' and 'you'll be running this place soon.'

'Yeah, and then I'll fire you Ow-*wine*,' I'd say with a perfect smile and he'd chuckle and chuck me on the arm in a ridiculous way reminiscent of an American high school football coach and his quarterback. I was just waiting for him to ruffle my hair so I could thump him.

I'd made a number of visits to see Jenny's flat since February, from outside at least. At first it was just part of my strategy to get a heads-up on any new information. But more and more, at odd times of the day or night when I had little to do, and the newsroom was more than I could take, I began to wander down there, along the path by the silted waters, staring at the ugly Millennium Stadium and up into the blank windows of what had been Jenny's flat. Straight into the heart of the new, unknowable, unfolding mystery story.

I would turn scenarios over in my mind about how Jenny and Mike might have gone inside, that night after Charlie's. I imagined them standing in the darkened doorway, him supporting her a little, then her inviting him upstairs, the light going on in the front window, seeing them taking their coats off, and then…..and then….

One darkening afternoon in April when the weather had returned to its customary gloom, I was mooching on the riverbank, collar up against the drizzle, cold-fingered, breath blooming before me, when I saw a battered red Vauxhall Astra pull up. The driver performed an inexpert parallel park that left more than a bit of the wing sticking out into the narrow street, and Jenny's mother, Mrs Morgan, got out.

I knew it was her from the police picture. She looked different though, as Jenny had in real life, older, and of course, tainted with that patina of grief brought about by random bouts of crying, broken sleep and unwarranted guilt.

She looked to be in her early fifties, tall and rangy with

greying black hair cropped short and severe. Her woollen coat looked expensive but her leather loafers were battered and bursting at the sole where they showed below her stonewashed jeans. She was wrestling with a couple of plastic storage boxes, obviously ready for Jenny's stuff.

I watched her for a moment or two, locking the car, balancing the crates, not at all sure I was going to approach her. But then she caught my eye as one of the crates tumbled on to the gravel. Out of instinct, I stepped across the street and bent to pick it up.

'Mrs Morgan?' I said. 'I'm Liz Jones from *The Mail*. We've spoken on the phone.'

Less than two minutes later we were standing in Jenny's flat. It had seemed perfectly natural to offer to help her with the crates so she could manage the two sets of keys she needed to get into the flat. She said she'd liked the tribute piece I'd done. At any moment I kept expecting her to say 'thank you, but I can manage now' and politely but firmly close the door in my face. But she didn't. She was a really nice woman.

It was obvious that someone was still living there. A half-eaten plate of toast and what looked like a clot of blackcurrant jam were discarded on the coffee table, on top of the weekend copy of *The Mirror*. Catching the line of my gaze, Mrs Morgan said, 'Oh that's Harriet. Nice girl, bit untidy though,' gathering it up along with mugs of tea or coffee slops and taking them through to the kitchen.

Harriet was new to me. Harriet was a flatmate and an unexpected wild card. Harriet had not been mentioned by the police. I'd assumed until then that Jenny had lived alone. I knew that a flatmate would normally have been the ideal person to get comments from, maybe a colour piece about her loved and lost friend, a touching tribute. But in this case Harriet could be big trouble.

'Do you want to see Jenny's room?' Mrs Morgan asked suddenly.

I wasn't sure if I did or not. All at once, the flat was giving me the creeps. I certainly had no right to be there and I didn't want to see anything that might breathe any more life into Jenny's spectre. Since her death I had been battling to keep the figure of Jenny that ruined our reunion, with her leather and high heels, quite perfectly separate from the 'tragic' and 'bubbly' and 'beloved daughter' Jenny, constructed by my news-speak and colourful yet sensitive prose.

Stepping into the flat was stepping over the line that took me from tabloid reality to the real thing. I knew I would now see irrefutable evidence of her true life, lipsticks lined up on a dressing table, ill-shot family pictures on the bedside cabinet, a pair of knickers hastily discarded over the arm of a chair that never made it into the washing machine.

But at the same time I was morbidly curious to see her room. To see the scene where something I didn't want to know about might have happened. Perhaps Mike had stood where I stood now, I thought, halfway between the door and the balding maroon sofa, jacket in hand as she fumbled to switch on the Ikea lamp near the window, gazing around at the homely clutter, commenting on the Nirvana *Nevermind* poster, that underwater baby, maybe whistling a few bars of 'Smells Like Teen Spirit.'

A moment's hesitation and then what?

Jenny's room was depressingly like I thought it would be. Fitted off-white MFI cupboards along the wall that had seen better days, dusty cream lightshade with tassels hanging from the ceiling, brown and white seventies flowered curtains and cheap green carpet. A round wooden kitchen table painted with untold layers of industrial white sat in the centre heaped with books and magazines.

Against the left wall, opposite the window that gave way to the street and the stadium's sharp columns spiking the sky, a double bed with a patchwork, countrified bedspread and four coloured teddy bears was squeezed. It was like every student bedroom I had ever inhabited, complete with candle stubs on the window ledge, sitting in hard pools of wax and a half-full bottle of Red Top vodka among a little gaggle of empties.

Then for some reason I wanted to cry. But how inappropriate would that have been? My sobbing and creasing and snivelling, while her mother managed to stay straight and dry-eyed, patient and upright.

'She was going to fix it up,' said Mrs Morgan. 'We'd bought some paint and everything, but there was never time. She was only here a few months, but she was determined to take on the big city. She worked so hard. The police went through everything and took away some things. I don't know what really, letters and things.'

Her gaze floated out over the roofs of the city and then back. I waited.

'I tidied it all up of course. It was a bit of a mess. And the police took the sheets for, you know, testing and things. Though as far as I knew she didn't have a boyfriend or anything.'

I knew all that.

'Someone might have been here that night. Harriet heard them talking. But she was drunk on vodka or on drugs probably,' the last phrase in hushed, exaggerated parentheses, 'and couldn't say who. She thinks a man. Said she heard a deep voice. Thinks someone, probably Jenny, went out again after a bit. Though it could have been him leaving. Why would she go out again at 2.30 in the morning? Harriet said she sometimes went to the garage for cigarettes. Cigarettes? I didn't even know she smoked.'

She said all this wistfully, as if finally realising that there were hundreds of things she did not know about her daughter, probably many that she would not want to know.

'Some of her stuff was missing, I think. Some jewellery I know she brought. Nothing expensive though, just sentimental I suppose. They've ruled out any kind of robbery thing. Guess he just took it because he could.' She looked baffled, confounded.

This is not the story of my daughter's life or her death, she is telling herself.

How did this become her story, my words, her ending? I could see it in the elastic gaze stretching out towards the real world, snapping back to this strange improvised scene she had never prepared for.

Meanwhile, out of habit I was mentally sorting it all into a news report with the hot stuff at the top, and there in the number one spot was *the* thing – *Man visited dead girl's flat*. It had to have been Mike. Who else could it have been? If I knew it the police would. That is, if they ever made a link between them, ever found out about that night at Charlie's.

I caught hold of the table and pretended that I was just examining the view out of the window as I steadied myself. Then I saw it. There was nothing suspicious about it. It was just an ordinary pen, no reason for the police to give it a second glance. But I recognised it. I had bought it. I had bought it with Cora. For Mike. For his 21st birthday.

It was resting in the pages of a copy of T.S. Eliot's collected poems, open half way through *The Lovesong of J Alfred Prufrock*. Several lines had been underscored.

'Do I dare
'Disturb the universe?
'In a minute there is time
'For decisions and revisions which a minute will reverse.'

The poem had always been mine and Mike's favourite. We'd quoted from it, finishing each other's lines, that day on the beach, several lifetimes and a death away.

I felt the wind and smelled salt for a moment before Mrs Morgan offered me a coffee.

I disliked Harriet immediately. She appeared at that moment in the open doorway. She was the sort of shifty-eyed, infuriatingly confident kind of girl I had always detested at college and would have hated to share a flat with. Clad in black leggings, black smock, too much black eyeliner and hair dyed and highlighted in every shade of black and brown.

She was at least a few stone overweight and spread herself across the settee displaying more than a couple of rolls of fat, jostling with each other beneath the smock, each time she shifted forward to tap her fag into a filched pub ashtray and flash me the tattoos winding around her wrist. The second thing she said to Mrs Morgan after the pleasantries was 'Jenny owed me £150 rent, you know, and that vodka's mine technically, can I take it?'

I could see at once where the jewellery had probably gone. And more than likely the clothes that the press release said had been taken when Jenny first went missing hadn't been taken far. She looked me up and down rather knowingly but was happy enough to tell me what little she knew. Eager, even.

She'd heard Jenny come in with someone at about 2am, heard them stumbling about a bit outside the door as if they were pissed, heard her laughing in the hall. But the delightful

Harriet had drunk about 12 bottles of Bacardi Breezer, then done some pills her mate had given her, thrown up in the bathroom and passed out on her bed. Intermittently waking, she'd heard a man's voice, a man's because it was deep, in the bedroom and later the door opening and closing, maybe a couple of times. She'd told the police. That was it.

'Will I get money for this then?' she demanded.

Good Colour

I liked the newsroom at night. The rows of empty seats squared up to the black faces of the PCs and the pulsing drone of the air conditioning leant it a strange, almost post- apocalyptic feel that appealed to me. During the day it was always drowning in the incessant clack of keyboards, the whirr of printers, the sound of the radio or the news feed and endless people, including troops of disinterested school children and only vaguely interested dignitaries, wandering or dashing through on organised visits at all hours of the day.

This stream of visitors, staring quite openly at us as they marched past our desks, prompted my ally in general cynicism, Aled, to erect a sign made from the lid of a box of photocopier paper reading 'Do Not Feed the Journalists' in bold black marker. It was propped against his PC for several months before one of the HR people happened past and had a quiet word with the editor about it.

But the general air of a chatty, overcrowded zoo dwindled at night and I liked to stroll the deserted corridors, listening to the sound of my shoes on the faded lino, peering into empty offices, sometimes borrowing stray magazines for an hour or stealing sweets from a jar or half-open packet. I would wander across the top floor, looking at the near and far night lights of the city through the silvered panes.

I was unsettled. I got the sense that perhaps I was no longer walking the corridors alone. I refused to look behind me, still sauntering along, not speeding my step, in defiance of what might have been back there, trying not to glance in the reflective panes of the fire doors and the magazine office, in its little island of glass and carpet above the humming print room.

I had gone to Jenny's funeral that day. They had taken a long time to release the body. Come, Mrs Morgan said.

'Go!' *that prick* had said. 'You'll get good inside colour stuff', so I had not resisted.

The May weather had swung back even further to the other extreme, producing a violently cold day with harsh blue skies and heatless, piercing sunshine. The funeral was not in Wrexham. Apparently Jenny's father was buried in the little Valleys' town he had never really been able to escape. The town where he had been born and the family had lived for the first 13 years of Jenny's life. It was small and depressing and ever so much more familiar than I cared to remember.

The Morgans had some family from there and a few from far away, up North. You could easily tell them apart, these people from different points of the compass. The southerners had sand-blasted faces, bleached by the weather and hard work into a uniform shape, the same jowls, same loaded brows beneath cheap, untameable spiked haircuts, above gold chains and once-good suits.

The ones from the North were polished and clean-edged, subtle lipstick and distinguished grey hair behind hearty handshakes, manicures and gluey, glottal vowels. Jenny was going back to her father's land it seemed, to lie beside him where he had lain for ten years, where Mrs Morgan no doubt wanted to go one day following husband and child into the relief of the waiting soil.

The chapel – severe, plain angles, whitewashed and picked out in dark blue – was barely peppered with people from the gallery to the narrow rear doors. Vulgar with empty seats, shivery with mourners. It sat in stately fashion at the top of a steep hill, double-lined with parked cars so the hearse had to reverse up the street, past the boarded-up greengrocers and the struggling chemist, bumping through the pot holes, making the wreath bearing Jenny's name shake and fall backwards behind the glass.

In the street the friends of family and people who had known her father, and those who had no doubt dandled the young Jenny on their knee as a child or given her sweets in the street, filed in, blowing into their hands and stamping their feet. Silently, they shook hands with the old vicar, gaunt and reedily Methodist in the best Valleys' tradition, a spark of coal fire still burning in his watery eyes.

Many of the hangers-on had just come along to be part of the official mourning, I think. Not much happened in Abersychan. In hoodies and baseball caps, grimacing with cold, defeated-looking but belligerently watchful girls were sharing a surreptitious fag on the low wall, lighting the match in hands cupped against the knifing valley wind, brown and rigid trees stretched against the high blazing hills.

They played 'Unchained Melody' – yes really – and it was awful, setting everyone off in fountains of tears, from Jenny's young cousins who had probably only met her once or twice to her two harsh-faced aunts wrapped in coats, black court shoes and an air of distaste.

Only Mrs M did not cry at all. She sat soberly while the

reverend read a few psalms, including the *The Lord Is My Shepherd* and a couple of things in Welsh.

When it was her turn to read her tribute she declined to be helped to the pulpit by the usher, spreading out a single sheet of A4 before her on the lectern and shaming them all with a steady voice. She spoke of a Jenny who had big dreams of becoming a PA to the stars, a journalist or movie critic, moving eventually to California of course, making or marrying millions by the time she was 30. This I could believe. It was what I had wanted at 18.

What I could not believe in was the Jenny who used to walk and talk and breathe along the streets of the city where I lived completely oblivious to her. I did not want to believe in a girl with an everday life, going to her nine to five job, haunting the bars and pubs and deciding to break up reunions of old friends.

More and more I was becoming a little afraid of her, despite what I'd thought of her on that single night, through a fug of jealousy and contempt. I also felt pity. The clothes, the flirtatious manner, the mean little room, the outsize dreams seemed oddly familiar. Even if this were not so, even if they were just the constructions of my mind, it seemed she had been at least a little bit in love with Mike. Even if he had told me the truth and there had been nothing going on. She had his pen in her room, just happened to like the same poem? It was becoming more and more obvious.

What had she seen in him? Well, I knew the answer to that at least. But had she wanted more than he could give? Had she followed on his heels to the city? Had she hoped he could love her if she persevered? Had she taken her hopes and beliefs and poured them into him from afar, making sure they ran into every corner, forcing them to fit where they resisted?

And what had he seen in her? He told me nothing had happened, that she was nothing, a few drinks once, a silly diversion that wouldn't take no for an answer. Five years her senior, had she made him feel younger? He had been in her flat, at the end of the night, when he ought to have been elsewhere. Maybe he'd even been there before. Perhaps this was so awful not because of the thought of Mike with Jenny, skin and breath and whispered promises. But the thought of Jenny with Mike.

There in the dark, if there had been a moment in the dark, had she thought it was a moment out of time? Did she think she knew the man she had pretended, maybe even to herself, not to lead there? Did she think she was the architect, the one with control? Before she came, if she came, did she deny to herself that she hoped there could be a next time? Before she died, however she died, did she think it would cost her nothing?

Couples

I suppose that was what I had thought. That it would cost me nothing. You see, after Mike and Cora returned to Cardiff there seemed to be many times that we, I mean Mike and I, could meet in all innocence again and it would mean nothing.

With hindsight, it was extraordinary the number of times we used to bump into each other at lunchtime or home time, while browsing through the bargain racks in HMV or pondering the merits of three-for-two offers in Boots. I was always genuinely glad to see him. Something would simultaneously lift up and constrict inside and I would feel like that first year student, seeing him for the first time. Only wondering now, if he really wanted to talk to me or was just being polite because we had once been close friends.

We were mates. Nothing more. Why should anyone think otherwise?

It's true that in our old student days, people who didn't know us had often mistaken us for a couple. When we were a foursome this confusion amused us – we liked to keep people guessing. It happened once when Stevie and I took Mike and Cora on a weekend to Tenby, Pembrokeshire. We had spent the day sprawled on the beach, spread on our colourful towels like stubborn crabs, fingers and toes dug deep in the sand. The bright boats to and from Caldey island shuttled across the bay, betraying glimpses of anoraked families huddled against the wind.

We had booked two twin rooms – girls and boys – all very seemly. While Cora and Stevie showered, Mike knocked at our door, face beaming, pink from his bath, huggable in a grey woolly jumper with saggy arms.

'Fancy helping me on the noble quest for cheap alcohol, oh great Lizzy? Stevie is taking ages.' So I grabbed my jacket with a shout at Cora over the pouring taps. And we had marched the streets, walking up close, looking for an off-licence, then, once we found one, considering the rows of shelves, counting the coins, laughing and shoving each other companionably, whispering, smiling.

While the shopkeeper was bagging up our wine and lager, I asked him if he could recommend anywhere nice to eat.

'Bit of a special occasion is it? Somewhere nice and romantic eh, for you two?' he'd said with a paternal smile, revealing a terrible set of teeth.

Mike and I grinned at each other and nodded to the man.

'Knew it right away. I could tell. For our anniversary, me and my wife always go to The Plantagenet, bit pricey but she's worth it eh?' A wink to Mike. 'You make a very handsome couple.'

We both smiled at that. It sounded nice – old fashioned. We followed his suggestion and ate in a candlelit alcove in the achingly romantic, cramped splendour of the 17th century town house.

Then, because we were sitting in pairs the staff had assumed we were two couples and Stevie and I must be one. And I pretended not to see Stevie swelling with enjoyment as the other men in the restaurant looked over, clearly wondering, by gazing just a fraction too long, how someone who appeared to be as ordinary as Stevie had managed to catch hold of someone quite like me. And to extend the joke I played with the hair at the nape of Stevie's neck as a good girlfriend might, making him blush and grin. Mike was beaming at me, throwing a wink over his scallops, while planting a kiss on Cora's neck. Priceless!

We were playing a game. It was harmless enough.

The next day we took the boat to Caldey Island, saw the Cistercian abbey, tramped the rutted tracks and admired the ruined church. Cora ate too much of the monk's special, island-made chocolate and made herself feel sick. We had cake and tea and roared with laughter when Mike said:

'How fucking Enid Blyton is this, *again*? All we need is a dog. Let's steal one for the afternoon.'

And he had succeeded in tempting a collie to play with him with the ham from his roll and then chased me across the grass, wrestling me for my last Rolo. And it seemed so natural, so uncomplicated. Cora didn't seem to mind. How could she really? She had everything else, all the other parts of him that counted, so what was wrong with me having little bits like this now and then? In plain sight.

We had been seven years apart, but once they moved back to Cardiff what could be more normal than for Mike and I to fall back into step? If Cora had to attend a parents' evening, or school play Mike and I would go the cinema together, usually to see a literary adaptation, the most innocent of all pairings. Always sitting in the darkness, not touching, just whispering and chuckling and sharing popcorn.

Afterwards we might get chips and walk home. I would be cheery when we arrived at their house and he would take me inside and call a taxi.

Cora would come sleepily from the kitchen in her designer

bath robe and make us coffee while I waited. Then we'd relate the whole film to her, highs and lows, choice bits of script, camera techniques, interrupting each other and bursting into giggles, with Mike slapping the table and saying *oh that was pure magic and you are so right, Lizzy*, his enthusiasm blazing through the room, expanding to tidal wave proportions, carrying me before it.

And Cora would smile, the perfect, patient audience. Then they would wave me into the taxi, she tucked under Mike's arm as he grinned after me, clutching his free hand to her waist as he closed the door with the other, head already tilted for a kiss.

And during those long newsroom days, with the TV and radio screaming and news lists rolling and routine police calls and press conferences and everyone bellowing into the phones at once and the crackle of the radio and the endless cycle of the news wire updating each minute, there were these renewed moments of Mike-centred brightness to look forward to.

That meant I was sometimes able to cope with the mornings I had to spend sitting in the pool car, ignoring the crumbs worked into the carpet and corners of the seat, parked up in front of a mean little terrace of houses, waiting to quiz the family of someone who'd just died an unnatural or unexpected death, knowing I had to ask for photos and tributes, drifting marooned in the Golf among a street-sea of wiry, hardy, brittle kids, battering a football with undirected aggression, thinking surely I could just pretend I had knocked the door?

I knew I could lie and say I'd tried my best to speak to the bereaved, asked why their son, daughter, husband, wife had killed themselves, how they felt two days after their father was killed in a freak road accident, what their eight-year-old had said just before the car hit her. Tell that prick I'd got nothing, that there was no story after all. But there was always a story for someone, and the endless revolutions of the newsroom clock knew no mercy.

At these times I realised I was making just a little extra effort to put on my make up, to choose my outfit, to arrange the curl of my hair. All because my friend's husband might prefer this to that. And I refused to admit that this made me sad. And I refused to think about Cora.

Friends

Let me tell you about the night it happened. Now that you can begin to really understand what it was and what it wasn't. It's important to remember that Mike was the first and only man Cora had ever slept with. That made it special, extra special, as she always insisted. Infidelity means more then, because it breaks a unique bond. Your entire adulthood, and the sexuality which defines it, is tied up in one man. No comparisons, favourable or otherwise, no between the sheets histories to hide.

So to believe he'd had sex with Jenny was the biggest blow that could rain on Cora because the expression was then reduced to just an act. Who knows what it meant then? Did it mean anything at all? He was the first man I ever had sex with too. Do you find that hard to believe? How I, we, could have been twenty years old, at university and so inexperienced? While it seemed everyone was fucking and sucking and screwing whomever they wanted when they wanted, in whatever acrobatic way they wanted, because that's what young people did? I don't know why it wasn't like that for us. I never even saw a porn mag until I was 23, or a porn film until I was 26, both times by accident.

I don't think it was prudery, maybe just lack of opportunity, or at least opportunities we wanted to grasp. Upbringing, fear of diseases beaten into us as teenagers, embarrassment, even worse, banality – romantic notions of something else and the fear of losing that? It hardly matters now. That's just how it was.

I'd never had a boyfriend at school. There'd never been anyone to arouse my interest. Besides, who wanted to date the class swot, the bookworm, the one guaranteed to get all the A's, be on the debating team, represent the school in the national quiz and get all the way to the semi-finals? The one who says little because she is afraid, not of embarrassing herself but of embarrassing you, of using a word you wouldn't understand, of seeming superior with her more refined version of your accent, with her profanity-free vocabulary, who didn't perm her hair, wear blue eyeliner, smoke, who couldn't share the spin the bottle stories, the cider party vomit boasts, who wasn't on the pill – what would have been the point?

None of that mattered when I met Cora and Mike and Stevie. No one knew anything about me other than what they saw and heard, in that minute, first hand. How often do we get the chance, not to reinvent ourselves, but quite the reverse, to reveal ourselves without restraint?

In that first year at university I could afford to be disinterested and choosy, not just pretend to be, while beneath I was bleeding and pleading. There were a few dates and dalliances, naturally. I wasn't a nun. There was that bloke from Ancient History and Tom from the rowing team with the floppy, sandy hair, taut arms and tight t- shirts. And the guy I met in the central library over Dostoyevsky, though, truth be told I'd never read any. An eclectic bunch. I was just trying to find something that suited me and not trying very hard.

Then it happened.

It happened on one of those nights out with Cora, Mike, Stevie and Tim in our final year as students. Not the night of the tangerine dress and the falling across the red sports car. But one very like it. I screwed Cora's husband when he was her fiancé, while we were all the best of friends.

If I'm brutally honest a small and silent part of me despised her for it. For letting me do it. For being so fucking tolerant. All those long months of her never minding the smiles and hugs and whirling on the dance floor and Mike holding my hand. We never hid anything. There was nothing to hide then, for either of us. But why didn't Cora ever draw a line? Why didn't she stop it short? Perhaps because, like me, guileless and stupid, she didn't see that it had to lead to anything else. It just was what it was. For itself. He and I were friends, and he and Cora lovers.

Part of me wanted what they had, of course, coveted it without ever saying the words, even to myself, that seemingly so trusting, tender, togetherness. I thought it was inviolable. I suppose a tiny part of me despised him for that too. For not being the man I imagined he was. For being just a man.

It happened because Cora would not let me walk home alone. She was always afraid of what could happen in those dark streets of Cathays, in the shadows between chip shops, kebab houses, sun bed parlours and chapels. If Tony the landlord had not been laying the mouse traps behind my bedroom skirting it could not have happened could it? Living together as we did?

But fate took a hand, or played a joke, or just dealt a wild card out of pure malice. Those mice. I was tired of their skittish feet that sounded like the talons of invisible cat-beasts scratching in the depths of the night. It was only for one night, until Tony could sort it out the following day. So I was staying with Tim in Tudor Road. He'd given me a key and I'd dropped off my night bag that afternoon.

Of course Tim got hammered and disappeared with some

dark-haired girl with heaving cleavage. His housemate Ruth was away for the weekend. I would have slept on the couch in our house but Stevie was there. I couldn't sleep in the same room with Stevie. I couldn't sleep in Cora's room with her and Mike, obviously. I could be back for breakfast.

Cora's feet hurt more than usual that night because of her new boots so she passed on the extra few minutes walk. She sent Mike to escort me that short distance, to make sure I was safe. Not Stevie, because he was the guest and had to set up the complicated camp bed he had brought. It was two in the morning, still warm and I was not as drunk as I could have been. As I ought to have been.

As we walked, Mike took my hand. To steady me, I suppose. I was not sure why, except it was something he had always done at such times. We were approaching the front door and all at once I did not know what to say, because I wanted to be inside but I did not want the part that came between, the saying goodnight. I was trying to be light-hearted about it because I was embarrassed by how warm his hand felt, by his comfortable silence as we stepped between the pavement cracks, the patterns of light cast by the orange streetlamps, as the night and the road and our lives stretched on forever.

On the doorstep I turned the key quietly so as not to disturb anyone who might be sleeping, though the place was dark with desertion. Mike was still holding my hand. I did not know how to break his grip. In a moment we were inside.

'It was a great night, wasn't it?' I said, meaning it. Because I had to speak, even if it was only to hear the most banal and normal of words signalling that this was just a banal and ordinary evening. 'Actually, it was better than great. I had a fantastic time,' and I meant it even more.

'I'm in love with you,' he said. Just that.

And we were still standing in the dark because I had not yet fumbled for the table lamp or taken off my jacket.

He was still holding my hand. His voice cracked in the gloom. I saw his face in the weakened light from the window, wracked with something that was halfway between revulsion and relief.

'Am I not supposed to say it? When you are here and you are so beautiful and so incredible? I've waited two years to touch you. Every time I see you I want it more. How can I do this? What am I to do?' he asks.

He expects an answer. He wants to be told to be strong because he was too weak to remain silent.

Suddenly I am no longer in the moment. We are not here. Not together. This is someone else's life and I can only just bear to say his name. I wish he had grabbed me, forced his lips against mine, given me the chance to resist, the excuse to be angry. But we were not those people. At once, it is not my hand that presses fingers to his lips to silence him. It is not me that pleads. Go home. Go home. Go home, before she wonders where you are.

And the other voice says: 'I do love her. You know that don't you?' and breaks off.

Someone says *we can't do anything about this* but I don't know who has spoken or what that means. It is not my face cradled in his hand and it is not his lips that press mine, desperate and unwilling but oh, so gentle.

As the warmth flows I know already what will happen, as we slide down on to the sofa among the magazines and newspapers. Wordless now in the soft darkness, breath quickening. Many streets away she waits. But she feels much closer.

'I'm so sorry,' he says.

There aren't fireworks as such. I wonder if he can tell that he's my first. He's gentle and unhurried but it's over too quickly and too slowly. We talk for a little while afterwards. He tells me of the hours spent thinking of us, and I, cradled in his arms, tell him that I do not love him.

He takes this silently, without protest, swallowing it down and digesting it wordlessly. I cannot see his eyes. My head is on his chest and I haven't the strength to look up. I mean it, but only because now I want him to leave. He knows that he has to. That he should. What has begun is already beginning to be over. Please, please go, I beg.

What in God's name will he tell her? He has been almost an hour, half a dozen streets away.

'I'll tell her I got lost,' he says. We know she will believe it. He reaches out and brushes his fingers across my cheek. He leaves and I sink to my heels with my back braced against the front door listening to his footsteps recede. I feel nothing that I should.

That was it.

Until the morning came and I felt so sick to my stomach I could have died. I slunk around the strange house in my last-night party clothes, hands never still, tidying, turning the pages of newspapers I did not want to read, channel surfing through a combination of religion, sport and post-pub youth TV. I did not want to go home. I did not want to see Cora. I feared I would look different, less like a girl, less like a friend.

About half past one, when I prayed that Mike would have disappeared back to Swansea, on the train, I kicked my feet all the way to the scene of the crime, the real crime that was about to take place. My lying to *her*. The other was no crime, I told myself. I said it over and over until it seemed to become true.

It was a small weakness, the need for acceptance, comfort, two people at the end of the night afraid to be alone and to lose the moment. There was no need to break the world apart because of it.

But what if he had told Cora? Got home, blurted it all out in a selfish bout of pathetic misplaced loyalty, shifting the blame and his own weakness sideways. I would deny it of course. Though how guilty could I look?

As I put my key in the door, feeling like a stranger breaking into someone else's home, Cora pulled it open, still in her nightie with Miss Piggy fading on the front. The image is in sharp-focus after all these years.

Her mascara from the night before rings her bloodshot eyes. For a moment I wonder if she has been crying and panic hurls itself into my throat but my face remains still. 'Alright?'

'I was sick,' she says sheepishly, picking her way back through last night's debris, collecting glasses as we head for the kitchen. 'God, what a night. The boys have gone back for the match. Want a sausage sarnie?'

I sit at the kitchen table playing with the ketchup bottle as I have a dozen times before. The garish daffodils on the plastic table cloth are very interesting, mesmerising. I am spot-lit by the sunlight arrowing through the corrugated plastic lean-to roof. Cora seems quiet or is it just me? My paranoia? We talk about drinking too much and our respective hangovers. We remark on Tim's whereabouts and state of health.

'You'll never guess what happened to Mike last night?' she says, sausage fat spitting.

And I, armed with my second glass of orange juice already, because I must do something with my hands, must respond.

'What?' I ask as expected.

'The berk I am going out with got lost on the way back from yours, pissed, of course, went all the way down City Road before he realised he was going the wrong way and ended up with a kebab. I was half ready to call the police when he staggered in at half past three.'

She is jaunty enough. But I can see that, if she accepted the story as she took him in her arms last night, she is no longer so comfortable with it. Spoken aloud it feels shaky, shored up on a weak premise, a shifting footing of an excuse. Flimsy. She looks to me for confirmation. As always.

'How did he manage that?' I say it with the usual tolerant smile we reserve for Mike's exploits, such as the time he sprained his ankle back-flipping for the benefit of the girls in the flat downstairs when we were first years, resulting in four hours at the Royal Infirmary.

Cora says she can't imagine what happened. She wants to ask me what time he left me at the house. I know she does. I see it there sitting behind her teeth on the back of her tongue. She wants to ask if we called in anywhere on the way, for chips, if I made him tea, if we talked about the night, talked a lot, talked at all. But she cannot because she recognises this implies a challenge. This is what it comes down to. What would she be suggesting? And what proof could she have? And how could she think such a thing of me?

For a moment something in the way she will not look at me makes me sure she knows. But if she did she would not be able to hide it. She would weep and demand to know all the things she has a right to know and ask why. And I could not tell her.

But, it seems she is only concentrating on not burning her bare arms and prods the sausage into the bread. She presents it on a plate and offers to put on the condiments. Cora sees only her friend's familiar, if hung-over, face. My eyes are direct as ever, the smile of gratitude one she knows well. She is reassured. We break the steaming sandwiches apart with our hands, licking the grease from our fingers and Cora begins to relate the vagaries of the drunken setting-up of Stevie's camp bed.

I nod and roll my eyes in all the appropriate places and eat, glad I do not have to speak for some time. And I know that as scared and guilty and dirty and twisted and torn as I feel, in a couple of weeks I will have got past it, over it, and it will never have happened. It will mean nothing and will no longer be worth raking over and lacerating each other with.

And I will no longer ache inside as I do now, nor down between my legs where a slow, stubborn burning sensation resides, evidence that everything has changed.

It will belong entirely to another life. A dreamy night of the dark street, still warm from the heat of the day, echoing with footsteps. And then the silent closing of a door.

Mike and I spoke of it only once, a few months later, the day before he and Cora got formally engaged. Cardiff had barely seen Mike in the eight weeks before. All at once he'd had a lot of projects, a lot of essays, a lot of football matches to play in. So Cora went there, to him – a sudden reversal of the last two years. Then Stevie had invited us to one of his pizza and plonk parties.

Mike had come down to collect Cora on the Friday lunchtime, mainly because he wanted to watch Cardiff City play some match or other at home with Tim. We would have ridden the train together, the three of us. But Cora announced she would have to join us later on, because she had to cover someone's shift in the shoe store. She was adamant we should not wait for her and waste a whole brilliant and rare sunny day. When Cora was adamantine we had learned not to waste words trying to erode her edicts. We would be company for each other on the journey, she insisted, almost as if we were children who might get into trouble if we were left to travel the 45 minutes alone.

Just before we shuddered into Swansea station Mike said:

'Are you sorry about what happened?'

We had been discussing the Swans' disastrous league performance that year. Mike and Stevie put the fanatic in the fan, or so they boasted, avidly lining the windswept crumbling mudflat of the now-vanished Vetch Field in full stripes, discussing the mascot merits of Cyril the Swan, bowling home, beer-filled and blustery, along the vast expanse of Swansea Bay.

Mike had been explaining all manner of complicated shots and goals scored, which I couldn't understand. But he was delighted by my attention because Cora always groaned at these times and told him not to be so very boring and blokeish. It seemed fine, comfortable. I half-thought I might have imagined the whole thing.

I found myself grinning and nodding, touched by his exuberance about something so pointless. As he ran out of steam, shaking his head in mock frustration, I started to gather up my bag and coat, squinting for Stevie on the grubby strip of concrete approaching.

That's when he said it, his voice soft, uncertain. *Are you sorry?*

I looked directly at his face without hiding it, studying the lines I had come to care about so much. More than ever, I wanted to kiss him. I knew the engagement ring was in his pocket. He had not shown it to me but I had seen him sneaking a look at it in its navy velvet box while I went to buy us cold drinks.

'Mike,' I said through the fist that suddenly seemed to clench around my throat.

I stretch out my hand to touch his and for a moment, there in the stifling hot, sun-strewn carriage among the chewing gum balls and misspelt graffiti, I half- glimpse another, wonderful life, where I can be adored in every second of the day, not just those fleeting stolen seconds hidden in plain view. It overwhelms me – strikes me dumb.

I know it is an illusion. I think I know him because I have watched him with her. I have seen the affection and the tolerance, the hurt in his eyes when she tells him to sit up straight and mind his table manners and stop acting the fool, his eagerness to please when she tells him how he can make her happy if he just remembers a few little things, for heaven's sake.

But in the same moment in space and time there is no room for this vision after all, because I know how Cora's heart would splinter instantly if she even thought she knew what had happened that night. And I can't do it. Sitting there, I can't pretend there is nothing between us, but I still say it:

'But there can be nothing else between us. You know that, even if you don't love her? She's my friend. It's not right.'

'But I do love her,' he says, gritting his teeth. 'It's just, she's so different from you. You let me be me and that's enough.'

I knew it was enough, but only because I had no right to expect anything from him at all. I also knew it would not be enough if I were Cora, how could it be? I could not tell him that he was weak and naïve because I wanted him then, more than ever.

'Show me the ring,' I say, instead of what I mean. Instead of anything that matters.

He shows me the ring and there is a painful flash as my

brain arcs back to the moment Cora told me Mike had proposed, right after they bought me concert tickets for the Crash Test Dummies for my 19th birthday.

Afternoons and Coffee Spoons was mine and Mike's favourite song then. If it came on the radio Mike would grab my hands, yank me to my feet and spin me into a dance. 'Bounce with me, oh beautiful Lizzy. Radiant Lizzy, in the afternoon light,' he would say. 'Let us go then you and I, When the evening is spread out against the sky.'

I did not recognise it as a quote from Prufrock at first, when we had pogoed breathlessly about the house, Cora, cross-legged near her stereo, bobbing back and forth, quite angelic, consumed by giggles. It was not until some months later I studied Eliot and I cried. Just as the Crash Test Dummies had sung, was not our love story, mine and Mike's, measured out, if not with coffee but with teaspoons?

When she handed me the tickets Cora had said, 'I have something to tell you. I know you're still getting over loser Tom but Mike and I have some news. I wanted you to be the first to know. We've got engaged.'

I was silent. I thought I was shocked because they were still so young. It seemed so sudden, so serious.

I had wanted to say something. Not just any old thing. The right thing. But I didn't.

Compelled to pick up, Cora had said, 'I know it's probably hard for you but I didn't want to keep it a secret. We haven't got a ring or anything. I mean he hasn't *actually* proposed. It's not like he could afford a ring anyway for a while, but he's going to – *at the right moment*. Make it special, you know, surprise me.'

'I'm so glad for you,' I said. Then I began to cry. Quite inexplicably. My eyes peeled open and out poured the wetness of a drowning world. It was foolish and unnecessary and humiliating. Between the sobs and the waving profusion of emergency tissues promptly pulled from Cora's sleeves I said:

'No, I'm very happy for you, I mean congratulations. I mean. That's great. I know it's what you want.'

Then Cora began to cry too, and putting her arm rather awkwardly around me she said, 'It'll happen to you too one day, Lizzy. Someone who deserves you. You'll find your own Mike.'

Nauseatingly, the unholy trinity of Sting, Bryan Adams and, God help me, Rod Stewart began to huskily belt out *One for All and All for Love*, from the Disney remake of *The Three Musketeers*, on the radio.

'Oh, this is our song,' mused Cora, sniffling with a dreamy, far away smile on her lips.

This is how I remember all of our moments now. Through snippets of music and sound and light, like a flickering TV show in the background of someone else's life, disordered snapshots of feelings made sense of through other peoples' words. All strung together in and out of time, in and out of order.

That is why, in the carriage, as the train rattles into Swansea station, I find myself thinking of Sting, as Mike releases the engagement ring, now apparently ready for the right moment from his pocket: the right moment? Is it already here, so soon? So soon after…?

Mike flips open the box to reveal the cold glare of the pale blue stone. We sit and stare at it. Two figures, heads bent together, almost touching, against the smeary glass window and a soundtrack of coughs and crying children and the tinny crackle of Suede's *Animal Nitrate* scratching at the air from a Walkman. I feel as if my brain has short-circuited.

He kisses me, lightly and gently on the lips, leaning his

forehead against mine for perhaps five seconds before pulling back to look into my eyes. There are tears there, I know, but he cannot see them. It's a romantic tableau with the wrong heroine.

'She'll like it.'

'She should. She practically picked it.'

'I'm glad for you both.'

'But are you sorry it happened. We happened?' he demands.

'No,' I answer.

'Neither am I.'

Then the scene is broken by Stevie banging on the glass with a muted fist, mouthing, 'Are you two getting off the bloody train then or what? The pubs are open you know.'

Forsaking all others

As I said before, Mike and Cora's wedding had been quite an affair. For all the other guests it was exactly as it should have been – the picture-perfect happy ending.

I was dressed in lilac; smiling, always smiling carrying a beautiful posy of cornflowers and white roses. No frills, no flounces, no tulle. Tasteful and sophisticated, thank God. Stevie was the best man, beaming in his morning suit, Cora the blushing bride, Mike the proud groom.

The hotel was plush but not screaming bourgeois. It was soft sandstone, mock Georgian, teasingly exclusive, set on a small island in the middle of a rippling lake, joined to the mainland by an ornate bridge spanning a watery carpet of exotic Chinese lilies.

We were blessed with beautiful weather after the early morning rain. I was sitting, freshly showered and sleepy-eyed in my dressing gown, in Cora's mother's room, just after dawn, nursing a coffee and watching the hairdresser twisting Cora's specially grown, curly mane into impossibly intricate knots, braids and tendrils that seemed to multiply under their own volition, growing small lilies and golden hair pins, a pre-Raphaelite vision in her dressing gown.

Outside the sky was lunar white, a mist lifting from the dark sheet of water. Everything seemed surreal and magical and unlikely, absurd and touching and right.

If she had never quite looked beautiful, she had never come closer to it than in her simple 1930s-style dress, plain-fronted with a little delicate beading, a wash of satin to the tips of her matching narrow shoes. No veil, just a crown of tiny white flowers across the bonnet of hair, irises and white roses to match those in the bouquet.

Waiting for the wedding car I was struck by the almost insurmountable urge to hold her, rock her back and forth like a child. But I was afraid I would crumple some part of her, so instead I took her hand and said, 'You look beautiful, Cora.'

Stevie was an absolute godsend that day, chivvying up the slow coaches, keeping the old, clucking and complaining aunties and uncles supplied with champagne and sandwiches until they were pliable as children, taking care of the multiplying presents, stopping the youngsters from paddling on the fringes of the lawn and trying to feed pebbles to the swan.

I remember seeing him flitting back and forth, sending me quick, flustered grins, distributing fresh glasses of bubbly just where they were needed.

I felt light-headed on no breakfast, champagne and wine before a late, rich lunch. I was so tightly wired with the occasion, with keeping my dress clean and making sure I smiled at everyone and took care of Cora that I was almost out of my body, beyond it, beyond thought.

By nine that night I was in the hotel room, taking five minutes to breathe and massage my aching feet. I tidied my hair, touched up my lips and powder, ready to rejoin the big performance. Suddenly in the dim hallway Stevie was there, at the door, as I was locking it. He was tall, and I could see he was tense, still in the dark navy morning suit and lilac cravat. He smelled suspiciously of vodka. I turned the key, ready to return to the dancefloor mob.

We had not really spoken since the wedding breakfast, since I had traded tales with Mike and his brother Jeff, who kept taking my hand and kissing it, and fended off someone from Mike's office who insisted on knowing my room number.

I start to say something about my aching feet before Stevie cuts me off.

'Why are you so damn beautiful?' he says, but not as a compliment.

For a moment I am confused, wordless. There was something harsh rather than playful in his voice. So I laugh from habit because at least it hides everything, gives me time to think. I thank him graciously and say 'It's been a fantastic day hasn't it?' My practiced playful smile, always for Stevie, is made extra affectionate.

I run my hand down his sleeve in a gesture of friendship, about to take his arm. He is the gentleman, I the lady. I pick the old comfortable game.

But Stevie isn't playing tonight. He has been playing the game all day, a lot longer, and he can't do it anymore. I realise he is more than a little drunk as he moves in closer, cornering me with my back to the wall.

'How do you feel?' he asks. And I know he is not referring to the heavy Empire Line silk dress, up-tucked hair so hard and biting with pins it is starting to hurt, or pinching sandals. But I pretend innocence and say:

'I'm in need of another JD,' adding. 'Oh, it's been a long and memorable day. They looked so happy.'

Even to me it sounds hollow, though it is the truth of sorts. But again, Stevie isn't playing, and as I half-stumble on my skirt, he reaches out to steady me, not kindly.

'Knock it off, Liz. That's quite a little court you've been holding out there. All those breathless admirers. You've quite stolen the show. You just can't resist can you?'

He is determined that I should listen it seems. I perceive in the low-lit gloom that he wants to say something else, something more important. And inexplicably, I panic. I want to push him away and scream in his face 'Stevie, for fuck's save leave me alone so I can get on with this on my own.'

I try to sidle past him, exaggerating a tipsy lurch for freedom. But he grips my arms so hard that I wince and he pushes me back against the wall, the dozens of hair grips in my stylish do sticking into my head and making me wince again. Breath escapes from me in a short hard burst. His face is close, suddenly buried in my neck as if he is breathing me in. I am almost glad, for this is a moment that will never come again – we both know it.

We are real now. In it as we truly are. The day has gone and with it the niceties that keep us civil. It is allowed now for surely no one will remember tomorrow. My heart beats faster as I am half-grateful it has come to this. I cannot escape his fierce strength. So it is not my fault from here on in, is it? Whatever happens, for once, is not my fault.

'Why do you always want what you can't have?' He asks this – a non-question. I know he is waiting only for his next line. But I start to say his name anyway.

'Stevie, you're drunk'. No one from the party passes. No one can hear. Why would I want to call out? I think I hear him sob slightly into my ear as he continues.

'You could have had me any time, you know that?' he says, with anger bristling in his voice, as I know it must also burn in soft, accommodating Stevie's eyes. But mine are closed tightly.

'Look at me, damn you,' he insists, gripping my face. 'For

once look at me. But you didn't want me, did you? That would have been too easy for you? Why is that? Why don't you ever see *me*?'

His eyes are blank now.

I hear myself starting to apologise. Kisses and lies, secrets and sighs could be ready at my lips but they belong deep in the night. And Stevie is not in the mood for fairytales. He does not want to hear anything I have to say.

Suddenly he hears a song he recognises. One of our old favourites.

'You want to dance?' he says.

I do not.

'But Lizzy, you love to dance don't you?' he snaps, failing to generate the playfulness in the familiar phrase he does not feel. 'And everyone's wondering where the bridesmaid and the best man have gone. We'll be starting a scandal.' He is a caricature of himself, cooing obligingly, the vitriol beneath his smile burning through the mask.

Now he fastens his hand around my waist with determination. His long legs are leading me through the adjoining door to the dance floor before I fully comprehend what is happening.

I try to pull away but I cannot. He knows this and he knows I cannot struggle as the door flies open with theatrical flourish and we are before the 80 pairs of delighted eyes that see the best man and enchanting bridesmaid head for the heaving floor. Still, I try to plead modesty, though it is not what I feel. I do not want to be up there beneath the disco glare with Mike and Cora swaying close and the new, steely Stevie unpredictable, close, turning the whole thing into some awful soap opera moment – an entirely different kind of domestic drama.

But he is not giving me a choice as he clutches me around

the waist, the dress rustling around us, tiara catching the rotating lights. He is hurting me. It is what he wants and the only way he can. And he knows that no matter what, I will not make a scene by pulling away. After all, the charade is now complete. The deliriously happy bride and groom and we, the old and joyful friends, doing our duty.

And then he says, 'He loves you, you know.'

Do I? I think I did once. That hardly matters now, I want to say. That is in the past. This is after.

'Not enough, though,' continues Stevie. 'If he did he couldn't do this to her. To you. He'd take a risk – he wouldn't let you go. *I* wouldn't let you go.'

Before I can answer the crowd begins to whoop its appreciation and, taken by the wine-numbed movement of the moment, fairy lights glittering along the bar, Stevie acts. With an energetic flourish he lowers me backward so my hair, if it had been loose, would have scraped the floor, bodies touching along their length, graceful and fluid.

'Remember this?' he spits. It is a challenge.

Upside-down, turning with a vengeance, I am at once angry and nauseous and I pray to whoever may still listen that I will neither vomit or slap Stevie so hard his teeth will rattle in his head.

Mike floats past, Cora in his arms, her back to us, but the recognition in his eyes is so painful that I long to moan his name. Quite without warning Stevie kisses me – hard and needy. In that moment it does not occur to me to protest, less still to participate and this is what finishes him, as nothing I could say would have. Our eyes lock, he sees my detachment, and sheer misery pours out of him. Mercifully the DJ interrupts it. Blaring and brash he introduces the next song and Stevie, off-balance, like a man underwater in a place he doesn't recognise, must return me to my feet. I am unsteady but no longer angry.

'I'm so sorry,' he whimpers, burying his face in my neck. I realise he is crying. The crowd applauds as Cora and Mike take a bow, Cora all smiles and Mike staring at Stevie. And I hold him. Glad it is dark. From a table almost hidden in the gloom Phillippa watches the scene through a glaze of gin and tonic and catches my eye. She has seen in the performance what the others have not, but apparently declines to comment and instead, reaches for her glass.

Before the end of the evening there was a great deal of drinking and wild, frenetic bouncing that passed for dancing. I was in fear of my now bare feet as I twirled from hand to hand among Mike's tall and rowdy, yet eminently likeable friends. Shortly afterwards, as the more formal guests drifted back to their rooms on sleepy feet, long after Stevie had returned to his room pleading too much vodka, Mike had stumbled across the grand piano in the foyer. Tenderly opening the lid his fingers trembled over the keys, softly playing a familiar tune.

I had not even realised he could play. How could that be? He played so beautifully, with surprising precision for one who had disappeared so many pints and was overflowing with champagne. Though Cora denied it afterwards, she fell asleep leaning against Tim, dreaming, I hoped, about a perfect day.

All day she had looked irretrievably happy. Mike had not touched me, of course. But he looked at me then, with the music rolling through the hall and upwards beneath the beds of already sleeping guests and he smiled, a million words passing between us on the melody he had chosen, carefully or instinctively, one we both knew. And it was almost enough.

A new line

At the end of July, six months after Jenny's body was discovered, the Curryman made his first attempt to blackmail me. As if I didn't have enough to think about. God knows I had little money. I was a poor target to profit from. Sky-high Cardiff rents, student loans and the pathetic paycheque offered to most reporters had seen to that. But a few hundred quid seemed a sensible investment to get him to keep his mouth shut, to keep me in my job, to keep Mike out of a prison cell maybe, to keep the edges on the world.

At first I tried to brush him off, deny that I knew even the slightest thing that he was rambling about. I even threatened to call in the police myself if he didn't leave me alone (bold stroke, that). But he was patient. I suppose he could afford to be, not, I imagine, having a great deal else to do all day.

The main problem with the Curryman was that he was polite and coolly persistent, not at all like someone you could pass off as a raving loony or a street-walking nutter who would grab at pigeons' tails, hail stray whippets like old friends or address random mongrels as Napoleon Bonaparte, mumbling under their breath. He demanded to be taken sanely and seriously. And sooner or later I would have to oblige him.

He was waiting for me outside the office. Not directly outside.

He realised how that would look. He might have smelled like cooked cabbage but he was smart. The car park was always busy and one of the office workers, not to mention one of the security guards, might intervene if they saw him waylay me.

'Excuse me miss. Is this man bothering you?'

'Yes, he fucking is. Please assault him with as much excessive force as you can muster. At once.' That would have been ideal. But he waited until I was round the corner and snuck up behind me with the question.

'Excuse me, Miss Jones?' Of course he already knew who I was. 'You don't recognise me do you?' He smiled.

I smiled back. Of course I did, at the same time registering the shabby brown woollen coat with bald patches, the moss of stubble crawling over his chin, (no moustache, definitely no top hat, a far more discreet kind of villain), the wetness of his lips releasing humid breath into the sharp air, coffee and cheap fags. Of course he had something to say.

'Saw you at court, didn't I? Not likely to forget a face like yours, am I, gorgeous? And I saw you one other time before that. You remember.' There was a half-knowing smile playing about his lips.

'You were mistaken then and you are mistaken now,' I said. 'Sorry, I have to go.'

'I saw him leave with her, you know,' he said, right to the point. 'Took home the little girl that died. The one with the red hair. I remembered him. He was decent to me. I remember the ones like that – not like the rest of them. They don't even see me now. Bet his wife doesn't know. That snooty one was his wife, wasn't she? Don't expect she'd like to know, would she? You covering that story so well and all, really moving like. Such a nice funeral. That bit with the playing of that song from the radio was nice. Do you think the police would like to know he took her home? Perhaps they'd like to know that you knew that too and didn't tell them. What is that, hampering police enquiries, perverting the course of justice or something?'

'Look mate, just go and bother someone else will you,' I said. Filling with horror from my boots up, I reached into my pocket and offered him a quid to go away.

That didn't help.

'It'll take a bit more than that, my lovely,' he grinned, but he took the pound anyway, polishing it between his thumb and forefinger ruminatively as if considering his next ploy. 'But we can talk again when you're not so busy like. I know where you are, don't I?'

I could feel him staring after me as I strode away. The whole encounter seemed to blur and waver way behind me. The words that had come out of my mouth had been automatic words, like automatic writing I suppose – the kind scribbled by mediums, who say it is the voice of another from the world beyond. I hoped the words that had actually hit the air were delivered by a coolly amused, faintly irritated, unflappable journalist who knew plenty about human nature and was not about to be inconvenienced for a moment by this pathetic example of it.

But all the time inside a small child was screaming, 'What the fuck is going on? What the fuck is going on?!' in helpless rage, knuckling its eyes, kicking its feet into the pavement, making its stomach knot with rage, hoping it would be sick and receive some sympathy from someone, bigger, wiser, able to make things right, make the right choices.

However, this type of rescue wasn't to be an option. The second time he approached me he was more direct '£150 or I'll go to the police,' he said. Just that. No smile.

This time I had to speak to Mike. I went straight round to his office and we sat in his car in the underground car park like two people who now really did have something to hide.

'It's never going to end is it?' he said. I wasn't entirely sure what he meant.

'If you mean is he just going to have a change of heart and disappear back into the gutter, I suspect not.' This was the tone I had adopted with Mike of late, that of a stern governess with an impossibly simple-minded child. Sometimes I could see why Cora employed the methods she did with him.

He shrugged, 'All right, so what do we do?' worrying at an invisible blemish amongst the stubble on his chin.

'I guess we pay,' I said, though the thought that we had somehow been bested by a weasly fucking vagabond left me so incoherently angry that I wanted to get to my feet, swing my arms like an outraged gorilla and batter Mike until his head pulped like a ripe mango and the flesh oozed out or he fell unconscious. I felt that he was the architect of this particular cock-up in more ways than one and he was the nearest target. I was tired. Very tired. But I wanted to hear what he would say. And I didn't see what else we could do.

After a moment's pause in which he ran his hands through his curly brown hair several times and chewed his lip he said 'Ok, I guess we don't have much choice.'

I was instantly incensed. No answer could have been the right one, but I was affronted by the ease with which he accepted defeat. It might have been inevitable, but did he have to acknowledge it so quickly? Accept my lead? But then why was I so surprised that he would?

'Oh, for fuck's sake,' I barked. 'For once why don't you make a decision? Just once? Do something, anything. What do

YOU think we should DO Mike? What do you think WE should DO?'

'Well, we can't not pay,' he said earnestly. A little hurt, he added. 'Don't shout at me, Lizzy. I know this is my fault. We could just bluff it I suppose. Even if he says something they might not believe him right? Just because I was there they can't say I did anything, because I didn't.'

I summarised starkly. I wanted him to hear it all in small syllable words that he could only confront, not chase in and out.

'You lied to the police. They questioned you at the office, asked if you knew her and you lied, didn't you? You took her home. You could have been the last person to see her alive. They haven't yet made a connection to her being at Charlie's that night. No one's come forward to say she was there. You withheld information. Why do that unless you have something to hide? All he needs to do is mention Charlie's and you and it all starts to fall into place, whether you did anything or not. What about Cora when she reads about you in the paper? What about me when they find out I knew? You said there was nothing between you, but she had that book. You said you'd never been in her flat, that you hardly knew her. But you were in a *dead* girl's flat. More than once, probably, eh, Mike? Long enough to leave that bloody pen.'

How much plainer could I make it?

'Pen?' he looked bemused.

'Yes, that pen I bought you for your 21st birthday.'

'The blue fountain pen? I haven't seen that pen in months. I thought I lost it at work.'

'And the book? The T.S Eliot? You me and Jenny just happened to share a love for T.S Eliot? Prufrock, to be precise?'

'How should I know? What book?' He stops and thinks. 'I

167

used to carry T.S Eliot in my bag. I lost it in the move from the office I think. Maybe Jenny saw it. Lots of people like Eliot. Look, Lizzy, for the last time, I did not have an affair with Jenny. We did not have sex. We were not in love. I don't know about that stuff, the pen, the book. She could have lifted the pen for all I know. I walked her home. I told her to back off, I left. That was it.'

'Well, that's not how it may look to the police.'

'I know.'

A silence fell.

'Remember that time?' he said, cupping his head in his hands. 'We never thought.....' his voice trailed away. I paused, swallowed, softened but still stubborn.

'How did we get here, Lizzy? When I think of what we wanted, who we wanted to be. Why are we like this? Shouldn't we be happy? Can't we change?'

Neither of us seemed to have any answers. When it was most important, when it was real, all our words fell away.

'Will we be alright?' he asked softly.

'We'll pay,' I said, though I suspected this was not what he meant. 'It'll be alright. He's hardly asking for a fortune. At least he isn't greedy.' (For now, I added to myself. Something told me there'd be time for more.)

I reached across and put my hand on Mike's shoulder. He raised it to his lips and cradled it as if it was a hand made of the most delicate and priceless fabric in the world.

Two days later I put £150 in ten pound notes in a brown envelope. I shoved it into the Curryman's hand in the ladies toilets at Cardiff Central station, end stall, the one with creative graffiti.

'Don't try for anymore,' I hissed, making my eyes as hard

and my voice as cold as I could, bearing in mind the stench of urine that was always hard to ignore.

'You've had your bit of fun and just remember you are now officially guilty of blackmail. You've been up before the Mag enough times, a few more strikes and you are in. If you get my meaning. If you make trouble for us you can guarantee I'll tell the police and I know a few of the judges, you know. I'll make sure anyone you know in this godforsaken world gets their name splashed across the paper too, so count yourself lucky, be a good boy and fuck off.'

Anniversary piece

A tendril of chill wind began to snake along Queen Street and the prickling on my skin, as the first leaf cracked underfoot, said more clearly than the shiver rattling me beneath my raincoat, that autumn had blown in.

After the payoff to the Curryman, August slid into a September which blazed by with almost Mediterranean heat-blurred splendour. It packed the beaches with the last desperate detritus of summer, kids and dogs and pensioners and parents all fading to pink with the fading evening light.

At the paper we did the usual Back to School articles, the Off to University articles that always follow the A level and GCSE results. Are standards falling? Are degrees useless anyway? These are the stories that fill the gap while Parliament and the Assembly sojourn and all the interesting celebrities are on holiday in Sardinia, the seasonal page fillers that mark the turning of every year. Round and round we go and where we stop...

I was experiencing the usual sense of expectation that seems to super-charge the air at this time of year, the cold, clear, chill wind sloughing free the sweat and dust ingrained in the skin from the summer, gulped fluidly into the lungs like water. The over-gaudy August plumage was being shed, the smell of burning wood and wind from the north replacing the sickly bloom of decaying summer, followed by the steady browning of the boughs. With it came the promise of being scoured clean, scourged down to the bone and purged, made pristine.

I went home that day with a welcome £50 a month raise, pulling out my scarves and gloves, cosy corduroy skirts, pastel polo necks and October-snug boots, thinking of stew and soups, hearty and nourishing in the close-curtained darkness. There would be parties and bonfires, hot chocolate and brandy, skating and smiling and a million other reasons to laugh out loud and stride gaily, rosy-faced through the frost-bitten streets.

I exhaled for what seemed like the first time in a year. Jenny, the doubts, the threats and the Curryman belonged to the old world. It was a new beginning. That night I slept like a child, adrift on a sea of pleasant pre-teen dreams of shiny lights and new shoes.

Unfortunately, I had forgotten one thing. Cora: her name in the mouth, full, wholesome, satisfying, safe, central.

Strange how we, Mike, Stevie and I, had always seemed to revolve around her preferences and whims; her dinner table, her choice of bars and clubs, her high moods, her low swings, her sensibilities, deferential in disagreement and discussion, appeasing in confrontation, eager to keep her happy. Perhaps we just did it because it was simpler, perhaps because we liked the role of errant children, throwing good-natured giggly faces behind a parent's back, playing an old favourite, the humouring Cora game.

Maybe it granted us a perverse power, but we genuinely wanted to protect her. We wanted her to be happy, and for our lives to be a little easier because of it.

That was why, after her initial reaction to the night at Charlie's, we had tried to shield her from the extended facts and business about Jenny. Neither I nor Mike had let on that he had known her in Wrexham or that she worked for his firm. When it was just an unfortunate incident there didn't seem to be any point in making it worse. The police hadn't made further appeals and didn't seem to have linked Jenny to anyone there that night at Charlie's. Jenny's movements remained a mystery. We seemed to have been granted a reprieve.

Cora had not seen the first article I'd written identifying Jenny's body. Mike was right, she rarely read or followed the news. Life for Cora was not out there among the death and scandal and public services in ruins, but in those around her, in her daily revolutions, tight and small and prescribed. This made it easy to keep Jenny outside, beyond the boundaries, where she belonged. Deep down I think we knew we couldn't keep it a secret forever. We were just biding our time and keeping things simple for as long as possible.

Months later, Cora had stumbled across the funeral report by chance, Jenny's picture on the coffin, in page-three Technicolour. She'd only bought a copy of the paper that day because one of her pupil's mums had made the education pages for a homework club she'd set up.

She saw the date of Stevie's birthday stated as the last night Jenny had been seen alive, knew it was that night at Charlie's, and there was my name on top of the story. The story also said that she had worked for a PR company – luckily it didn't connect hers to Mike's, as they traded under different names for branding reasons.

'It's her. It's that Jenny isn't it?' Cora's voice crackled down through my mobile phone, wavering with agitation and poor reception, but I only pretended not to understand. In a tight, unacknowledged corner of my chest I'd been dreading this inevitable conversation. I'd thought of how the sentences might form and what I'd say, the neutral tone and expression I'd adopt, but how I'd writhe inside, caught on Cora's sharp pin of accusation. At least she'd called my mobile so I could seek refuge in a quiet corner where we could not be overheard and hide my face.

'Cora? I can't really hear you. I'm moving into another room. Say again?' I shouted, taking my phone out of the office and into the empty news conference room.

'That Jenny. It's *that* Jenny,' she yelled. 'You knew about this? What happened? Did something happen to her? How come you're writing this? You never said anything about this? Can you hear me? Lizzy? Lizzy?'

I sat down heavily in the editor's wing-backed chair, ready for business, gathering my reserves.

'Yes, that's better now. I can hear you. You saw the report then?'

'What happened to her? How come you didn't say anything about it?'

Prepared response number one came easily. 'Well, it was sort of last minute when I was asked to write it, and to be honest I didn't want to upset you again.'

'But when did you know she was dead?'

This was the trickiest question. I had given it a lot of thought, so I knew what I was going to say. 'Well, to be honest I've known for quite a few months. I saw the first reports when they found her body but I didn't mention it as I knew how upset you'd been about it all. There didn't seem to be any point raking up bad feeling. There was nothing we could do about it, so far after the fact, anyway. I hoped you wouldn't see it at all. I know you don't realise it, but it's the sort of thing I see every day. It's not that uncommon.'

173

'But, from the report, the family, the police, they seem to think something bad happened, that maybe it wasn't an accident. They haven't said she fell in the river or anything. They don't think there's something suspicious about it, do they? You know, maybe, *Foul Play*.'

That was quick. She'd made that leap far faster than I had expected her to. (Foul Play? Oh, how I hated that phrase with its Agatha Christie overtones. Well, now you come to mention it Cora, it was Mr X on the riverbank with the blunt instrument.)

'Well, it doesn't say that, does it?' I replied without hesitation, patient, calm, not prompting, providing neither cues nor clues.

There was a deep but emotive silence from Cora's end. It suggested the possible gathering of fierce energies, an outburst for sure. It lasted so long I half-thought we'd been cut off. Then, from the sudden hitching of her breath, I realised she was not preparing to explode; this was not hurricane Cora about to make landfall with me directly in her path. She was struggling not to cry.

I was surprised. Tears were somehow worse than the flurry of questions and accusations I'd imagined. But they did make it easier to justify myself. She'd reinforced my point without prompting.

'You see? I knew this would upset you. I knew it'd bring all this back. That's why I didn't mention it. I'm sorry, Cora. There's no need to take it to heart. '

Silence surged back again from the end of the line then Cora cleared her throat, wiped her nose and recovered her voice.

'I get it. You didn't want me to lose it again. And I have. But I'm ok. So what do they think happened? You must know. You pick up stuff that you don't put in the paper, right?'

'Actually, I don't think they know,' I said truthfully. 'They don't seem sure about where she went or who she was with that night. It's a mystery.'

'How can that be? How can they not have found out? The police, I mean?'

'This isn't the telly Cora. It's not always neat like that.'

'But it makes sense that someone from that night must know her last movements or something, right? That's why the police have made an appeal with the funeral.' There was a silence, worse than the others because I knew for sure what was next.

'We were with her. *We* saw her. Shouldn't we have said something? I mean should we have told the police? We know when she was at Charlie's. Mike.....' she tailed off and the high-pitched breathing began again. This time she couldn't control it. I could hear the tears I couldn't see. 'Dear God, she was only 22. I thought she was older than that. I thought she was older.'

She was talking to herself as much as to me. I suddenly wondered where she was, glancing at my watch. It was 3.30pm.

'Cora, are you at school?'

Bloody hell! Are there kids and teachers and parents around? Some end of term parents' evening thing with all the mummies and daddies wondering why the nice teacher is weeping and snotting into her newspaper?

But to my relief Cora said: 'No, I *was* at school. I was on my way home when I got the paper to see Susie's mum's project in there. I'm in the car now.'

That was something. At least no one could hear her.

'Well, look, please Cora, don't get upset. I was upset at first too but these things do happen. It's sad but I guess I'm more used to it than you.'

'Yes,' she gave a wry half-laugh, half-sob. 'Yes things do happen. Just not usually to people who we know.'

'Well, we didn't know her really,' I corrected at once. The last thing I wanted was for Cora suddenly to go all maudlin over youthful, lost Jenny whom, until 30 seconds before she knew was dead, she had detested and derided. 'I mean. We saw her briefly but we didn't know her. That's why we didn't think it was worth saying anything to the police. It's months after that night. We don't know where she went or what happened after we left. It just seemed like it would create a lot of fuss for nothing, since we couldn't help.'

'You mean fuss with me and Mike? Fuss between us? Mike knows too, doesn't he?'

'Yes,' I said cautiously, knowing it would be far too easy for her to catch me in a lie. 'Only recently though.' The minute she put the phone down she'd be calling Mike. We'd agreed a sort of holding statement to say that, if she asked, he'd only found out about Jenny's death just before whichever article it was that tipped Cora off. That seemed the least complicated fib.

'Right. Of course. Yes.' A shade of self-possession edged its way back into her voice. I sensed her withdraw slightly. Her calmness said she was irritated and a little hurt now. She didn't like being the last to know. I suppose she had a right to be annoyed. At least that was better than angry or hysterical.

She ended the call quickly, assuring me she'd be fine, it was just a shock and I should let her know if I heard any news, and of course she understood why I'd not mentioned it before, she knew I was trying to protect her, and I wasn't to worry, she wouldn't get all upset about it.

But as I lowered my phone and slumped back in the editor's chair, I realised we'd made a mistake.

Though it had initially made things easier for me and Mike, my omission, *our* omission, if not exactly a lie, now obviously made her suspect a cover-up. I could hear it in the tone of her voice at the end of the conversation. A cover-up could only be for Mike's sake. And it didn't take long for Cora's niggles of doubt to warp into something closer to home, something more self-serving than the tabloid-friendly 'tragedy' of the death of a girl none of us had really liked.

After a week or two had passed Cora began to raise the old refrain that there was more to that chance Charlie's meeting with Jenny than she had first realised. She knew Jenny was from Wrexham now and the PR world there was small.

Mike and I consistently denied there was anything else to tell. So she was dead? That didn't change what Mike had said happened that night. But instinct told Cora that the man she loved and had lived with for years was holding something back. Even if she wasn't sure what was being kept from her, a seed of suspicion began to sprout, roots fastening it down in her heart, promising the bloom of a dark, blighted flower.

As high summer rolled in the police had no new information and the publicity began to die away. Nothing would be revealed about Jenny's fate until the outcome of the inquest. The passing weeks helped to dull the edge of Cora's doubts and questions. As routine reasserted itself and made everything appear normal again, she appeared to have settled into a grudging holding pattern.

It was easy to believe this because we wanted to. We wanted to go back to before, before Jenny. So Mike made every effort to spoil and please Cora and convince her of his undying and undivided devotion. It had been a blip, a bump in the smooth track of their relationship, now lost under the rails as they moved forward in their happy married life.

Over the hotter months of the summer when the days spun out and melted into endless evenings, Cora was not in school and we could be lazy. With my rolling shifts we were able to go out and about together, more or less as we always had – to the eyes of the world, nothing more complicated than a group of good friends.

Mike, Stevie and I were careful at first not to mention *you know who*. Then as the weeks passed we forgot to think about not mentioning *you know who* at all.

The four of us took trips down to the pebble beach at Southerndown, ate ice-cream, resolutely cheery and even tempered, Stevie regaling us with stories of work. I followed suit, with tales of colleagues' imbecilic newsroom cock-ups. We wolfed down pre-packaged sandwiches, melting in a slather of sun cream in the grass, retreating to the gothic shade of the old walled gardens and ruined manor house when the sun was most merciless.

At night we would hit the shady, lager-swilling terraces of the city's Mill Lane, the new crop of jaunty café bars with tables outside and exotic alcopops, well away from Charlie's. Here we could drink and people-watch, feeling superior to the flabby, polyester shorts and crop top-clad crowds with their bulging bellies, big hair and thick necks.

All was well with the world and the world was the four of us.

But, as I look back, I can see how, sometimes, Cora regarded me watchfully from the corner of her eye, when she thought I was lost in a doze, engrossed in building a sandcastle, reading my book or swigging a cocktail. Something was building in her very silence, her reduced tendency to cluck and fuss and gently bully us. These, always her trademarks, the very core of her Cora-ness, were diminishing with the dying August daylight.

We assumed she was relaxing, and happily plied her with wine and Martini which she rarely refused. We took this as a positive sign, a triumph of our liberality, our optimism, infecting her. It gave us peace and quiet and we were glad of that. We could forget.

But Cora never let go of Jenny. She was incubating her frustrations in the warmth of July and August, ready and waiting.

At the start of September the new school term began. And, without our noticing it at first , Cora continued with her summer drinking habits. This was the second sign I ignored as I eagerly broke out my woollies and anticipated the delights of the oncoming winter. Cora, who considered it a big night if she drank more than three Martinis and a glass of wine, now downing glass after glass of vodka, faster than I could order them, leaving me struggling to keep pace, should have triggered an alarm.

By October, Cora would rarely refuse a lunchtime glass or two of wine or a quick one after work. I see now that she was fuelling her own quiet paranoia with whatever bottle came along. On two separate evenings I had to help Mike shove her into a taxi, stumbling, legs pitching as if she was picking her way along the deck of a rolling ship: neither was a really late night or special occasion.

The anniversary of That Night, Jenny's disappearance, Stevie's birthday, was approaching. I had to write a year-on piece – a murder/death/mystery-still-unsolved piece. A renewed appeal by the police was issued, hoping it might jog someone's memory. I thought this was a bit pointless so far after the fact, unless they'd uncovered some new evidence – if so, they didn't release it. To my intense relief the diary they had found in her room seemed to have led them nowhere. The mysterious "him" from work that she had written she would meet that night had never surfaced.

As my article hit the shelves, page two with a picture and tribute, more nice words from Mrs Morgan, Cora began to go into freefall.

I knew she and Mike had been arguing a lot since the end of the summer. Her moods were becoming unpredictable. The subject of Jenny had crept back into every conversation, insinuating itself into a moment's silence, a lull in laughter. Something had been going on between Jenny and Mike. The hints then came in public, when the four of us were together, the accusations and questions when she and I were alone. In a flash she could switch between melodrama and martyrdom and after a few drinks the rage of a jilted lover flashed on and off with the accelerating flash of her vodka glass. It was very tiring.

Her increasing Arctic silences in the face of my patience and her occasional blank bouts of watchfulness, began to irritate and needle me more and more, scoring my flesh, marching up and down on my nerves, boring me to tears.

Slowly, she was turning each moment of peace into a penance – the penance of being in her company and then a belated guilt for feeling it. And Mike began to seek me out, like a penitent, baffled and saddened when, try as he might, he was quite unable to understand why she was so irritable, tearful and brutal, why he was unable to pacify her or coax the old, pliable Cora to return.

As we rolled through October she began to fire her suspicions about Mike and Jenny at me again and again, what they might have done, at lunch, at coffee, on the phone. She started ringing me at odd hours of the day and night, sometimes even at the office, leaving long and plaintive messages on my voicemail when I recognised her number and clicked divert. Sometimes the sound of her voice on playback, or even just the sight of her number flashing stridently on the caller ID, was enough to trigger a response akin to fingernails raking down a blackboard.

When we were together she began to bandy the dreaded word itself as a weapon, sabre-sharp, to slash the skin. Fuck. Had they fucked? That night, sometime before? The word, the thought, the belief had become so corrosive she could not clean it off – it had worked its way through and under her skin.

The more time passed, the more she drank. The more she drank the more petulant and aggressive she grew. Then at other times she'd fall under the shadow of a different cloud, becoming weepy and taking hold of my hand saying, 'You're my best friend, Lizzy. You really are,' as if desperate to make me believe it.

This then, was Cora a year on, falling to pieces and bent on shattering everything else around her.

It led to complications for me. Cora's moods made it harder than ever for me and Mike to bump into each other by accident or arrange those little theatre outings. Every time he went anywhere alone he had to endure an interrogation. This frustrated me to the point of insanity. I couldn't understand why she couldn't let it go. I had almost managed it. It was all so long ago, wasn't it? Why all this now?

A week before Halloween she and Mike had a major argument. Another one. He had finally said he wanted her to go to the doctor, get some anti-depressants or something, anything, but they couldn't go on like this. She'd flown into a rage, screamed that he'd like that and it was all his fault anyway and why should she make it easy for him? They'd barely spoken for days, he said. Mike had been looking perpetually harassed for weeks. I'd thought he was exaggerating, playing for sympathy, but now I suspected the reverse.

I'd seen Cora work on him once for a minor transgression, for his failure to book long-promised concert tickets.

I had watched, fascinated and, I admit, impressed by the sheer precision of the torture. For a week she had sawed on his nerves with her brittle withdrawal, in person and on the phone, and I watched him over-compensate, froth, plead with his eyes, fawn with gifts of sweets and chocolate as she allowed him, little by little, to thaw her out, earn back her good favour – it was almost medieval, courtly and a bit sad.

But this was worse. Less contrived, more unpredictable. I could see why Mike, usually so well-versed in the language of wordless apology, was at a loss.

Even though Cora was now trying my very last nerve I didn't really want her to be so unhappy. She was still my best friend, after all. So, for Halloween I thought I'd cheer her up, we'd hit the town. I'd make an epic effort to be a good friend. I felt virtuous.

Trouble was, the Currryman had started to lurk around the building again. The possibility he might ask for more cash was foremost in my mind and, tired and preoccupied, I made a stupid mistake. In a rushed attempt to win back Cora's trust I told her about the blackmail.

I was quite circumspect. I just said that a man had said he thought he'd seen Jenny leave with a group of people, spotted us all talking when he'd sneaked inside the foyer to get warm and threatened to tell the police we'd all left together. It had an element of truth, just enough, I thought, to get her on side.

'But why would that be bad? Couldn't you just deny it?' she'd said, clearly puzzled.

'Yes, but then they'd need to come and speak to us all, find out Mike and Jenny had been in PR together for a while. It might look bad that we hadn't come forward earlier when we saw her that night and we all got split up.'

'But, before you said it didn't seem important because we didn't have anything to really tell.'

'Yes, but it's not so much about how things were as how they look now.'

'But *we* were together and Gabe would give Mike an alibi wouldn't he? He was there all night at his party?'

'Well yes, if Gabe wasn't too ratted to remember who was there, but there'd still be time between his leaving the club and getting to Gabe's they couldn't be sure about. Time enough maybe, or they'd think so, to do something – it might seem suspicious, that's all.'

'Yes, they might think that I suppose. It is about how it looks,' said Cora, a faraway look in her eye.

'I wanted to tell you because I don't want to keep any more secrets from you,' I said. 'You always seem to think I'm not telling you everything, so now I am! I was trying to keep Mike and you out of all this.'

At that moment, I half-believed this was the truth. I thought if Cora could be convinced that I still cared for and trusted her, she'd feel part of the circle again, integral to it rather than excluded. Alright, perhaps deep inside I just wanted to feel better because I knew I'd been a poor excuse for a friend.

Cora thought about it for a while then asked. 'Did you give him any money?'

'Well, only £50 to get rid of the hassle. Just seemed easier than getting involved.'

'What if he tells someone?'

'Then it's just my word against his isn't it? It seemed better not to piss him off for a few quid.'

'You don't think it makes you look like you've got something to hide?' Put like that, of course it did. It seemed that way to me too, now that she'd said it. It seemed glaringly incriminating. But we were getting off the point.

'You don't have to worry about it, Cora,' I said soothingly. 'You can let me worry about it. I'll make sure it's all ok for us all.'

James's lightbulb

We met early, straight after my shift finished, for the grand *cheer up Cora* outing. The George is a semi-regular haunt for journalists, probably because of its rather heavily-layered air of faux Fleet Street decrepitude, worn dark wood, with little partitioned stalls at the back. But there was also The Goat Major with its pictures of the goat, mascot of the Welsh guards, and its roaring fire and all the new places that seemed to be spawning under the Edwardian eves of old St Mary Street , with wooden floors, extortionately priced glasses of wine and rich creamy cappuccinos the shade of the comfy leather sofas. The real media types, the broadcast hoard from BBC Wales in its Llandaff suburb, preferred the more upmarket vibe of leafy Victoriana Pontcanna, the little bars and restaurants growing over-priced but somehow more popular for it.

It was where the true Welsh-speaking middle classes from S4C and the artistically incestuous drama department liked to gather in little cliques, nattering deliberately and just a little too loudly in Welsh so everyone would notice them.

At seven o'clock Cora and I had downed our drinks and talked about my Curryman encounter. She seemed mollified for a while and it was shaping up to be the night I'd planned; a night of confidences and cocktails, some bar food and reminiscing, and me soothing her with shared stories, events and places and times long lost, morphed into our own myths, making her laugh and reminding her that we were great mates who trusted and took care of each other.

But by nine, things were starting to shear off in a different direction. Though Cora insisted she was fine I guessed she had drunk some wine before leaving the house and was well on to her fourth or fifth vodka. It was as good as winter now, cold as hell, biting and dry, the city cloaked in darkness. People dressed as sexy witches in suspenders and basques and others wearing the mournful Munch masks from the film *Scream*, had a habit of popping up out of side streets and pub doorways, whooping, reeking of vodka. October 31st. When evil rises.

Seeing Cora's glassy eyes I thought it best to flee The George in case my colleagues were getting off the late shift. Bar Risa was new and fairly cheap and I might get Cora to have a few snacks or a Panini to soak up the drink.

Then fate took a hand. Just as we were drinking up we were ambushed by James. Beautiful James…tall, lean, dark, louche, good-looking, on loan from the London office, awash with cosmopolitan promise, flush with money, radiating smooth, wide-grinned confidence.

James, with his laconic charm, elegantly waisted in a long dark raincoat, was oddly reminiscent of a Nineteenth Century European vampire. Milk-skinned, aristocratic, charming, untrustworthy, an easy lay. In tow were two of the boys from the business desk, Phil and Will, both funny and bright, with trendy bookish glasses and, despite a shared penchant for checked shirts and floppy student haircuts, worth lingering over on a dull Tuesday afternoon after first deadline.

But in James's wake they were floundering, struggling for

even a stray glance from the two exquisitely lip-glossed girls from magazine sales that he had somehow acquired since five o 'clock when I'd refused, for the second time that day, to have a drink with him.

'Ah, Elizabeth,' beamed James as he caught sight of me, in his frightfully posh but soft English voice that always made me tingle slightly. 'It must be fate that has brought us together after all.'

Reaching out with a strong hand he clasped my neck, drawing me in and planting a long kiss on my cheek, as close to my mouth as possible without touching it – cheeky bastard. He was already slightly drunk. The two magazine girls wilted visibly in their Kookai tops and tightened their metallic glossed finger tips around their bottles of WKD Blue.

Two minutes into the affable mutual insults, bitching about overtime and the general decline in the standard of *Newsnight* and *Timewatch* he said:

'Seen your stuff on this river girl, Liz. Good story. Good colour piece with the mother pouring her heart out. Poor cow. You've really kept it going.'

A bolt of electricity, dark green and sharp as a laser seemed to leap into the gap in the conversation, straight through Cora's hunched shoulders, cracking her spine upright, setting my senses on alert as she leaned in slightly, eyes narrowing.

'You have a light touch for that sort of thing,' continued James. 'Nice, all those little details about the girl's primary school ballet dreams and the class picture, young hopes destroyed, moving, not too sickly, good human interest.'

I continued as normal, not looking at Cora but feeling her. The prickle of static electricity, nervous energy passing across the air between us, the precursor of a storm.

'Human interest ? What would you know about that, James daahling in the big bad smoke?' I responded, flicking back his immaculate jacket, brushing his shirt with my fingertips. 'It's all sex scandal and cash for questions isn't it? Where's your mini tape recorder today? What was that story you did last week on the gay MP and the rent boys? Now *that* was full of lovely human details. But how did you get the inside track on that? How far did you go for the scoop, the hot line? In character?'

He grinned, 'You know I'm not that kind of guy Liz. My lips are sealed.'

'They are now, but what were they doing then? That's what bothers me.'

'Ohhh, what have I done to deserve this slur? How can I convince you of my red-bloodedness tempered with essential decency, Elizabeth, when every time I come down to share quality time with my colleagues in the provinces you are too busy to spare me five minutes of your valuable time?'

'Well, I'm here now. You could start with a Jack Daniel's and ice please sweetie,' I minced, cocking my head towards the crowded bar. He grinned again, even wider. 'And I'm sure your London allowance will allow one for Cora.' I was also sure that by the time he'd returned he'd have forgotten the subject of Jenny, now hanging in the air between me and Cora, the invisible corpse, the soundless death knell of the evening.

'Hard, hard. You'll go far,' he replied without even looking at Cora. 'You should come to London and hone your negotiating skills with me.' The magazine girls smiled weakly in the background. Glancing at Cora I noted the slight glaze in her eyes, the hard set of the mouth. 'Two JDs coming up.'

'Vodka please,' said Cora, but he was already gone, her voice below his register of recognition. She returned to silence. Relieved she hadn't said anything else, I felt a bit sorry for her. I was hardly being attentive, prattling and trading nonsense with the beautiful James when it was her night.

'We'll ditch him soon, don't worry,' I whispered.

'Why are you talking to him in that stupid way? You sound like idiots. He's an idiot!'

She wasn't wrong. I had slipped into the easy, luvvie, media routine. It was simply second nature between us. I did not usually speak like this to anyone outside the hack niche – it was all exaggerated media prance and parry – satirising our own profession a bit, that was the point. Not that the magazine girls could sense sarcasm or self-deprecation – well, they did spend their days talking about whether a round or pointed toed shoe was the look of the week. They just thought we were flirting.

Cora knew the difference, though. She'd seen me switch it off and on before but she didn't seem amused this time. I made a mental note to fight the urge and fuss her a bit, ward off any moods before they became too pronounced – that had been the point of the night. The great *Cheer up Cora* mission. I mustn't get side-tracked.

So I quizzed her about school, her mother's forthcoming birthday and if she fancied seeing anyone in concert, bitching a bit about the other girls until I coaxed a smile.

But when James returned with the drinks he was a man on a doomed mission – to get laid. With me. I must admit that, after the JD, I became a little distracted, admiring the soft pink shade of his lips. I liked the slight shadow of stubble beneath his chin, the smooth swell of his forearm on the table next to mine, so slender by comparison. I began to wonder how his fingers would feel closed around my wrist, tightly.

This did not alter the fact that I would not sleep with James if he fell on his knees and begged me. But I could still admire him, as he changed tactics, only half-listening to the conversation he was now politely and expertly conducting, looking at the soft hairs near the nape of his neck, trying to identify his undoubtedly expensive aftershave. James was an unashamed brand snob.

'Were you, Liz? You never told us that,' said James suddenly.

I was aware that everyone was looking at me. I wasn't sure why for a moment, trying to fight the warming blur of JD heating comfortably behind my eyes.

I thought back through the previous half-heard exchanges.

'You must get to mix with unsavoury characters in London,' Cora had said.

(*That aftershave? possibly Givenchy Gentleman*)

'Murderers, paedos and con men to a man, and that's just the journalists.'

(*Or Hugo Boss ?*).

'Yes, but you don't have to go to London for juicy stories. Liz could have her own murder mystery right here. Right from the river Taff.' Cora pauses, 'And to think we were there in the club that night that girl died. Weren't we Liz? As close as we are now.'

The stupid bitch! She couldn't resist it, could she?

I saw a challenge unspoken in her slight smile. She was waiting for me to blanche, stumble, stutter. As if!

'Were we, Cora?' I said with a perfect air of vague boredom.

'Fuck, Liz, were you *that* drunk?' laughed James.

'But of course we were there,' insisted Cora, ignoring him, her voice a shade stronger. 'In fact I think we even spoke to her.'

'Wow, really? Wouldn't that be, like, really creepy,' said one of the magazine girls.

'Whoa yeah, absolutely,' said the other one. 'I mean you

could've, like, been one of the last people to ever see her alive. You are like, witnesses, because someone she went home with was probably the one who did it – killed her. Last one to see the person alive is likely to be the killer and all that. No, the first one to see the person dead is ....' Having thoroughly confused herself, she stopped.

'No, it's the person who reports finding the body is often the last one to see the person alive? Isn't it?' said James. He paused. 'That's something from Inspector Morse or something isn't it?'

The drink was affecting everyone. Except magazine one, she was always that stupid.

'We don't know that she was *killed*,' I said impatiently. 'She could have just fallen in the river, pissed.'

'Oh no, Liz, that's not half as good a story, get with it,' reprimanded James, grinning his huge grin. 'It was probably someone she was shagging. Lover's tiff. Guarantee it. Grand crime passionelle.'

'Is that in the Magnum limited edition choc ice range?' I quipped weakly. He grinned more.

'Or a stalker,' said magazine one.

'Or a psycho,' magazine two.

'Or a lesbian lover,' one.

'Or a jealous wife out for revenge,' two.

'Or that bloke she was with,' said Cora. It took perhaps three seconds for the grin to dim and the light to click on in James's head, the little journalist's light that, like a bare, energy-saving bulb, dangles from a flex in the roof of your brain.

The kinetic energy created by a given combination of words, in a given scenario, with a given person flicks it on, illuminating a line or phrase in a shadow-splurge of speech. The light makes a little invisible pen fidget into action, the more the words marry up to a story, the more the pen scribbles and the brighter the light gets.

'Did you see her with a bloke then?' James asked, his eyes flicking like tracer fire to Cora's face with real interest for the first time that evening.

'Well,' said Cora, rather playfully, to my astonishment. 'It was very busy in there you know.'

'Well, good God did you or didn't you? Who was he? What did he look like? Do you remember?'

'There was a lot of smoke. Everyone was dancing, but,' she eyed me carefully, 'I'm sure she was talking to a tall guy, floppy brown hair.' Suddenly she was coy, but willing more questions with her upturned eyebrows and slowly spreading smile. Everyone looked at her. She was the centre of attention now.

'It could have been anyone, Cora,' I said, deliberately indulgent, with a faint roll of the eyes towards James, inwardly flaming with repressed rage, forcing it down from my throat and fists into the deepest pit of my stomach. 'She could have been dancing with George Clooney and you wouldn't have recognised him, the amount you'd put away,' I smiled placidly.

'No Lizzy, the amount you'd put away. I hadn't drunk that much. I never really did then, did I?'

'Still, did you see him, Liz?' said James, something troublingly alert in his gaze, the glow growing a little behind his large dark, lager-softened eyes. 'Does Owain know?'

'There's nothing to know. I can't even remember for sure if I saw her. There were hundreds of people in the club that night. Don't suppose they thought it worth mentioning either.'

'Yes, but if it was definitely Charlie's she was at that night, they might do another appeal for the bloke. Even if they don't, it would make a great colour piece wouldn't it? I mean, in the first person, you inside the club on that fateful night, her last hour, a glance across the smoky floor, little did you know she'd be dead before next morning. Great after the inquest verdict either way.'

'You hack. Don't be so fucking melodramatic,' I laughed. 'And don't you dare suggest it to *that prick*. He'd love the idea, work of fiction or no.'

'But maybe you should tell the police if you know for sure that was the last place she was, where she was last seen' he said. 'My sister's husband is a copper.'

For a split second a faint twinge of morality and social responsibility broke the surface of his news radar, interrupting the smooth stream of imaginary columns of newsprint and blurred pictures screening through the front of his brain to the headline at the top.'

'Oh, perhaps you should. I mean, what if they find out later and you've been writing all these stories? I mean couldn't you be disbarred or something for not disclosing information?' magazine one.

'She's not Rumpole of the Bailey, you fuckwit. You can't disbar a journalist,' sneered James good-humouredly. 'Though, I suppose if you actually killed her yourself they'd probably be within their rights to fire you.' The light went out. Any real interest had vanished with a swallow of Corona and the impressive cleavage of a passing overflowing blonde in a cut off halter-neck. He'd be back in London tomorrow.

'Or if you knew who might have done it and covered it up,' offered Cora, seeing his attention waver.

'Done what? We don't know anything was done to her!' I repeated with a huff of exasperation. I'm going to throttle her.

I really am going to throttle her. Right here, right now, throw her down and wring her neck!

'Or paid the murderer for his story,' grinned James, joining in with what he thought was now the old game again. 'Or it turned out you'd been involved in a lesbian affair with her, mmm…' he continued, getting carried away, that beautiful grin erupting, eye on the halter-neck.

'Or paid someone to keep quiet,' said Cora with a hint of desperation, knowing she had lost him.

'Oh yes, death, kinky sex and blackmail. That's a front page. Well, if Liz isn't game for the inside story, what about you, Dora? Fancy a freelance piece on your last hours in the death club then? If it turns out it was murder you might even get into one of the nationals − on a quiet day.'

Cora laughed, sneering at James with unveiled disgust. 'First person? If only you knew. That would cost you money James, daahling. More than just a couple of JD and cokes.'

'Oh, she's learning from you,' he crowed, still thinking she was playing the game. 'What a bad influence you have had on her. See if you can't make her more wicked − as long as I can watch.'

The music surged and the volume of the crowd buzzed to overcome it and I tried to breathe normally.

'Come on to a club with us Liz, pleease,' said James in the next breath, his electrifying grin back on maximum wattage. The death of some PR luvvie was no longer of the slightest interest. 'Oh come on, we'll have fun. What do I have to do to convince you I'm crazy about you?'

If I hadn't known that he was a shallow tart I could have accepted his offer, and everything that accompanied it, that is if I hadn't been fighting back the urge to strangle Cora with my handbag strap until her teeth rattled free of her head and she told me what the hell she was playing at.

But I did know. So we parted company with kisses. The next day I heard that he had indeed snogged one of the magazine girls in the pub then gone home with the other one.

'So?' I demanded. I was barely controlling myself and I didn't want to lose it. I didn't want Cora to know that she had rattled me. We were out on the street in the thickening dark, streetlights glowing in the low drizzle. I was tugging on my gloves with channelled violence.

'What was that all about? Are you unbelievably stupid or what?'

'What?' said Cora, smirking.

'Do you realise how unsubtle that was? How dangerous? I work with these people. They might not really give a toss unless there's a good exclusive in it but they're not complete idiots. You can't just go around saying things like that. They'll think there's something to what you said and they'll think it's a story just for them.'

'Lighten up, Lizzy. I was only playing – testing the water. We *were* there that night but so were lots of people, like you said. Don't blame me for your guilty conscience.'

'Guilty? Don't be childish. Why should I feel guilty?'

'Why? Why?' she looks incredulous. 'With what you do every day, making stories out of people's misery? A girl is dead and you turn it into *'good colour'*? You're selling your soul every minute of every day you click away on your computer, and what's more, you know it!'

'Oh don't be so fucking naïve, Cora!' I exploded. 'It's the way of the real world and I do what I have to do to get along in it.'

'Yes. Don't we all?'

For a moment she seemed lost in thought. I took the opportunity to change tack and hide the fact that my fists were clenched to stop my hands from trembling.

'Do you want your husband to be arrested, Cora?' I asked as calmly as I could.

'Michael? No,' she hesitated, 'of course not.'

'Do you want me to be arrested then? What is wrong with you?'

'I've asked myself that, Lizzy. I'm not so sure. Maybe we should go to the police? Do the right thing. Tell them everything.'

Pure panic surged inside me, my stomach lurched. My grip on this conversation, on Cora, was slipping, I could feel it.

'Everything what, Cora? Tell them what? For about the 100th time, we don't know anything. If you mean about us seeing her there and about that bloody tramp you must be mad. He didn't really know anything himself. You'd just end up dragging us all into it. You'd end up screwing yourself because you have this paranoia that you can't trust Mike.'

'But of course that would be you screwed too, wouldn't it, Liz? Yes, it could be messy. I see that now. Loose lips sink ships,' she smirked again.

'Don't joke about this, Cora. We're all in this and you'd better pull yourself together and keep your mouth shut. Why invite trouble?'

'Don't tell me what to do, Elizabeth. I'm going home now.' And with that curt dismissal she turned on her heel and marched off, in a fairly straight line, shoes clicking on the wet pavement, vanishing into the darkness of All Hallows Eve.

And there it was. A thought. A terrible thought, surfacing for a fraction of a second, as I watched her retreat into the night, springing from a dark recess in my soul. Jesus, if only she'd get mugged. Or hit by a car. If only I could bloody do away with her. That would solve everything, wouldn't it?

Startled, I bit back on this snarl of a thought, surprised by its ferocity. I didn't mean it, of course. It was just my brain lashing out, the verbal equivalent of kicking a car door or throwing a coke at a dog. A reflex action, a response to the feeling that I was losing control. I took a deep breath, told myself to get a grip, get a taxi and sober up.

But later that night, at home, unable to sleep again, as was more and more often the case, I found myself sitting at my PC, squashed into the alcove before the bedroom window, in my flat that was not really mine because it was rented, checking emails, reading over my latest Jenny update. But really I was thinking about what Cora had said – and what it meant.

Looking out into the two houses whose gardens backed on to mine, each was a theatrically-lit scenario against the dark night, curtains wide.

There in the window on the right was the middle-aged lady with her never-ending stream of half-completed jigsaw puzzles, seated at the table in her pink velour dressing gown, alone, comforting in her predictability, saddening in her predicted loneliness. Maybe she wasn't lonely, though. Maybe she was just contented, piecing her pictures together, enjoying the satisfaction of making them fit.

Next door her neighbour, the prematurely bald man, was picking up his son's toys at the end of a long day. Sometimes the boy, all four or five years old of him, would climb up at the table to eat his dinner or to slump in his dad's lap for a story. He was the man with the old motorcycle. He restored it in the rickety side garage come rainy or shiny weekend. I saw his wife, pegging the washing aloft when the wind was right, or standing at the sink, soapy to her elbows.

These were normal people with normal lives – safe, flowing constant, just a window-pane and a few paces away.

Lit only by the PC screen, my face was strangely distorted, blurred by the double glazing into an overlapping oval of itself. I did not recognise it. The two sets of reflected eyes swam into focus with a little effort but still combined strangely, as if through water. Then the dark thought came again – behind this face, between these ordinary lives. And I wasn't able to rein it back.

Transfixed for what seemed like hours, I tried to make that window-face my own again, tracing my blurred fingers around its lines, fingertips in slow motion, across the brows, across the lips, trying to smooth sense into them again. One by one I watched the lights of the city go out, and a little more of that gaze darken as my features blended into the night.

Dream newslist day

The following day I had one of those weird, freaky shifts in the newsroom when there are so many great stories around that the news editor is almost orgasmic while planning the pages. They happen occasionally, the chance, the fatal and the macabre combining to create the most surreal tales of human life and death.

You could certainly invent it but no one would believe you. Half the time you can't even fully report it. What you do is apply the process to make the product. It's a little like painting by numbers. There's a pre-prescribed pattern to the printed word. There's shade and fact and colour and comment in fairly equal amounts. Look at the facts, find the news line, work the angle and the emphasis. There's artifice to it, if not art exactly, there's skill and precision in making those words fit. Accuracy is required, a little flourish here and there adding texture to the basic facts. What comes out at the end is a more or less faithful picture of an incident, an accident, a crime, a life lived or lost.

It can't always be complimentary of course, or comprehensive, for that matter. You're not giving anyone the opportunity to take stock, straighten up their tie and smile. It's still life, not real life. No matter what they try to tell you it's not truth, it's not real time, it's not reality. It's a carefully constructed impression, from a certain angle in a certain light, a snippet, a sound bite.

It has to be this way. The media doesn't report the news. By sifting events it generates it, prioritises it, trims it, dresses and fashions it into the fluctuating product that the viewers, readers and listeners buy into.

Listen to my day. Think if you later read the stories or have read hundreds like them.

On a city housing estate a man died of a heart attack. An everyday event, until the doctor realised there was no way in hell they could get him out of the house and into the funeral director's van. He weighed more than 47 stone. The fire service had to remove the front window of the house, then winch his sloppy carcass (he'd lost control of all his bodily functions) up and out with the aid of a special A-frame. Ten men struggled for two hours to load him into the van. He was 34. He had twin daughters. It was their 8th birthday.

In the delightful suburb of Splott, a pensioner was knocked down and killed by a car. Her son had been killed by a car in the same street three years earlier and we had file pictures.

A woman was raped in a Grangetown alley. A man hanged himself in Cathays. There were two road accidents in the town centre.

Six miles from that centre a man died in his bath after an electric convection heater crashed from the bathroom wall, bounced off the bathroom cabinet and into the water. In Llandaff a man hanged himself from his banisters. He lived in a three-storey Victorian house. It was a long drop to the hall. His head popped clean off and rolled under the stairs, where it lay for 20 minutes before the police found it among the outdoor shoes.

The bizarre, the pathetic, the mundane, the horrific. This is any day and every day and all in a day's work.

This is what I did not say to the fat man's girlfriend, as I stood on the pavement with my note pad and she pleaded with me to leave him his dignity. I did not tell her that was impossible now. That Big Bill would always be this giant object of pity and fascination. Nothing more.

In nine and a half hours I visited three police scenes and two private homes, spoke to two grieving relatives, two police officers, a local councillor, four neighbours and a binman. I turned out three page leads and hit every deadline with just minutes to spare. It was a long day.

And of course, behind all this, every minute, there was a bigger story, a better story, with closer characters ticking behind my eyes non-stop. The story I now appeared to be part of, was playing a prime role in, and seemed to have less and less control over.

So for once I really could have done without a call from Mike, at 7.30pm, as I left the newsroom. I was empty as a hollow egg, head vibrating with a million words, clattering round and round as fast as a Gatling gun, struggling just to put one foot in front of the other to make it to my car.

'She seems to think this is a game,' he said in bewilderment, half an hour later, almost in tears, in my big armchair. He'd never been in my living room alone before. It was almost too much to process, the image and the idea. Mike in his grey work suit and black shoes. Mike, his hands on the table in front of me, one over the other. Mike speaking.

Only a comparatively thin sliver of time had passed in the outer world since that morning but that day, a day with a headless man for God's sake, it was enough. A crack had opened inside me and a void whistled in.

I watched the little vein above Mike's left temple pulsing at an amazing rate. He was almost hyperventilating. In the week since our disastrous pub encounter with elegantly wasted James, Cora had apparently imploded.

Mike explained how she had refused to go to school twice, almost been arrested at the Tesco Metro on Tuesday for swearing at the cashier who refused to sell her more vodka, spraying chocolate bars from the till stand into her face and across the counter in a shower of coloured paper. I'd been unaware of all this. Cora had left me a dozen messages over the last few days, some angry, some pleading, but I'd been too busy, and too resentful, to speak to her.

'She said she's going to the police, to tell them about that night,' continued Mike. 'She says she can't stand the guilt of knowing. Knowing what, for God's sake? But Lizzy, I think she wants to punish me for that night. For Jenny. For what she thinks I did. In her eyes I've made her suffer and now she wants to make me suffer back.'

He heaved a great room-shaking sigh, letting his head fall into his hands. 'I don't recognise her anymore. She's so different. She's angry all the time. She doesn't believe anything I say. If I'm five minutes late home from work she's accusing me of all sorts of things. She goes through my stuff, I know she does.

'She thinks you and I are meeting up behind her back, like there's some sort of conspiracy. She calls me at work half a dozen times a day. She drinks at home. She's got some tablets from the doctor but she won't take them. I don't know how much more of this I can take. I got home today at five thirty and she'd been drinking. For hours, it looked like. She hadn't gone to school again.'

For a moment he hesitated, as if trying to decide whether

or not he had anything else to say. Silence flooded into the gap between us.

What the fuck do you want me to do about it, Mike? said the voice inside my head.

She's your wife, I wanted to say. But the words stuck in my mouth and I continued to watch from across the table as Mike spiralled down into his monologue, unstoppable.

'She was drinking whiskey or something when I got home, for God's sake. And we started to row about that, or something else, I'm not sure now. Then she's crying and before I know it she's hurling a bloody mug at me.' He lifted his floppy fringe to reveal a large red welt turning a slow, sour purple. 'A mug, for God's sake. She could have had my eye out. I can't take this shit anymore.'

From my observation point far, far away in the other chair I was coolly appalled, but also impressed. The blood-stained badge of Cora's newfound fury in physical form was mesmerising. She had good aim. Absent-mindedly, I reached out to brush my fingers across the welt, wanting to touch the livid flesh, feel the wound, the first physical truth for a long time. But Mike deflected the gesture, gripping my wrist with sudden ferocity then checking himself, taking a breath and setting his hand on top of mine on the table.

'Are you listening to me, Lizzy?' He paused, almost at a loss. He was close to tears.

'Was it tea or coffee?' I enquired. Across the great distance from which my mind was observing this conversation it seemed like a reasonable question.

'What?'

'In the mug? Cora doesn't drink tea.'

'Lizzy! What does that matter? Haven't you heard what I've

been saying? I don't know what to do!' He heaved a great and room shaking sigh. 'What's wrong with us?'

Us? *What* us? Apart from the fact that you are a spineless passive-aggressive who refuses to take responsibility for anything you do, your wife is a psycho who is trying to set you up as a murderer, which you could very well be I suppose, come to think of it, and I'm probably an amoral manic-depressive thinking about killing her. Is that what you mean?

That's what I thought. I didn't say it. (*Thinking about killing her?* Had that really been in the flow of those almost subconscious thoughts?)

'Lizzy? Lizzy, what do we do?' pleaded Mike.

When he became aware that I was not answering he hesitated, then said: 'That's not all. Look.' He pulled a folded sheet of paper from his trouser pocket and handed it to me. 'I found this in her notepad two nights ago. I was just looking for something to write a phone message on.'

I opened it slowly, fearful of the look on his face. I was right to be anxious. It was a short letter. It was direct and to the point. It began, 'Dear Inspector Collins'.

It read, 'I think you should know that Jennifer Morgan was at Charlie's nightclub on the night she died. She was there until closing time.'

It was signed, 'a well-wisher'.

Inspector Collins was the investigating officer quoted in the colour pieces.

Horror pricked in my throat. My withdrawal cracked, as Mike must have known it would if I saw the note. He'd been waiting to see if he needed to use this last nudge to appeal to me. 'Dear God Cora, you stupid bitch,' I muttered. I closed my eyes.

'I think she meant me to find it,' said Mike sorrowfully. 'I don't think she would actually send it. She's just trying to torture me. She's doing a good job, too. I don't know what to do. Help me, Lizzy.'

In the next second I became aware that he was squeezing my hand painfully, as if his life depended on it. All at once I could almost feel the bones and blood of it connecting to mine, melting, fusing, bringing me back across the gulf of detachment, becoming impossibly distracting, so I couldn't pull my gaze from it, from the bitten down thumbnail, the three freckles near the little web of the skin at its base and the strong fingers.

I was concentrating on trying to breathe and I realised he was staring at me, puzzled, concern in his eyes.

Seconds passed. Then I said, 'I'll talk to her. Not tonight, though. I can't talk tonight. I can't think. Tomorrow. Stay at Stevie's tonight. But have some dinner with me first. I've pizza and wine. And I need some wine. I need a lot of wine.'

He nodded.

So the pizza was heated and the wine poured, without the need to say anything more about it. An untroubled peace reigned as we ate and drank in front of the TV, chatting as if there was no world outside with its trouble and strife waiting. At some point I fell into a dreamless warm slumber. When I woke I was covered with my old cardigan and little note on the arm of the sofa read:

'Thanks for always being there for me, love Mike x.'

I looked at the note for a long time.

The smack came right out of the blue. No one had ever slapped me across the face before. The crack sounded so loudly that for half a second I thought it had originated somewhere outside the room. As Cora's hand returned to her side, her eyes widening, a fiery bloom spread across my cheek. I realised my mouth had fallen open and I hinged it shut, so dumbfounded I had to suppress both the urge to laugh and the urge to belt her back as hard as I could. That would be disastrous, of course. With my blood up and my hands set free I could quite easily beat her to death. I took a step towards her involuntarily and she drew back in fear.

It had started badly from the minute I arrived that evening, the day after Mike's visit.

'Did he send you round? Where is he?' Cora had demanded, when the door was barely even open. 'I expect he told you I'd lost my rag or something. Course, it's all my fault. It always is with Michael, isn't it?'

She smelled strongly of vodka and had been crying. Now she was heading for the kitchen, wrestling with the lid of a bottle of pills, failing to defeat the childproof cap and slamming it on the counter as if to force it into submission. Grabbing it from her, I surveyed the label. Valium, for God's sake.

'What are you taking these for, Cora? You are obviously pissed. Are you trying to kill yourself or what?'

'You'd like that wouldn't you. Right now that would be perfect for you wouldn't it? A good story? Not that you need another good story, do you, Lizzy?'

'Actually you wouldn't be that interesting, Cora, unless you turned out to be having an affair with Catherine Zeta Jones of course.' I was trying to make light of the situation and moved to put the kettle on. 'I'll make you coffee shall I? Something to eat?' I grabbed the bread knife and started sawing a loaf with bustling practicality.

'Coffee, sure, coffee, that'll solve everything. My life's falling apart and your best shot is coffee. Lizzy, who always has all the answers. Lizzy, so in control and coffee is all she's got? You must be slipping.'

'*You* are falling apart, Cora, not your life, and I don't know why you are so determined to make sure it happens,' popping the slices in the toaster and pulling open the fridge.

'Look at you, as if butter wouldn't melt in your mouth. Always the same, isn't it Lizzy? You must feel very superior to me. Cool, calm, capable and oh so beautiful. Everyone listens when you talk don't they, Lizzy? But you don't listen to me.'

'It's hard to listen to anyone who's as pissed as you are these days. What are you trying to tell me then, Cora please? I'm not a mind reader.'

'You know well enough, you just don't want to admit it.'

'We are talking about Jenny right? Cora, why can't you just let this go? It was a year ago. She's dead. She's *dead*. Even if what you think about Mike and her was true, what difference does it make now?' I wanted to pull her stringy hair back and scream into her face, 'you stupid bitch, why aren't you happy?'

I realised I was barely containing my anger. I said: 'you are both here together, now, Cora. Why isn't that enough?'

She stared away into the limitless distance of the inner fridge, for perhaps ten seconds, fighting back tears.

'Because I have to *know*. I have to know if they…if they were….it makes all the difference you see…all the difference in the world. What if he… that night… he was drunk. You don't know what it's like. What he can be like. Oh why did we come back here?'

'You are making absolutely no sense,' I snapped, slamming the fridge door, losing my patience.

'You don't understand, you don't understand.'

'I don't understand why you belted him with a mug. Why you're writing little notes to the police? How did you expect him to react?'

'He told you about that? The note? He asked you to come because of that?'

'Yes, he did. Of course he did – to try to calm you down, to get some sense into you. He doesn't understand. Why can't you let this go?'

'Let it go? Let it go? You haven't let it go have you, Lizzy? You're making a bloody career out of it. All that stuff you've put in the paper. The tears, the heartache, the poor suffering family. It couldn't have worked out better for you, could it? No thought about us. What it would do to us, to me?'

'It's nothing to do with you is it? It's just a story, made up for the papers. It fills pages, that's all and all that crap is just part of it. Someone else would have done it if I hadn't. You know that.'

'Sure, but would they have done it half as well as the breathtaking Elizabeth wonder-girl? A ticket straight to the BBC for you, then? Am I spoiling that for you? Me and my pathetic marriage breakdown? Would they still welcome you with open arms, Elizabeth, if they knew what you'd done. Paying that guy to keep quiet. I'm not so stupid, you know. I'm not so dumb and stupid. I know you're in this up to your pretty neck and all the big blue eyes in the world won't get you out of it. Keeping quiet about meeting her in the club. Keeping quiet about Mike knowing her. Paying that man to keep him quiet. You were right when you said it's not about how it was but how it looks. How does it look now? Nothing to hide? How fast would your haloed Llandaff dream disappear if someone was to let the cat out of the bag about just how many lies you've told? And for what? Why? What have you got to hide?'

'Cora,' I warned. 'Be very careful. What you're saying is very foolish. Mike's your husband and he's the one who could come off worst. Do you want to point the finger at him? Make the police suspect something he didn't do? This was to protect him and protect you and to be honest, you could at least be grateful.'

Her eyes looked glazed but I could feel the hum of anger beneath the surface. She was working herself up into a full hurricane force while I was cooling glacially into something hard and sharp.

'Grateful? Grateful? This was not for me, Elizabeth. This was never about me was it? You must think I'm stupid. You always did. But I'm not stupid.'

'Seems pretty stupid to me, Cora,' I said steadily. 'If he wasn't having an affair before, he probably feels like looking for one now. Who the hell wouldn't?'

It was a cruel thing to say, I know.

Then she hit me. Not a cinematic slap, all ladylike sound, little fury, but a full-on, arm recoiled, ungainly, followed-through belt with the palm of her hand.

It took me a minute to accept that she had done it. Each part of my body was clenched tight. I didn't know if I was tempted to laugh or to strike back, or both. The moment of choice stretched out in stunned silence. Cora broke first, her anger dissolving wetly into a burst of weeping.

'Oh Lizzy, please. I'm so sorry. I don't know why I, I don't know what I'm…..Please Lizzy, forgive me. I'm so, so sorry. I'd never have sent that note. It was just to make him…. please forgive me.'

But I couldn't move or seem to say anything. I realised I was holding the bread knife in front of me in a tight, white fist. It had been lying on the counter while I waited for the toast. Cora saw it. Her eyes moved from the blade to my face and back again, as mine did in reverse. The room held its breath.

'You could, you know', said a very small voice, up to the left, at the back of my brain.

'Could what?'

'You could. It could be self-defence.'

'Why?'

'Think how simple it would make everything.'

'What would it look like?'

'She's depressed, she's on tranquilisers, she's paranoid, she could have attacked you and you had to defend yourself. It would be understandable, too. She attacked her own husband.'

'But that's ridiculous. Isn't it? You couldn't do it. Really do it. You'd never explain that away.'

'But you might if you smiled just right, if you told it just right, and then think what you could do...'

I didn't move. For an eternity. There was real alarm on Cora's face now. She could see that my stillness and silence was a cover for something deep and reasoning, the whiteness of my fingers and knuckles gripping the knife handle a testament to the idea's grip on me.

It was only the sound of Mike's key turning in the door that broke the invisible, elastic piece of time stretching out towards breaking point. The sting of its recoil made me wake to the scene we were almost acting out. Reflexively, hearing Mike's tread, I stepped back and laid the knife on the kitchen sideboard next to the loaf, moving away towards the cooker as he pushed open the door. Turning away from Cora. Rearranging my face, my voice.

'What's going on?' Puzzled by the silence he gazes from Cora to me, back again as I turn to say hello.

'Lizzy, your lip is bleeding. What's happened?'

'I bit it,' I said calmly, another reflex, reverting to a plausible lie without thought.

Cora's mouth is still hanging open. She pulls it shut only with an effort. He glances between us.

'What is this? Have you two been arguing too? Oh please, come on. Please? No more arguments. Please, Cora I can't stand it.'

She rushes into his arms, for refuge or in remorse.

'I love you. I love you,' she blubbers and he holds her, stroking her hair.

'Lizzy?'

'No, we are not arguing,' I say convincingly. 'We are making tea. I was telling her about my news story. Not a nice one. There was a decapitated man in it. I shouldn't have been so graphic. Cora pass me that kitchen roll, will you please, and the jam? I'm starving.'

I should clarify that I didn't really hear a voice in my head – not like a schizophrenic or someone who might hear an actual, full-on voice that wasn't their own. It was just my mind, rationalising, challenging, questioning, suggesting.

Still, I realised that was the third time I had thought about killing her.

Afternoons and Coffee Spoons

Of course, that smack alone would not have been enough to make me think what I told myself was unthinkable. Nor were Cora's public indiscretions, or the sheer irritation of her endless self-absorption. I may be many things but I'm not petty, or casually homicidal. It was something else. I suppose I haven't been exactly honest about how I felt during much of that year I spent denying I was more than just unhappy, more than just unfulfilled. And how Mike's return revealed all that, shone a light into the hollowness at the centre of my life.

A few days after the mug incident I remembered, or perhaps realised with perfect clarity, exactly what it used to be like when Mike reached out a hand to touch me.

It was one of those awful, dark, brain-rattling days when I would sit in the newsroom and get wired up so tight on coffee I'd have to silently will myself to breathe in and out, to dull the dark flashes on the edges of my vision. On the worst days it would seem like my skull could, at any minute, fly open, spraying bone and melon pieces in a glistening arc, and the only way to keep it intact would be to kneel down among the always busy shoppers of Queen Street, lay my forehead against the cool, rain-slicked ground, and try to exhale myself into the earth.

I wondered if, with the seas of feet spreading out around

me on my curled, trembling, embarrassing island of failure, anyone would reach down and say 'are you alright love?' Or, 'are you feeling ill?' Or, 'can I help you, darling?' And I would say:

'Please, please help me. I don't know why but I just want to go home now please, because it's too loud and too bright and too much the same. Every day. Every *single* day.'

Without my realising it, the days when I was like that had come to outnumber the days when I was not. I had made upwards of 20 phone calls that morning, trying to get some desperate-for-publicity "expert," in whatever area that day's news feature was on, to give me comments on something inane and vacuous. Are teenage girls magazine's too graphic? Are celebrity dads making fatherhood trendy? The return of sausage and mash? Again? Question mark on the question mark? And the deadline approaching, tick,-tock, tick-tock, 1000 words to go and no expert.

And 'that prick' was flirting with me, openly, clumsily, making everyone else grin into their keyboards sympathetically. And I was insisting, **no**, I can't swap my shift to the Friday overnight because you've fucked up the rota AGAIN and Claire says if she has to work the weekend it'll be her fifth in a row and she'll have a nervous breakdown. Is that my problem?

Two o'clock and *still* no expert.

2pm was when I'd usually decide to take lunch and try to calm down by going for a walk along the high street. But there was always the chance that the bustle, and the shop windows screaming with clothes and electrical equipment, spewing hot coffee and bread and cakes and books and computer games and high-end, high-price TVs, would make my brain short-circuit and I'd get the urge to lie down in the street again. Of course,

I never did. That would have been too, well, crazy. Openly nuts, instead of normally, quietly and invisibly insane.

So instead I'd stumble along as fast as possible, heading nowhere in particular as long as my stride was purposeful. And I'd find myself standing with frightened perplexity in Boots or M and S, trying to choose a sandwich and wondering if anyone else really wanted to pick up one of the litter bins at hand and hurl them through the nearest shop window, just to break the cycle, just because it was something to DO! *Breathe*. In. Out.

But on that day, Mike phoned at half past one. He asked me to have lunch with him, because he just happened to have finished 'doing lunch' with a client early. 'Doing lunch?' I had crowed in my best uppity accent. I was smiling instantly. 'Oohh, la-di-da, you utter yuppie. How eighties are you? Bet you are wearing braces today, then.'

'You can twang them later if you want,' he said lasciviously. 'Come on. They can spare you for an hour. I can't!'

My step was lighter as I hurried to meet him, smoothing my hair, pinching my cheeks. He had brought me a book – a new favourite of his, to share. But he had forgotten his gloves. I walked up to him, spotting him, head above the crowds, grinning already. He said something banal like, 'whew, my fingers are freezing, feel.' So I put out my hand automatically as I came to a standstill and our fingers closed around each other and the book.

We stood that way under the statue of Aneurin Bevan, his brass head splattered with seagull droppings, as a motorised rubbish cart clattered past, its little brushes spinning litter into its innards for what seemed like a lifetime.

The street faded out and became calm. The turmoil in my head was stilled and I smiled because of it. Mike smiled too, and I was back, with a jolt, in my own body. Right in it, again. For the first time in how long? Months, years, decades, aeons? I could feel my shoe pinching the toes of my left foot and the cold of the street seeping up through the thinning sole. A strand of hair tickled my left cheek. My nose was preparing to run.

He said, 'Your hair looks very nice today, Lizzy.'

We were not talking about Cora.

And I said 'Thank you Mike.'

We were not talking about the other night.

'I can't wait to hear what you make of this one,' he enthused, waving the paperback. *An American Tragedy*. It's fucking marvellous. Starbucks?'

I nodded gently and said 'why not?'

'Why not indeed?' he said. 'Globalization may be evil but consumer choice is the new religion.'

And I said, 'Give over, you twat.'

And there it was – the frisson of being in the moment, shocking its way along each limb from each of the tiny, blonde, almost invisible hairs on my hand, to my heart and down to somewhere deeper, warm and clean and frightening and guilty and wonderful.

Somewhere between the time when we left our student flat, full of novels and posters, promising visits, blisteringly young and unscarred; somewhere between that and the last court case before I qualified as a reporter, the really awful sexual assault that involved utensils and rape and margarine, part of me that I hadn't even realised was poorly and ailing, gasping and screaming, had died. A part he would have swept into his arms and lifted up, above the world, just by smiling.

Why had I never stopped to think that simply knowing Mike

made my life so full of things that I was able to touch and taste and smell and think and feel and fuck – slivers and all of everything else – all at once and not at all? With the melody that runs through my head, as it did on their wedding night with Mike's fingers on the piano keys, runs the knowledge of the many times I could have unfolded before him, opened out to everything he was and was everything he offered.

Why did I not acknowledge this until after Jenny? Until it was way beyond too late? Was there one moment when we could have changed it? Seized each other and run full tilt in the opposite direction, feet flying, breath bursting, over the earth, under the sun and through everything else between?

Perhaps.

If so, it was this one.

One weekend, while Cora and Mike were still living in Chester, Mike had come to Cardiff to see Stevie. It was a few months before the wedding. Pulp were playing the Cardiff International Arena. How could we not get tickets to see the band that had provided a soundtrack to all those times when we had played ourselves and other selves?

At the last minute Cora had cancelled to prepare for a school inspection.

After the show Mike, Stevie and I staggered, elated, into the heart of the city, arm in arm, doing our finest Jarvis Cocker impersonations, wiggling imprisoned elbows and fingers as best we could without breaking the link.

We all said that Cora had missed a great show and I said it was a shame that she could not be here too and it really wasn't the same without her.

Mike took my hand as we strode towards Sam's bar. That long-lost tatty and terrifying place that, caught in its own peculiar time warp, reminded me so much of the pubs of my Rhondda home that normally I'd have fled, screaming.

But even the tottering women with back-combed, bottle-blonde hair, crisp at the edges like twisted tissue paper and the men in too-tight T-shirts and chequered shirts, necks and arms and bellies bulging, tattoos screaming, couldn't spoil my mood that night.

I stayed at Stevie's, in the study, on the camp bed, with Mike set up to sleep on the plump sofa. Nursing late-night JDs, we had talked a little about their upcoming wedding, but not much. Mike seemed a little overwhelmed by all the plans and arrangements. Or perhaps he just didn't want to give too much away. Cora was determined it should all be a surprise – top secret until her big moment. She had been waiting for it all her life. The starring role, centre stage, no spoilers permitted.

Mike and I were seated at either end of the squashy settee, backs braced against the arms, legs crossed, sock toes almost touching. Stevie across the way, sprawled in the armchair, formed the third part of the triangle. We worked well as that

triangle: easy, smiling, knowing, indulgent. It was fine.

Then the song started playing. Blur – Damon Albarn's voice in the half darkness, suddenly sliding down the walls and beneath our sock feet, between the wine glasses and out under the doors, drifting slowly as the world began to peel away. *To the end*.

It was all I could do to swallow a sudden, unexpected rush of tears, my throat boiling. The wedding was just three months away. How much closer to the end could we be? The faintly absurd, dizzying carnival carousel of the tune sent me spinning back in time. And as I listened to the words of the song it seemed it must have been written for us, for me, its resonance so cruel that I couldn't help *but* look at him.

'Dance with me,' said Mike, as if he knew I would say no, stretching out his hand, fingers extended. There was no one to see us except Stevie, so arguably there was no real need to hide from anyone but ourselves, for once.

Neither of us spoke. Where there had been so many words from so many centuries between us, which Cora could not share, where she could not go, there was nothing to say about this moment. I rose to my feet.

Up close he was so warm, so unlike anyone I had ever known. The scent of him lifted up through every pore, through the soft fabric of his shirt. I felt dwarfed by his tall, square-shouldered presence, the sharp angles of his body. Safe. My cheek reached only to his shoulder, which surprised me. At a decorous arms' length he usually seemed smaller. Slowly, as the tune rose and fell, our feet moved in smaller and smaller circles, as if in a shrinking spotlight, until ultimately we had to come to a stop, in danger of disappearing into each other altogether.

He clutched my neck so firmly, the other hand clutching my waist, that I imagined us melting slowly into the carpet or descending achingly into a little heap of flour-fine dust then and there. It was like wanting to be smothered, breathing nothing else, ever. How much easier would that have been? Our fingers locked, opened and closed, fluttering like the wings of a butterfly trapped between closed palms. He muttered something. My name, I think.

When the last drum rolled away we stayed that way, realising a door to somewhere else was still half-open. Stevie was not there.

Was that it? Was that the moment we could have changed it all? Stopped the wedding? Seized the night and all those after?

Eternity ticked by in what must have been only a minute, echoing in my head.

Eventually I said, 'I'm going to bed'. While we were still standing in each other's arms. While I could still manage to speak. Mike said nothing.

So I left, praying for something – but at the time I would have said it was for him not to follow.

Which are the worst lies? The ones we tell others? The ones we tell ourselves? Or the ones we simply live? We had been alone together, really alone, perhaps five times in our lives. Never once had I said 'I love you'. So we had done no harm, had we? Hurt no one but ourselves?

My grandmother used to say 'Give people just enough rope to hang themselves.' But how much is that? I can see her now, sitting plump and comfortable in the old weathered armchair by the window, grey Sunday light behind, white hair, cream knitted cardigan, her feet barely touching the floor.

'Never juggle with people's hearts Elizabeth. The one you drop is likely to be your own.' But she was so old. What truth could she tell me then of love?

Did I ever sit in the darkness of the night and wonder if I was in love with him? Not really. There was nothing so specific, so self-conscious then. We were too deep inside the veins of the life we thought we had to fashion those feelings into an affair. Not without breaching and breaking and tearing, inflicting wounds that life would not survive. That's how it seemed.

Did I ever think of telling him how I felt? Of course not. I hardly knew it myself. Besides, it would have seemed improper. The word seems bizarre now, with its connotations of stiff collars, starched shirts and a glimpse of ankle beneath scratchy petticoats.

But it was appropriate. He was Cora's, that's all. She had marked out her territory all over him. He was occupied land that did not require barbed wire fencing or a vulgar flag fluttering overhead, against the backdrop of a changing sky. He could be annexed only for a short time, those brief and blissful moments when hands reached out in plain view, promising other histories. He could not be overrun and conquered. Naively, for much of the time it did not occur to me that he might want to be.

I did not envy Cora as such. I could never be jealous of Cora in the way I realised I had begun to be jealous of the imaginary Jenny – because Cora and Mike were the universe's constant. They belonged to each other, in all senses, all ages. True, I could not be privy to the secrets of their bed, their hands and mouths in the dark, the sighs and promises given life in the black-red friction created there.

But at the same time Cora could not go into the paper-deep places of mine and Mike's shared seduction, the worlds within worlds generated with instinctive alchemy between the first paragraph and the last full stop of the books we cherished. It had bloomed and rambled and played in the dirt and hyperbole of fog-ridden Dickensian London, the extravagant garden parties of the imaginary Monte Cristo, made fireworks before the finale, tasted intimacy in Thomas Hardy's market places with maidens and sheep and slow meandering corn fields. It was in the spare metallic slices between Sylvia Plath's pleas and Dostoyevsky's sibilant dilemmas, including all the territory between Thomas's ugly lovely town and Don Quixote's dust-blasted plains, swept into the heart of a Holmesian mystery, the litter of coffee cups and hypodermics.

It was just as real as anything else.

In this way I hugged the idea of what Mike and I had with

sticky, nostalgic affection, petting and polishing it from time to time, nurturing it darkly with invisible hands where it would never need to change or face the questions of daylight.

After that single long ago night together, sex, making love, whatever you choose to call it, when we broke our own rules, I was angry with him for the first time, for breaking this accepted pattern, for misleading me, for painting on a dishonest face, for not living up to my expectations. By betraying Cora he had also betrayed me, and my idea that love could be inviolable. I only wanted love that way. If he wanted less with her he could not hope for more with me. It was only later I learned what it could be to long for a little violation. And by then it was far too late.

Capital Letters

I suppose I am just trying to explain why I finally decided to kill my best friend.

If Cora had merely threatened me, to expose me, hurt me, I don't think I could have stomached the idea that had been taking shape over those late winter weeks. But she was threatening to ruin Mike, or at least take him away. Take *us* away. I only had such a small part of him, and most of that was memory, but I couldn't let it go again, go back to before – not after all this.

It would be like cutting deep into my own wrist and going about my daily business dripping gore, the trail bloody and sticky in my wake, reminding me of what I was losing. Ultimately, I realised I'd accepted that Mike *had* had an affair with Jenny, or at least slept with her that night. I also had to accept that maybe, just maybe, he might have done something worse.

He had taken her home – then she was dead. Could that really be a coincidence? The surprising thing was that by then I didn't care. Cora, not Mike, had become the deal-breaker.

I know that was partly my fault. I shouldn't have told her about the Curryman. Because in that one, simple half-confession I gave her something she had never had before – power. How could she be expected not to use it? With that knowledge in her

222

hands it did not matter, as I knew it must have all along, that I was by common consent beautiful and she was not, that men whistled at me in the street and turned to look at me in bars and shops, that I had a burgeoning career everyone assumed to be exciting and lucrative, that I was bright and funny and shared literature and the theatre and art and music with her husband.

All these things meant that I could humour her and advise her and be her friend, quite comfortably without the ghost of a threat, without a burnish on my confidence. Why should I ever have cause to be wary of Cora?

But the confession of the payment to the Curryman had implicated me in a crime, petty as it was. This was a weakness, a crack she could dig into and exert a little pressure. I had paid someone off to keep him quiet about my proximity to Jenny's death. Perverting the course of justice? That was not so petty – and I was guilty of it. I *had* withheld information about Jenny's whereabouts, her last hours. '*Award-winning Journalist in Blackmail Scandal*'. It was an unwieldy, unlikely headline, but it could be a good story – on a quiet day, of course.

If nothing else it meant I could lose my current job, and, more importantly, the one that was in the offing. THE ONE. The one I had waited for and fought for with pen and paper since I was 16 years old, sitting my GCSEs – the one that would really get me out, on, up, away.

You see, Cora was right. My work on Jenny's story had won me a nomination for the BT Regional Journalist of the year award. I was only the runner-up in the end, smiling as I gracefully accepted my plaque, clad in a black, slinky evening dress, blooming beneath the lights, the men loosening their ties after too much champagne, coming over to eagerly chat with me at the free bar, offering me business cards and invitations to call.

The first prize, unbelievably, went to some god-awful little weekly paper deep in the closed heart of West Wales for a story about allotment wars: it was published in Welsh, and, as it happened, an English-language journalist had won the year before.

But the important thing was that three hours hobnobbing at the Cardiff Park Thistle, and a little write-up in my very own paper, had prompted an offer of a job at *BBC* Wales, squatting beneath the dreaming spire of Llandaff Cathedral. Broadcast news – the gateway to the promised land!

When speeding over the flyover north of the city, I often glanced across to Broadcasting House, squatting in the Cathedral's shadow, the clouds routinely parting over its towering antennae like those over a Thomas Hardy landscape, to bathe it in golden beams. And when I mentioned it to my colleagues I could see them looking at me differently, with more reverence, with an acceptance previously denied. I would not say it was respect, for that is something all journalists lose before their first year in the field is out. But at the very least it was envy.

The glow of those three iconic letters, *BBC*, stretched out to cover me in corporate light and half-blinded them with their own ambition. It was so bright and brilliant I was sure it would melt and fade out everything that I had spent my school years trying to escape. The past could be written anew, creating a new me who could finally say, 'I told you so. I told you I could do more. I told you I belonged somewhere else as someone else' – even if there was no one really there to listen.

This all seemed far too sweet, too essential to give up. Cora wanted to dash it from my hands, then stamp on whatever broken pieces were left. I don't know if she fully understood the consequences of telling the police we had all met Jenny at Charlie's that night and then gone home without Mike. But on some level, she must have. She *wasn't* stupid and I tended to forget that. She said she just couldn't bear the not knowing anymore, couldn't bear the secrecy.

I suppose she felt that, even if he could lie to her, Mike couldn't lie to the police. It would all have to come out and she would have her answers.

Trouble was, I couldn't live with it anymore, either. The not knowing if she would crack and plunge us all into God knows where, snatching Mike and the rest of my life away because she could. *And would,* to hurt us both, even though, in the process, she would hurt herself far more.

And there was something else. Something that meant I would have to act quickly. It's always the little things, isn't it, the last or smallest thing, even just one single letter, one consonant even, that force your hand, make the decision for you?

James had paid a fleeting visit to the office to say hello and make one more bid for some drinks and sex. He was off to London that Friday night, back to the big, wide world and all it promised. And he asked me to go with him. For the weekend of course, not for life. Nothing that romantic. He was persistent but not deluded.

Part of his persuasion technique involved the promise of tipping me privileged information. A bargain – information for flesh. 'Owain's having an affair,' he offered, along with a cappuccino.

'With Cath from design?'

'No, Paul from design.'

I burst out laughing. 'No-go I'm afraid. Not sufficiently interesting.'

'Simon is going to get fired for selling stories to *The Mail on Sunday.*'

'Bollocks – *The Mail* wouldn't touch our shit.'

He sighed, 'Granted. I could tell you a real secret though, if you promise you'll keep it to yourself. You can't print it. I'll get my nads ripped off. Deep background only. Deep Throat stuff,' he grinned suggestively.

I grinned back. 'You've been watching *All the President's Men* again, haven't you, Jamie? Oh, all right, Woodward and/or Bernstein, you can try, but I'm not promising anything.'

'Well,' he leaned right in, unnecessarily close, conspiratorial and hushed. 'I was speaking to one of my contacts down in the police station yesterday and he said that the mother of that river girl, what's her name, Morgan, had been going through some of the girl's stuff she took away after the funeral, you know, ready to chuck out, and she found something new.'

'One of your contacts? You mean Phil, your sister's husband, the sergeant?' I clarified feebly, but I couldn't raise enough of a smile. I dreaded what might be coming next.

'Well, yes alright,' he conceded, 'Phil. That's why I can't tell anyone. Marie'll kill me. Well, round about September, Mrs Morgan was going through one of her daughter's old books and came across a note – a love note or something, arranging a meeting with a man. They are sending it for fingerprinting. And it was signed....' He waited, leaning in even closer, drawing strength from my bated breath. An ocean stretched out between us and I was drowning in the middle of it. 'Just the letter M.'

My heart collapsed.

'Yes, exactly, isn't it wonderful? The mysterious Mr M. Or Mr M something? *Dial M for Murder* etc.'

'What did it say? The note, the letter? What else?'

'I don't know. Just something like, 'can't wait to see you. I know we shouldn't be doing this but I can't help it.' Sounds like a married man, maybe the man from the club is M? Remember, what your friend Nora said. It's all coming together now isn't it? Little tart fools about with a married bloke. It gets out of hand. Well, he must have done something to her or otherwise why didn't he come forward at the time when they made all those appeals? It'll be bloody murder before you know it! Bet you could leak it or get it confirmed through one of your contacts? Great exclusive for you, Lizzy. That has to be worth your *quality* time?' he ended triumphantly.

I had to keep up the disinterest, couldn't let him think there was anything significant in what he'd told me. 'Maybe. But not today,' I swatted his arm and pushed back the chair, rising as steadily as I could to signal the end of the negotiations. 'It's pure storytime. Mysterious Mr M indeed. No Pulitzer for you Jimmy. And no shag. But thanks for the coffee.'

He smiled graciously; he'd never really expected me to accept. 'OK Liz, don't believe me if you don't want to. Callously break my heart again. It's your career. But if you use it you owe me, eh? Next time the coffee and the story's on you.'

Storytime

Storytime. Quite.

The next day something happened that made me think perhaps James's version of events was more than half-right. Threads of plot had started to intertwine and the implications were compelling.

At 11am I was perched on the edge of a worn-shiny seat, toast-coloured terrier attentive at my feet, and the old couple opposite, he with the inhaler to hand but not using it yet, not wanting to in company, she sitting at a thoughtful distance, close enough just in case. Both were markedly smart compared to the shabbiness of the old fashioned room, where heavy 50s furniture and handed-down china stood its ground against the prickly orange and brown nylon fabrics that marked the last gasp of the 70s.

They were clad in cardigans, slacks and slippers, a non-threatening audience. I had the folder open on my lap, carefully guarding the loose leaves to prevent a landslide. Page after page was covered in sprawling, maturing handwriting, sagging under the weight of immaculate cursive forms here, sloppier there, but unmistakably all by one hand.

'She was always writing stuff when she was a kid,' said the old man.

'Reams and reams of stuff, bits of poems, stories about people in the street, always making up things. Tried to write a play once about life after the pits, you know, social implications like, kids on drugs or in the pubs, you know.'

Yes, I did know, all too well, so I nodded.

'Oh yes. Lots of cursing in that one. Lots of the F-word in it,' she cut in. 'I said, 'Jenny, is there any need to have it full of all that f'ing and blinding? People don't talk like that, with all that filth,' but she said 'Nan it's not filth, it's realism'. She was only about 11, always ahead of her time.'

He picks up. 'When she was about eight she wrote this story about a boy who falls down an old mine shaft and goes back in time to the Victorian era and all that. Won a prize for that at the school Eisteddfod. I helped her with the details of what it was like down the pits. She said, grampy, tell me what it was like because you was there. I said Duw! I'm not that bloomin' old little 'un! Ha, Ha! Won a prize for that, though. It might be in there somewhere, in that lot. Have a look then, one with the little rosette thing on it, on the top, by there.'

He points shakily with an unopened Twix finger his wife has provided on a plate for us, with some Jaffa Cakes and thin slices of homemade fruit cake, fanning out around the iced centre of a chocolate Mr Kipling cup cake, an alien orchid against the demure pink roses of the best china. The terrier's eyes follow the wavering treat in the hope it will drop and he can salvage it.

I rifle gently through the sheaves of A4 and pull out the one with the withered, once-red rosette, desiccated as the paper that is stiff in my hand, as he reaches towards me with the gnarled fingers of the other hand – to the past. She waits a discreet moment or two then takes it from me and puts it in his hand across the last few inches of space. As she does, two big fat tears slide silently down his cheeks, one from each eye, despite his resolve, despite his pride, despite the fact that women are there.

'It gets him like this now and again,' she says apologetically, as if he is deaf, not merely weeping. 'Come on now, Glyn, drink up your tea,' she dabs at his face as if he is a child, dirty from the street, with a hanky from his cardigan pocket, 'before you need the gas. Do you want the gas?'

He waves her away. 'Don't fuss Vi, don't fuss.' Sips his tea. Concentrates on his breathing, with his black lungs under his baby-blue cardigan.

'I'm sorry Mrs Morgan. I didn't mean to upset you both.'

I had gone to see them in the hope of getting some better pictures to freshen the appeal about Jenny, generate some human interest, cull some family memories, a heart-warming anecdote featuring the dead. You know how it is. But I was already regretting it. They were so bloody nice. An old-fashioned nanny and grampy in an old-fashioned world, dealing with their old-fashioned grief, with cakes and dignity.

'That's all right m'dear, talking about her keeps her here with us doesn't it?'

She lands a few affectionate dog pats on her husband's thigh and a few more on the dog. 'You know what men are like. They try to be all strong and then they just crumple up. She was our only granddaughter, you see. Got three grandsons on our other boy's side, and love them all to bits of course, but she was always grampy's girl.'

'Aye, she was, she was,' he wheezes. The dog gets a Jaffa Cake.

'Course we lost her dad young too. Only 47. Jenny was just

13. Then Lynne took her back to Wrexham, though we still saw a lot of her like – all the school holidays and university holidays. Fair play to Lynne, she made sure we all kept in touch. Could've been funny about it, like. You know they had an up-and-down marriage. She never liked it here much, but she wasn't funny like that.

'Last time Jenny was here for a stay was the summer she came down to Cardiff while she was looking for a flat. Hard to think that was only just over a year ago. She was all excited, you know, first proper job, going to live in the big city like she always wanted. We were worried about her of course, in a place like that. Well, you read all that awful stuff in the papers. You know about that of course. But what can you say? Can't wrap them in cotton wool forever. She didn't really know anyone but she said she'd make friends and it was part of the same firm she was with up North, so that was something. We thought it would be alright.'

She leans in a little bit, conspiratorially, lowers her voice to a loud whisper.

'I think she might have had a boyfriend down there and wasn't wanting to say, you know. Like we'd never been courting or something, never had a bit of fun. But Jenny was a bit shy like that, not really into boys you know, late bloomer.'

Suddenly she's wistful. I fear she will start to cry too, just as he's drying off, then we'll all start. But the moment passes and in the next one she sighs and concludes :

'Still, she's with her dad now.'

There it was. The shut down. The switch off. The resignation of the poor and the humble. The resolute acceptance that life, their life, could not but be filled with loss and struggle. How could they hope for anything more? The resolute acceptance of a higher plan, because it negates the necessity of asking the real question – why must it be so painful and who keeps it that way? This acceptance had kept whole communities running for decades until the coal ran out, until the chapels were boarded up and then turned into flats that stink of piss and community centres that ring with the clacking of line-dancing classes. For a moment I envied their simplicity, their ignorance.

'Do you mind if I look at some of this stuff for a few minutes? I mean, just to get a sense of her for the background piece, to go with the tribute, you know,' I wheedle. It's the classic way in for people like me to get those personal bits and bobs that people like you like to read about.

'Of course, love. Actually, if you want, she left a load of boxes upstairs in the back bedroom if you want to look through it. More writing stuff in there I think. Been up there for years.'

Normally I'd say no. What's the use of rifling through boxes of that sort of ancient junk once you've got the photos? But she is proud now, pleased that anyone still cares enough to ask and I don't have the heart to tell her it won't survive the edit. Besides, part of me badly wants to see where and how Jenny began, to solve part of her mystery, to see something of what I was sure Mike had seen.

'There's other stuff, too, in the boxes. She meant to come back for them when she was settled in the new flat like, only ... she never did. Never did come back.'

He wobbles. Another tear sploshes down his cardigan.

'Go on up, lovely. Up in the back. I'll be up in a bit now. I think he needs a bit of the inhaler,' she whispers loudly. 'Give us a couple of minutes.'

It was just the usual junk upstairs, in the box room at the back that smelled of Yardley Tweed. A few soft toys, a couple of handbags, a pair of winter boots, some plastic kitchen saver boxes of assorted sizes, a wok. Student leftovers. And books. Literature student staples and clichés, cheap and cheerful paperback classics, an Arden Shakespeare, a Norton Anthology. There, on the top of the box, was a crumpled copy of T.S. Eliot's *The Wasteland and Other Poems*.

I smiled in spite of myself for a moment, a fleeting memory causing me to reach down, take its crackled cover in my hand to thumb the well-worn pages. Then I remembered the copy I had seen at Jenny's flat, with the pen and the underlined verses. This was a much older, crumbling edition, and it naturally fell open on the pages bookmarked by a postcard, placed, of course, at the opening of *The Love Song of J. Alfred Prufrock*. The postcard was a dog-eared reproduction of a Monet from the National Museum and Gallery in Cardiff, the indistinct blotches of one of the lily ponds instantly recognisable.

I stared and stared at it for a long time before I was able to turn it over, afraid of what I would see. On the back were scribbled these lines:

Words in the creases and cracks
    Fill the places inside where we lack
    The open years in the silence
    The promise of stories
    Comb out the truths
    Catch them with teeth
    Rook them with fingers, before they fly windward
    Stealing the ending with our stolen voices
    Again.

Stroking the words with my fingers, feeling them hum, I fought the tears rising inside. My words. A 19-year-old's attempt at poetic profundity, coming home. Full circle. From the past. Into my hand. In this back bedroom, miles and years from home.

It was something I had written one afternoon in the sun-dappled university library, cramming for Part One Poetry, doodling on the edge of a ring binder, thinking about the conversation I'd had with Mike in the dining room an hour earlier about Eliot, while Cora peeled potatoes.

I had never shown the words to anyone. I would have been too embarrassed. But I had leant many books to Mike and vice versa. They passed between us as a currency of acknowledged affection and unconscious lies, weekly, sometimes daily, like the pouring of water on to a parched land that could never drink enough. In the bottom corner of the card another hand, not mine, not Mike's, had added 'by Michael Matthews.'

'One of her poems,' said Mrs Morgan, wheezing up behind me, catching her breath in the doorway, arching out her back, knuckling the joints with her bony fists for relief. 'A sad one, I bet.' She's squinting at the writing but she can't see it without her glasses.

'She wrote a lot of stuff. Sad stuff really. Can't say I could understand all of it of course. A bit literary for the likes of me.'

'I understand,' I say. She's shrewd enough to see the glisten in my eyes. But she thinks it is for her dead granddaughter. 'Well, why don't you keep that one,' she says. Gripping my hand with her lumpy, bumpy one, a comradely squeeze is bestowed.

'Feels like, in a strange way, and I don't mean nothing by it, but if you'd met her in the city you might have been friends. She'd've liked to do what you do. Good with words and all that. Can see you like your books too. Funny, you're not like I thought a journalist would be. You don't sound Valleys or nothing exactly but, the way you talked about things earlier. You're not one of them city types. Am I right?'

I am transparent, it seems. Even without her glasses she has seen something of me, through me. Not everything though. I nod.

'See, I was right. You can always tell the ones as are nice and down to earth. Take your time looking, take your time. Want some more tea?'

An hour later she sends me away with a slice of fruit cake in a paper napkin, a photo of Jenny aged four on a rocking horse, a sad poem written when Jenny was 12. She waves from the doorstep until I have wound my way out of sight.

In my bag is the book she offered, burning a dark hole in the fabric of the afternoon.

At the head of the hill between the two valleys I stopped the pool car, pulled off onto the grass verge and pulled out the book. I took the postcard between my hands, intending to tear it to shreds, free it on the racing afternoon winds, destroy the evidence that Mike and Jenny had ever met, erase the image of Jenny taking a pen and reverentially writing Mike's name on the words she had taken to be his own – maybe the words that had made her fall in love.

Did it matter so much that Mike had given her the book? Yes, it did.

The thought of what the book might have meant, what *she* might have meant. The thought of him opening her up, page by page, using a practised key, a familiar sequence, the debut she offered, part of a tale already told but about to be retold in a way where we, he, did not know the ending. Maybe first in Wrexham, then maybe in Cardiff , night after night, in the dark, between the lines, in a place where Cora and I could not go.

I could smell longing in it, darkness and silence and the end of time. The promise of two worlds in one. In one word – Jenny.

I stood there for a long time. Each far-off ribbon of terraces turned gaudy painted faces to the roadside. White with the weight of still-heavy frost, the trees marched as far as the hill crests, its white powdering for once hiding the dust and the soot and the poverty and forgotten promises just below the surface. Boughs, branches and bushes were glittering in the emerging low-slung sun, pretty as a postcard, vibrant and reflective as a hymn that would once have echoed across it on a Sunday morning.

Yet all I could feel was the inevitability of the oncoming deep winter. In my nostrils I caught the faint scent of decay through my tears. This time the tears were for Jenny, as well as for a girl who had, once, long ago shared her hopes and dreams. And her love.

Methodology

On the journey back to the office, thinking of that slap in the face in Cora's kitchen, thinking of the book and postcard, of the diaries in police hands, of Cora's little note to the Inspector, of the love letter signed M, of my job offer, of the police, of the rest of my life, and of Mike either in it or not, I began to formulate a plan.

It wasn't much of a plan, as plans go. But then I knew from experience, even though it was vicarious, that the more complicated a crime is, the more things can go wrong – the more likely you are to end up on pages one to three of our newspaper.

It wasn't exactly that I sat down then and there and drew up a scheme to murder my best friend. It was more that I played with the idea in spare moments and minutes, turning it over and over in my mind like a Rubik's cube, discarded with demonic frustration time and time again but always stubbornly retrieved. Tantalising, impossible to solve, but there was still the possibility I might get lucky.

Could I? Dare I? What if? Did I dare disturb the universe?

One word from Cora would do it now, puncture my world of Mike and promotion – join the dots through the diary and the letter, with its fingerprints and initial, and any other evidence the police had kept to themselves, creating arrows that led straight to Mike. And maybe that was where they should point.

I had to act, for once, for good – to protect what I wanted and what I loved.

At first I toyed with the idea of pushing Cora off something. A railway platform, or a balcony, perhaps, like the one in the shopping centre. That seemed the easiest way. But there are so many CCTV cameras around these days, dark-eyed and impassive. I didn't fancy my chances of not ending up on Crimewatch.

Idly, as I ate my lunchtime sandwich, or dawdled on the court steps, I'd think of the places that might do, busy and brimming with people, all intent on their own business, but ideal as an audience to the aftermath.

But with each such train of thought, I'd have to eliminate a location for one reason or another, as I saw possibilities of detection. Plus, I wasn't a doctor. I wasn't sure how high the fall would have to be to finish it properly. I didn't want Cora to survive, crippled and martyred or anything like that. I wasn't a complete monster. And frankly, I seriously doubted that when the moment came I would have the guts to do it. You see, I'd have to be as normal as possible right up to the last minute or she'd be suspicious, then, somehow, summon the strength for a forceful, perfectly-timed shove.

It would be difficult. And she was my friend, after all, and that might make it hard to coolly coordinate the exact moment, the exact amount of force required, speed versus pound for pound multiplied by distance. Simple physics.

It couldn't be too hands-on. There couldn't be blood or violence. I realised, too, that staging an 'accident' would be unpredictable and risky.

I couldn't break into their house and fake a burglary, not just because Mike would be there, but I didn't really know how. Not how to do it quietly without waking the whole street. There were too many variables. It would be too easy to mess up royally.

It had to be plain and simple and Cora had to be compliant or complicit, even if she didn't realise it. Clean and tidy and beyond suspicion, beyond salacious headlines, beneath what would interest any hack worth his or her PC. I thought I had settled on just the thing.

That night after work I went home, drank a bottle of wine, listened to a favourite CD and realised that I was going mad. Completely mad. What was I thinking? What the hell was wrong with me? I couldn't do this. I couldn't really be contemplating this?

I needed to pull back, cling to some perspective. But I couldn't get it in the city. So I did what I always do at the point of system overload. I called in sick, told *that prick* I had women's problems, and then spent a whole day watching old movies and drinking tea, eating toast, letting my brain slow, speaking to no one, thinking of nothing.

The decision then came naturally. There was somewhere I needed to be: the place where I had always gone when I needed to really think things through. So I started on the journey home – to my real home. Back to The Valleys.

Time Travel

This is how it always goes. Turn into the valley at its gateway in Porth and almost immediately you begin to travel up hill. Before the Relief Road snaked out its tendrils of tarmac and shiny metal from North to South, the old road would decrease in width and quality while people drove at impossible speeds through double-parked traffic and fleets of buses.

As you ascend, the villages cluster in parallel rows. Behind, the hills rise up like tidal waves on either side. The bumping and grinding through potholes, and heart-in-mouth, slamming on the brakes, near-misses, are part of the expectation, as you weave beside sturdy stone terraces, leaning onwards and upwards.

Keep driving north, ever north, turning neither left nor right, ignoring the clans of bomber-jacketed, shaven-headed youths, until you begin to wonder if you can possibly go much further. Remains of ancient woodland cling to the mountainsides, that in autumn are a dazzling montage of yellowed grass, burning orange gorse and ferns and glowing heather, shining black slate peeping out from neat fir-striped patches of forestry that smoke in the summer, and in their nearness brush the sky. It's beautiful, of course. If you look only casually, take in a glancing view.

To the right side of the road the houses fall away to factory units, discreetly camouflaged in summer by a row of leafy trees.

TELLING STORIES

The valley's under fit river snakes through the ravine below. For a while it was black and then it was clean and became clear as the hills became green.

My old school is perched high above this river where a colliery used to stand. It is square and black and white and grey, seventies boxes of prefabrication on three floors and two sites, perched on the place where the houses slide to one side, giving free view to where the last town ends. The mountains take over, and miles further on, the sun sets in the cradle they form.

It was bloody cold there. Always. For half the year waves of rain and rivers of wind washed and blasted every inch of building and playground.

But there would always be hockey after English on Wednesdays. And I was a hardy, outdoor child, lugging my books and violin and gym kit home in all weather, riding my bike in all but the snow, sliding down the mountainsides on pieces of cardboard when the summer grass was worn dry and slippery, into the feathery-dark evening, until the mams summoned everyone in to tea.

Cora and Mike knew nothing of this life. I had never taken them there, taken them home. Not because I was ashamed, as I had long suspected, but because in going back I could not be sure who I was anymore. While there I would often feel that I had forgotten the true sound of my voice. I had become too expert at flattening it, sharpening it, smoothing it as required.

My name at home was Beth – never Lizzy. Cora started that and I was happy to be renamed. Beth had little to recommend her – under-confident, overachiever, aching for friends, fearing to belong to the lager, litter, lipstick, rugby and redundancy all around that stretched far beyond the pits and the closing factories, delving into books for salvation. Drowning in them.

From the day before Beth's 14th birthday when Evans English tossed her Stephen King book into the bin stating 'You shouldn't read this rubbish,' things changed for her.

Evans English, five feet and a bare few inches, stern over his black rimmed specs, the embodiment of every Welsh school master, belonging to another age and drowning in this one, disappeared into the dusty, overcrowded storeroom from where he doled out the exercise books and pens, and stashed his whiskey bottles, returning with *Tess of the D'Urbervilles, Jane Eyre, a Tale of Two Cities, 1984, Vanity Fair.*

From that moment words accessed other worlds, permitted dreams and allowed words to become armour. Perhaps Lizzy was born that day, and from then on was just waiting for the moment to show herself.

The park, my park, sits alongside this school beneath Evans English's old classroom. Its ancient glacial lake is set in a hollow formed by ice and water, millennia ago, before the people came and became miners, steep sides wooded with watching trees, water deep, black, listening, longing.

The lake seems to exist outside time. It, unlike anything else, is unchanging, save for the odd new bench or litter bin and the sliding of the year which dresses the canopy with each new season's colours and polishes the water. Birds explode from their hiding places and their voices echo off the cliffs. Time after time I have sought its silence and solace.

Watching through the trees I had never failed to feel that, if I had only arrived a few seconds sooner, I might have seen something occurring, something elemental and unearthly. It carries the feel of the just-happened, just-missed action in the corner of your eye, glance over your shoulder. I expected to turn to see bearded faces watching me with burning eyes, peering, peeping people from pre-history, side by side with flat-capped, petticoated families, for this lake has watched all our history, watched before the community was even founded, and remained unmoved by the struggle or the laughter.

If it could talk it might spin a few tales about black, body-breaking work, broken backs, broken lungs, broken promises, food bought on account until pay day because you had to stick together, stolen Saturday night kisses after the pictures, choral singing, 24 hour washing cycles, reds in little Moscow, first free primary education for children in Britain, strikes and marches, drugs and blowjobs, levelling of coal tips, truancy and domestic violence. In no particular order.

This is where I began to be made and where I always go for answers. Where Beth and Lizzy would make a decision. Beth might admit defeat, but what would Lizzy do?

On that dark December day as I wound through Porth and up to the heartland, I met the valley brooding beneath the full weight of its winter gloom. Soaked with grey and twilight, the houses and hills undulated like soiled sheets in the washday wind, splinters of brown and black wood and stone pinning the edges precariously to the land, the ragged pines clinging to their stubborn water-heavy wintergreen.

Even the multi-coloured twinkle of Christmas lights could not banish the sense of seasonal defeat. Some houses were putting up a fruitless fight, festooned with hundreds of glowing bulbs, Santas scaling ladders, snowmen in plastic hot air balloons, giant reindeer grazing in the odd front garden.

It was gone three in the afternoon by the time I walked down the steps, past the steamy-glassed classrooms of the lower school to the water. It felt as if night was already gathering below the crest of the hills, pushing downwards, waiting.

There was ice clinging to the water's edge. Two ducks and a drake were idling near the bulrushes at the far end. A middle-aged man in a red baseball cap, pulled down low, walked a golden retriever. 'How be?' he nodded in customary greeting.

I sat on a half-broken bench, pulling my coat under me to keep out the damp, avoiding the bit of splintered wood where the seat had fallen, or been kicked through. Within minutes my lungs were cold and my mind was empty, as I'd hoped.

This was where a decision would be made, an answer offered, without the trappings of thought, without the insistent stream of consciousness that was my own voice – somewhere in the background, beyond all that, where it mattered, I was tuning in to something older, darker, cleaner.

I was lost inside for some time. When I surfaced it was nearly dark.

Then something unexpected happens. I see Sal.

Yes, it is Sal. With what looks like a six-year-old girl. And a toddler. And a baby. I know it is her at once, without doubt. She's wearing jeans and a pink anorak, snug in a matching scarf, rosy-cheeked, same shock of curly ginger hair clashing with her clothes. She is 100 yards away but I'm in no doubt. I suspect she has been looking at me for some time. At once grins are spreading out across the thirty or so steps between us, the pram wheels crackling on the wet ground, closing the gap.

All at once we are awkwardly gripping each other's hands in the way of the once intimate. We are saying each other's names and laughing, like we used to. The years close around us in that instant.

'Beth? Beth! Bloody hell, it is you. Bloody hell.'

'Yes, it's me. Hello, Sal. Hello little Sals. God you've been busy.'

'Bloody hell, you look great. You look really smart. I thought it was you from all the way over there. Miles away as usual, you were. Wasn't sure you'd recognise me, with the babies and all.'

I think she means she wasn't sure if I'd acknowledge her. Ten years and ten lifetimes onwards and upwards from where we once stood.

'Don't be stupid you daft bugger. Course I knew it was you. I was just, well, you know, coming to see my parents and I thought I hadn't been up here in ages…..'

'Visiting the old stomping grounds,' knowingly, she nods. 'It doesn't change does it?'

I sidestep. 'And who is this?' I squat to say hello to the chunky toddler clutching Sal's leg, same ginger curls.

'This is Lauren,' she says, hiking the toddler on to her hips. 'This is Catherine. And this,' cooing a little into the pram 'is Elizabeth.'

'Good name.'

'Yes, it's my middle name.'

'Yes I know. You and Darren still…?'

'Oh yes. He's with the council now. I.T. Still haven't the faintest about all that myself.'

We smile at each other, easily, in a way that silences a thousand words. I don't like to ask if she still plays the cello, if she ever got a job teaching music.

'What you up to now then?' seems neutral ground.

'Well, not much time with these three. I did start my PGCE, remember I wanted to do music? But then Catherine popped up, sooo……Seen you in the paper though. You did really well, Beth. Knew you would. Left us all behind. Knew you could.'

'Hey, there's this new thing called Facebook someone told me about. It's this new site where you put a bit about yourself on the net and you can look up old people from school. Loads of people are on there. I was thinking that I might go on it if Darren shows me how. Maybe time for a reunion, like? Ten years. Good God! You don't look a day older. You sold your soul to Satan or what? Got a painting mouldering away in the attic up your mam's? Wonder what everyone's like. Fatter I expect. Course most of them are still around anyway but people like you...' She stops, realising that this line of thought goes nowhere.

I smile at her and shake my head a little. 'Don't think so, Sal. Just don't see what I would say to anyone.'

'No, you're right really. Not much point. Want to walk round with us? Too cold to be standing around.'

So we walk, and she talks about the children and asks me about the paper, and if I'm seeing anyone, and relates the to-date histories of the people we knew: Lucy Fisher had three kids and one of them is 12, Tony Nicholas is in prison for nicking cars, Dan Andrews overdosed four years ago, Nadine Baker works in the sweetshop, Susan Earland manages the bread shop, Darren Davies teaches geography in Ton Comp, Paul Peter's mother had a stroke last year and can't speak or recognise anyone. And we talk a little about who we used to be too. Not too much – just enough. And I see that Sal is living a life she likes, with kids she adores, and she smiles a lot and is very like the old Sal I remember.

Who am I to judge her for that?

As we reach the gates we must separate and we grip hands again, then hug.

'It's really good to see you, Beth.'

'Yes it is. It is,' I say, and part of me means it.

'We must go for a drink or something sometime, you and me. Over Christmas. There's a do up the Rug as usual. Be like old times. There's the disco and the raffle.'

'Yes, of course, of course. I'll call you,' I say, knowing it would be exactly like old times and that's why I will not call.

As I turn all I can hear are her words. 'You've done really well for yourself, Beth. Left us all behind.' As I walk away I am crying.

I don't go home. I drive straight back to the city. Away from the life I chose not to lead. Remembering why. I've made up my mind.

After the store

The next day was December 21st. Cora and I went Christmas shopping. We went to the toy store and wandered among the bright-eyed, watching teddies. Afterwards, over coffee, she told me quietly and calmly with more self-possession than she had shown in a long time, that she was going to *do the right thing*.

Mike was on the last day of his training course. He'd be back very late that night, early the following morning in fact, from Leeds, for the Christmas holidays. I knew Cora would be home alone, probably drunk, and I knew where the spare key was, tucked between the inner and outer pot of the magnolia planter in a tiny plastic envelope.

'All right, Cora,' I'd said. 'We'll wait for Mike to come home tomorrow then we'll all go to the police, together. Make a clean breast of it.' She stared at me for a few moments, as if the words were taking time to fully register. 'We'll go to the station and tell them everything. Whatever happens, we'll do it together. We can get through it together.'

She believed me, you know. It was the word 'together' that did it. I reached across and took her hand, giving her my best reassuring and practised, sincere smile. The end-of-interview, of course I'll write this responsibly, you can trust me I'm a journalist, smile. She looked so relieved I actually felt sorry for her. For what she and we had become: and failed to become.

'Will you, Lizzy? Really? You think we could? You'd do that?'

'Of course. I can't bear to see you like this, Cora. This unhappy. It has to end somewhere. We'll talk to Mike in the morning. Whatever else happens, at least you'll have your answers.'

She lunged across the table, threatening to up-end it, slopping cappuccino before her as the cups wobbled, to lock her arms around my neck. If I had been able to feel anything like a human emotion at that point, my breath would have left me and perhaps the force of what I intended to do would have ebbed away, slipping into the swirls of slush and snow settled in the streets and gutters outside. And it might have been different.

But I was beyond that. In the spot-lit precision of the moment I was emptied out and so calm, oh, so calm.

'Come on,' I said, gently loosening her grip, breaking the embrace. 'Let's go to Old Orleans. We'll have cocktails like we used to, one of those Christmassy things with the cream you always liked. Then we'll go and see a rubbish film. There's bound to be something out. It's been too long since we did that.'

So we did. And Cora seemed lightened immeasurably, smiling at me and taking my hand in the street, sipping the cocktail and having a little sing along to the usual Christmas tunes. I remember her like that, head thrown back, wailing tunelessly to *Hey, Mr Churchill*.

I remember a hundred other nights when we had done exactly the same thing at a dozen different bars along St Mary Street, how we had talked about everything and nothing while the Baileys or the Martini or the Archers flowed. I tried not to remember them as we giggled like school children, all the way to the new multiplex.

In the darkness of the theatre I was painfully aware of her closeness, the flickering of the screen reflected in her woozy, drunken, laughing eyes. Her hand reached out awkwardly for mine, resting on my wrist and squeezing it for a moment. Then I drove her back to her house and we wrapped up some gifts together, sitting on the floor in a sea of shiny scraps and scissor ends, adding the little bows and bits of twine Cora had bought. Finishing touches.

We talked about Christmas past and Christmas presents, of six stolen chocolate reindeer and cheap turkey rolls. As we talked I topped up her glass, again and again.

'It'll be alright now, Lizzy. It'll be alright now,' she slurred. 'It'll all come out, about that night, and then we'll know everything.'

She waved me off at six, eyes glassy and gleaming. I headed home to wait. I made a pit stop at the teeny Tesco Metro and arrived at Cora's again around nine thirty. I parked in the next street, my woolly hat and scarf obscuring my face as I walked to the door, the only sound the wet, metallic crunch of snow hardening in the night chill.

The lights were out, except for the one in the back kitchen, glowing through the length of the hall. No one moved in the street. Windows were filled with brightly lit trees and neon salutations of the season. Getting no answer to my soft knock, as I'd expected, I let myself in, heart barely beating, now, freezing like the slumbering street, breath almost invisible. If Cora was still awake the pretence for my return would be the shopping bag I had left behind the hall door earlier.

Still in silence I climbed the stairs, clutching my heavy shoulder bag, calling softly through the house room by room, ending with the bathroom. In darkness, I opened the door.

I still see the blood. In the dream I sometimes have.

It pools out across the floor, over my hands and clothes, down the stairs and across the slick hall floor, peppering the banisters, flecking the walls, soaking the carpet, dampening the air.

Though Cora is dead I try desperately to scrabble away from her vacant but accusing stare. The more I try to haul myself up to the second floor the more I slide and lose my footing, the faster my hands slip and my shoes scud down a step at time.

In reality there wasn't that much blood. Most of it was in the bath and a lot had gone down the plughole.

She beat me to it, you see. She slit her wrists.

I opened the bathroom door and there she was. For a second that seemed to unwind as slowly as a winter Sunday, I had thrown the thought into the air that I might just slip away, back out through the bathroom door, moving silently in reverse, through the hall and out the front door, backing down the neat street to my car and driving away into the late evening. A simple trick of time travel, and then, I'd never have been there at all.

The thought floated softly towards the red Victorian tiled roofs, ambling like a snowflake with all the time in the world, but disintegrating in one touch. This was it. I needn't carry out my plan at all. I could just walk away now and everything would be different. Cora would slip away. The future yawned before me, an immense stretch of darkness between the door and the scarlet edge of the bath.

But I moved forward.

If I hadn't called the ambulance I don't know if she would

have died, probably not, or not for a long time anyway. More than likely Mike would have made it home first.

The cuts were half-hearted for such a spitefully bright kitchen knife, no long-blunted blade dulled by the tough skin of potatoes and apples for Cora. It was brand new and sharp as a scalpel. She would not have wanted to endure pain and would probably have worried about germs on an older knife, clinging to microscopic imperfections in the metal.

I remembered when we had bought the knife, part of a set of four on offer from a Scottish sales rep in a department store in Swansea. It was the kind they promised could cut a can in half, and the rep had indeed done this, and many more fascinating tricks, like throwing a beefsteak tomato up in the air and slicing it in half in mid-flight, seeds, skin and juice separating wetly before the bored and fidgety audience. Cora had been transfixed. She made me chip in so we could get a pack.

She kept the fillet knife because frankly I thought meat came frozen or in breadcrumbs and would never dream of filleting anything. I'd thrown one paring knife in the kitchen drawer and then proceeded to try the bread knife on various unyielding objects to see if it would slice with the precision promised.

It was one of the paring knives lying in the bath, next to her left wrist, which bled fitfully. The bathroom was icy cold because the window was open and my breath was quite visible, as was Cora's, though mine was hard and sharp, little dragon-like snorts, and hers was more like a puff of flour settling after a sneeze.

On the edge of the bath, running down the enamel, was a small trail of vomit. No doubt Cora had retched at the sight of her own blood after making the cuts. She looked quite pathetic, reclined at a shallow angle, no water in the bath. But at the same time, considering she'd gone through with it, I was quite impressed. It was the most decisive thing she'd ever done.

She wasn't naked. She was wearing one of those balcony push-up bras in rather good quality red silk and matching high leg knickers. Probably something Mike had bought her for one of their numerous special occasions. Nothing tarty.

She started to cry when she saw me. It was a moment or two before I realised she had opened her eyes and was looking right at me. Tears were leaking down her face, her features twisting in such self disgust that I wanted to turn and run. At least I think it was self disgust.

'Why you?' Was all she said.

I thought she meant why did I have to be the one who found her that way? I suspect she had intended Mike to find her on his return, cold, martyred, blue-tinged, black-blooded, her own photographic negative in silk and sacrifice.

I pulled a towel from the handrail by the door and gently covered her red and white form, not realising right away that tears were slipping down my face.

Sliding one arm beneath her cold, cold shoulders, and fishing out my mobile phone with the other, I rocked her almost imperceptibly saying over and over 'please don't cry. Cora. Please don't cry,' until the sirens came and the scene ended.

After the House

In the hospital bed a few hours later, Cora is pale, cleaned up and washed-out. The only colours are the off-white of the sheets and curtains, the dull worn khaki of the institutional peeling walls and the dark rings that halo Mike's eyes.

Cora looks remarkably perky. Her face peeps out above the folded bedcover, eyes bright and watchful, and she talks to him animatedly in a persistent whisper.

I cannot hear what she says. If it is the truth, or a portion of it, or another tale altogether, I do not know. But I watch through the glass partition from the night-lit corridor for a signal, pacing and stubbing my feet against the scratched skirting, moving and standing, drumming my fingers on the fire extinguisher, shying away from nurses' eyes. I am half-irritated, half-sulking, exhausted and wound tight inside, pacing, watching.

He takes her hand now, gently. I see her respond with a smile. Now he is crying. Simple wet tears, falling easily. His face is full of indulgence, as if he were looking at a child. His other hand strokes damp hair from her brow, soothing. After maybe 20 minutes he gets to his feet and looks for me through the glass. Rising, he holds her hand until the last length of arm and finger run out as he comes to speak to me.

'Thank God you arrived when you did, Lizzy,' he said.

The words shattered something inside. Hope exploded. I suppose I had wanted him to at least indicate in some unspoken way, some subtle form, that he realised if Cora had succeeded he would have been close to another life, one with me, one that he could, just for one second, on the dark side of himself, grow to want, or want to grow. If only his wife had killed herself.

Instead he said: 'I've made such a mess of things with Cora, with everything. I drove her to this. I knew she'd do anything for me. I just didn't realise how badly she meant it. She said such strange things, such unbelievable things...' he trailed off.

He looked as if he was grappling with a difficult maths problem.

'She said she actually thought I had loved that girl Jenny. I know I've done some things that weren't so smart or so kind, but really? How could she think that?

That's why she did it. She said she didn't know me anymore – who I was. Didn't know what the truth was. She's not who I thought she was either, but then, who is?'

His eyes drifted off somewhere, out above Cora's bed, out into the dark and through the years, away. 'But I have to make it right now don't I? After this? If ever there was a time to make it right.'

He spoke the words almost with pride, with unmistakable awe. Her strange courage, her decisive act, had overwhelmed him, revealed her adoration and her dependency. I could see it. His naivety led him to believe it was for him only, as everything was, and could only be, for him.

In another life this was the moment I would take his face in my hands and say, 'I love you, Mike. I know that now. Please be with me instead. We can leave all this behind us and go on, or go back, to each and every night we didn't touch each other because it seemed so wrong, because we had ideas about what was decent and right and possible. We can have the life we should have had – even if we don't deserve it.'

But instead I felt sick to the place where my soul had once been. And I could see from the look in those familiar blue, beautiful eyes that the moment was long gone. I wanted to grab at his clothes, beat at him with my fists, beg, scream, cry, wail, tear at my hair, howl in anguish. But the idea of Mike was becoming more and more insubstantial before my very eyes.

The toll of the years was getting harder to shoulder, the pressure pushing the breath from my body as he looked at me, begging for understanding and absolution, as usual. I didn't care much for what I saw. Did he accept what he had done to Jenny, to me, to his wife, out of weakness and ease and vanity? Where once there had been no intention to cause harm, now there was no recognition of the damage done.

'She opened up her wrists for you. You must be very proud. I guess that's where I went wrong. I would have killed for you but not died for you. That's the difference. All the difference in the world,' I said calmly.

He looked at me with genuine sadness and puzzlement. Thankfully, he does not fully understand.

'Oh, Lizzy,' he croons, reaching forward to cup my face. 'If things had been different. If I had met you…'

I pull away so violently he actually recoils, and a janitor replacing loo roll in the disabled bathroom a few doors down stops and stares.

'She's my wife.'

'Yes. Then you should go back in. Be with her, she needs you now.'

'Lizzy,' he begins, 'you know, I can't explain….'

But he was speaking to my back. I was retreating, fleeing, as the bright light of the ward gave way to the unforgiving wet drizzle of the car park and everything after, leaving Stevie staring after me from a green plastic seat in the waiting room.

After the hospital

At home I wanted the dark to come, warm and comforting and soft, lapping around my feet first, moving upwards to wash myself from myself.

I should have thought of Cora, I know that. I should have tried to feel what she had felt but I could just feel him. All those times we had sat close yet not even touching and I had longed for him to look at me, make me real to myself by taking me in with his eyes. And the little accidental caresses, the invisible fluff and strand of hair he would spot and smooth, out there in the open. And the dance of days that passed between.

It would have been a relief to cry but I couldn't. Hollowed out as I was, scooped and scrubbed clean, not looking any different from the outside, yet torn right down the middle. And further outside the other kind of darkness listened and watched and waited.

It was around three that I first thought Cora might have left some sort of suicide note. As the shock wore off I woke to the idea with a picture in my mind of a single sheet of good quality paper, folded and tucked somewhere not too obvious.

It occurred to me that she might have written something that would screw us all. Had someone picked it up or was it

258

lying there waiting for a stray hand to collect, ticking silently like a little pile of explosives, rolled up and bound in a ribbon?

Of course the policeman had taken a quick look around. But she probably wouldn't have left it in plain view. She would have wanted me to find it, or Mike, more likely.

Once the idea of it had popped into my head it stubbornly refused to let me sleep. I didn't want to go back across town at that time of night in the cold pre-dawn damp. To tell the truth I was a little scared to go to that empty house, where the blood would still be clinging to the bathroom like a bad memory.

I turned over among the tangle of sheets saying it would keep until morning. Half an hour later I was starting the car and shifting into gear. A note? A note? Why hadn't I thought about it while the usual questions were being asked and the paramedics were dealing with Cora? I suppose I was trying to get over the surprise of seeing that the policeman who appeared at the door was the one from Jenny's inquest. The one from the court café, Mr *You Can't Print This, But...* A coincidence?

He recognised me, of course, and gave a small, almost sheepish smile, but was otherwise very businesslike. He led me to the armchair by the window, where I could see the ambulance in the street below, and the usual gathering of ghouls hoping for a glimpse of a mangled body. In any other circumstances I might have been among them, asking what they had seen or heard, frantically scribbling down all the details I could squeeze out. The policeman saw my glance and drew the pink velvet curtain across. 'Don't you worry,' he said. 'It'll all be fine now.'

I was so unsettled to see him again it didn't even occur to me to wonder why he was there so quickly. Just a minute after I called the ambulance. He had followed me you see, first to my house and then along the empty road to Cora's.

But the police had gone by the time I got back to the house. The weary Inspector who had perfunctorily taken the PC's report had long since departed to the warmth of his home. If he had spotted a suicide note he would surely have said something at the time, shown it to me. *What's all this, then?*

I used the spare key again. It was still in my pocket – forgotten in the unexpected scene that had confronted me. I'd meant to wipe it clean, return it to its pot once my work had been completed.

There were signs the police had had a bit of a poke around at Cora's dressing table, in the work bureau, the mantle-piece, but not much was disturbed. It was too late and too cold. There'd be more questions tomorrow, surely, but it was an obvious case of a self-inflicted injury.

Still, I had to be sure they hadn't missed anything. I found Cora's diary among a pile of exercise books on the living room table. It looked like one I had given her, along with one of those little address books and a pen, for her first University birthday. It was a sort of joke, because Cora had accidentally boiled hers in the laundrette washing machine. Pulling it out I realised it *was* the same book. Inside the front cover I had written in blue biro, 'For Cora, Queen of the toads, who on August 11 defeated the bread rolls single-handedly and vanquished the ironing board with a single blow.'

This didn't make much sense. I had forgotten most of the references.

Inside the back cover was a photograph. It was the one of us all that had been hidden behind the wedding picture I knocked over in Cora's bedroom, an exact copy of the one on my pin board at home. Cora in the tangerine dress, the Tom Cruise poster, even the vibrator is in shot.

Folded neatly alongside it were a dozen newspaper cuttings about Jenny. The first two reported her missing, long before I even knew she was, before I'd been given that heads-up by Owain. Then there were the 'Body Found' cuttings, before Jenny was identified, and then all the story cuttings up to the one about the inquest, when Cora was, supposedly, oblivious to Jenny's fate.

I stare at Jenny's face in one of the official pictures. She stares vacantly back. It looks like one of those taken at a family birthday party, maybe her 21^{st,} and Jenny has been caught off guard. She is less polished than she looked that night at Charlie's and younger, I think. Her hair is a little lighter and longer. At least I think it was. To tell the truth I could barely remember what she looked like anymore.

But that wasn't all. In a plain white envelope was the earring I had seen that day at the dinner party from hell. It had stabbed me in the foot in Cora's bedroom and I had placed it in the trinket box alongside Cora's wedding ring, assuming it was hers.

Without warning, something crackled up my spine and into the front of my brain. I saw the pieces fuse together. So this is why she did it, then. With the knife. All those weeks of wringing herself out to me. It was because it told her what it now told me. Where Mike had been, at least, and what he had probably done.

How else would the earring be here? Jenny's earring. The mate to the one found on her body – the other assumed lost to the waters of the Taff.

Was there more? Perhaps Mike had told Cora something after all. Something he had not told me. She had thought her husband was not just an adulterer, but a murderer. And not knowing had taken her apart.

In the pile of stuff was also a photograph of us all, that

night at Charlie's. I had been so drunk I had forgotten that Cora had taken her camera. There we were, the four of us. I don't know who took the picture – just a random bloke we had press-ganged at the bar I think. We all look so happy, me, Cora, Mike, Stevie. It must have been taken before Jenny appeared, surely? Mike's arm is round Cora's shoulder, grinning. Stevie's arm around me. Two couples, all smiles. I am laughing.

Happy birthday, it says wordlessly. We are all lovers and friends and we stand against the world.

I know now that there are no real lives, no real truths, only, in the click of the shutter, 100 possible explanations, identities and answers. They dwell in the soundless laughter frozen in mid-flight, in the light that glances off a cheekbone, gleams on glass, the world of promise in the freshly slicked lip-gloss. I see my face, flawless, glowing, drawing in the eye, promising a wordless bargain. I am young, I am beautiful, I can make you part of my dreams. I can be your reason.

I tucked away the photos and cuttings and left the house quickly. It was as I was bumping down the stairs I realised I still had the bottle of vodka and the sleeping pills in my shoulder bag. I knew I'd have to get rid of them the first chance I had. I never drank vodka. I dropped them in a wheelie bin at the end of Cora's street.

Would I have used the pills and booze for the purpose I brought them? The night that I found Cora? Would I have plied her with deliciously strong glasses of vodka, each glass laced with a few crunched up pills the doctor had given Cora for sleeplessness, more and more, convincing her it was just like old times, it would do her good to relax, get a solid night's rest? Would I then have laid her upon her bed, tucked in warmly, knowing Mike would not be back until at least morning? When she passed out I could have run a bath. Hauled her in and just let her sink slowly under the water. I wouldn't even have had to stay and watch it happen. I could have left and let fate take its course.

I wouldn't even need to wipe my fingerprints off the vodka or from the rest of the house, only the pills. Why wouldn't we have had a drink together? Cora had already been prescribed the Valium, had been moody and unstable. Everyone could vouch for that, especially the cashier in Tesco's who she'd showered with sweets. I would put on exactly the right horrified and teary, vulnerable performance for the police if they had wanted a statement.

Would I have done it to protect Mike? I asked myself that on the stairs, pausing in the darkness. Had he already killed to protect Cora? Then I went home. And slept like the dead.

After everything

Two weeks later I was round at Stevie's for salmon and potato gratin. Cora was home, recovering well. It seemed all was right between her and Mike and thus all was right with the world.

'Why would she do it do you think? Try to kill herself? For him? I mean for fuck's sake, is he worth it? Is any man? I mean anyone? And that Jenny, was it worth it for her? What the fuck is it with people?'

I was unloading on Stevie, half-saying what was expected, to hide what I suspected. Stevie boiled the kettle and banged cups around in a reassuring bout of activity, the afternoon silence displaced by my aggression and his tea-making, in the mellow-lit bachelor pad. I hadn't told him about the earring or the clippings. My suspicions. That would make it too clear for him.

'Did he, you know, sleep with her do you think?' I asked, almost in spite of myself. This was the final question, its answer the puzzle's one missing piece. Because no matter what had happened, whatever else Mike may have done, somehow it was still the hardest thing to deal with.

The thought of him with her, opening her up inch by inch. She was the blank space that Cora and I had feared most, because if it was true, then she could go into both the places we had occupied – the worlds of the real and the imagined. She could be everything where we had both failed. Where I had failed more it seemed. Why risk it all for Jenny if not for me? *If* they had fucked.

Stevie would know. I realised that at last. Mike shared everything else with him. Why not this?

I was on my feet, grabbing the cup into which he was splashing milk and setting it down, and the silence was unbearable.

'Stevie, did he tell you? For the last time, was it an affair? Was it worse? Did he do something, something bad?' There, it was said. I expected silence, outrage or at least denial.

But Stevie burst out laughing. 'Something bad? Oh baby, you never change do you? Bad? As in, did he kill her? I wondered when that might occur to you! I was waiting for it. Mike hasn't the guts and you know it. That girl was unlucky, that's all. Probably had half a dozen dodgy blokes after her. Did he fuck her? That's what you really want to know isn't it? I doubt it. If so, he never told me about it, and he told me *everything* else. The real question is why the fuck do *you* care so much who he sleeps with?'

He had never called me 'baby' before and I didn't think I cared for it much now. Nor for the strange smile on his face as he spoke.

I bristle before his amusement. I would like to slap him hard but instead I turn away. Then without warning, without a smile or a trace of it, Stevie says:

'I thought if Cora knew, he would stop. So I told her.' Just like that.

He looks as if the weight of his guilt is about to wash him to his knees. The kettle boils hysterically and after a moment I look him full in the eye. I know what he means without any further explanation.

'I thought if she knew what had happened he would leave

you alone for five minutes, then I would have the chance to show you something real.'

He stops, then tries to continue his defence. 'She had a right to know. Or I thought so then. I thought she'd rein him in, in that typical Cora fashion.'

He sighs, as if the pressure of speaking might crush him if he doesn't fight it with all his strength. 'But it didn't work did it? Nothing changed. I don't think she ever even raised it with him, even asked if it was true. That's love, isn't it?'

There was a faint sneer in the words, but not in his eyes. He hadn't the heart to raise it there.

'Seeing you together that night, in the street, him holding you over that stupid sports car,' he broke off. A million words tumbled out in the silence between. He paused and said carefully. 'After that night out it was clear to me. It hardly takes that long to get from one house to the other. He was riddled with guilt of course, but he was so happy. He had to tell someone and that was me. Though he must have known what it would do to me. How could he not? He thought it might mean something you see. You might really want him. Lucky bastard, I said.'

I was frozen.

Stevie had told Cora. He had told her about our single dark night. Maybe even in our shared house, while making tea perhaps. It didn't matter exactly when or how soon after. Days? Weeks? Years even? The outcome was the same.

He had taken her aside one afternoon, in his quiet, well-mannered way, taken her hand perhaps, and told her he didn't know if he should say anything but he thought it was for her own good.

Or he had at least dropped a hint, a well-chosen word, or a word spat out in anger, in spite, in disgust. A word, a gesture, a touch, a kiss, a dance, a blow. Kind or cruel, drunk or sober, in earnest or in play, wasn't it always all the same? The meaning had been undeniable. Not so nice, not so sweet, not so tolerant, not so stupid Stevie.

'But it didn't work, did it?' He continued. 'Not in the right way.'

He is close now, tall. I see the sinews of his shoulders flex, cannot but remember the Stevie of the night of the wedding. My instinct is to step back, make room between us for what he is saying, but I resist the urge so he will not know that I am suddenly afraid of him. I say 'What are you talking about, Stevie?' What else could I say?

'She loved you too much, as much as she loves him. But you knew that all along, right? That's why you were always that way. Because you could be. You knew she'd forgive you anything.'

There is a glint of amusement in his eyes and something harder, older. We are both much older now.

And to be honest I *had* known it. My affection for Cora was real but could probably have been put down if had to be. It was not that way for her. Cora – carrying her armfuls of commitments and attachments through life like a jumble of old clothes from the back of the wardrobe, odd socks poking out of the top, faded T-shirts, the occasional flash of colour, a tangerine dress well-worn and well-loved. That was clear enough to everyone, a rainbow jumble of emotions – just Cora. She wanted to belong as much as I had, more, evidently.

I was in that jumble somewhere, tumbled up and entwined with Mike and her dad and mum and Stevie. To put me down, cast me off, she would have had to shed so much more. And even if she had wanted to, her arms would then have been empty and she would have been left holding nothing. So she had known all the time and carried it inside – and never spoken of it.

It must have been a raw, seeping wound every time she looked at me, feeding on each smile and touch, paradoxically growing larger and yet more brittle, threatening shard upon shard. How does it feel to be invisible to the person you adore in plain sight when your friend appears? How many moments do we live, waiting to be made real by a gaze, by a look of approval, of admiration, of love, as the eyes turn elsewhere and the body follows?

I thought I knew. And I thought I knew something else that perhaps Stevie did not.

Cora couldn't bring herself to hurt me, not then, all those years ago. So she had hurt what she could, who she could, years later, probably for nothing.

Suddenly it all made sense. Too much light and motion. The room reeled. What I, he, we, Stevie had done. How could I ever have thought that Mike would have had the guts to kill someone? To do anything, except allow things to happen around him?

It was about me. And about Cora. How had I been so blind?

'What have you done, babes? What have you done?' I said under my breath.

I imagined Cora going to Jenny's flat by the river that night. Jenny had invited us to her birthday while we were at Charlie's, so Cora knew where she would be; the exact flat wouldn't have been hard to find. She thought Mike would be there. But she hadn't found Mike. So she'd waited. Or had she seen them there, seen him go in or come out later?

She needed to be sure. Hadn't Stevie and Mike suggested she'd thought maybe something was going on with Mike in

Wrexham? Maybe there was a girl? Was that reality or just Cora's worst fear? What had she felt at the prospect of the move back to Cardiff, here, to me?

How had it happened that night after Charlie's when Cora's worst fears must have been whipped into a maelstrom of jealousy and bitterness, ten years fermented?

Did Cora follow Jenny to the garage when she left her flat to get fags? Confront her? Demand to know if Mike was inside or if she was screwing her husband? Either way, Mike was gone by then, collapsed at Stevie's, both too drunk to do anything but fall into sleep.

They met somewhere, anyway. Jenny and Cora. On the bridge, most likely, when Jenny went to get the cigarettes, like Harriet said. Just a few hundred yards from home. Upstream from where she was found. It would have been very late, long after the last taxi had disappeared into the night. No one had seen them.

What would Cora have said to her? Was that when the earring had been wrenched out? Harsh words turn to blows, grasping fists, Jenny's haughty stare, failing to see in Cora anything but a drunk and jealous wife? Cora would have screamed that she was a slut, a bitch, a whore, a no-good fucking cunt. Jenny was wearing Mike's leather jacket – what more proof did Cora need?

Or Cora might have been calm, as ice-cold and determined as the black river winding in the shadow of the stadium, alongside the watchful walls of the castle and the naked trees. Either way I was sure it wouldn't have taken much force, Jenny being so small and dainty and tottering, wine and heels and the wind against her. Cora couldn't have meant it until that last minute, could she? A shove, an explosion of rage, a few seconds struggle, a momentary thought or lack of it? A need to strike out. To actualise the words 'I hurt.'

Jenny would have laughed at first, either way. Maybe right up to the moment when she realised she was going to fall, down over the low railing into the glassy, waiting water. Who would hear her cry, the eddies filling her throat, stealing her scream, the cold clutching at her clothes, pulling her down? Cora could have called for help, phoned for help – but she didn't. She went home.

This may not have happened, of course. I could not know for sure. I could never ask her. And Jenny could not tell me, for she had no voice. I had forgotten the sound of it, heard only on that night, straining above the club music. Her mouth opens but she is now mute.

I remembered the state Cora had been in the following morning, remembered vaguely, deep in the small hours, hearing the front door open and close as I lay fogged on a Jack Daniel's sleep in the spare room. The sound of the car that was not a taxi. Cora had started to collect all the newspaper cuttings before I even told her about Jenny because, before she was missing, even, and before she was named, Cora knew who she was. And knew that she was dead.

When she had asked me, that day in the toy store, if I thought sins committed in a previous life could come back to haunt you in the next, perhaps she had not meant what I thought. At the time I thought she was asking if she must have been very wicked in a previous life to be haunted by such troubles as these. I believed it was her melodramatic way of trying to deal with the fact of Mike's faithlessness. I realised that, at the moment she spoke those words, she was already planning to kill herself. She just wanted to be free of what she'd done, but only if she knew she wouldn't be damned for it. And as ever, I had given her the answer.

'*Don't be daft Cora – that's nonsense,*' I had said, anxious to avoid a scene. Even though I didn't believe it. Even though I had thought, 'Yes Cora, we deserve everything we get.'

I'd made a last grand gesture too. I'd shown myself to be on her side. I'd said I'd go with her to the police. No matter what the consequences. I'd chosen her over Mike. For once. At last. That was enough. She could let go.

At that moment I knew all our lives, as we had come to know them, were over.

The Verdict

So Cora got what she wanted. Mike would be hers forever, because of what she had done. And he was happy enough with that. I'd seen it in his eyes that night at the hospital, the look that almost amounted to one of admiration.

And it worked out alright in the end for me too. I was sure Cora had told Mike the truth and now that he knew, and was manacled to her by it, she did not need to threaten anymore, she seemed to have forgotten that she ever had. She no longer feared me or wanted to make me afraid – Mike had made his choice. So she never again mentioned the police or the Curryman or the bribery, or wanting to go to the police, and I got my promotion in the first week of the New Year.

And what happened to the Curryman, AKA Mr Rhodri Lewis of no fixed abode? He never came back for a second payment.

At first I continued to edge uneasily out of the office, expecting to see his too- bright eyes and outstretched hands awaiting me. Each time I fumbled with my car keys in the dank and shadowy car park, twisting my head at each footfall, I anticipated his grubby grip upon my shoulder. But slowly I scanned the street less and less, the impression that I saw his face above the filthy raincoats of the town centre's restless rough sleepers becoming rarer, until I saw him not at all.

I found out why he had gone quiet at the inquests in March. That was how I heard his real name for the first time. I remembered it from his other court appearances, though I'd never made the link at the time.

It turned out that Rhodri Lewis, aged 51, had died just before Christmas. He was a former schoolteacher who'd taken to the streets following the death of his aged mother seven years ago. He'd drunk an entire bottle of vodka and downed a packet of sleeping pills. The night had been cold and wet with old snow. Despite the new anorak he was wearing, the drugs and drink soothed his body into a dark fitful sleep. He had lain down behind some bins at the end of Cora's street and drifted away.

He was found the following morning by a man walking his corgi, ice cold, his hands twisted in an unbreakable grip around the empty bottle.

To my surprise his sister turned up at the inquest. This was clearly the last in a long series of embarrassments her brother had inflicted upon her. She was a brittle and black-clad secretary in her 40s, with painfully high heels and neatly pinned auburn hair, the roots in need of a re-touch. The whole time she spoke she clutched a fake leather bag tightly across her body as if warding off the intrusions and indignities of public death. She strongly objected to any suggestion he had tried to kill himself despite the fact it was an obvious conclusion to draw. Why would he have bought a new jacket? Where would he have got the money? How could he have got hold of sleeping pills?

Clearly it had been a mistake, a misjudgement, a fatal combination of factors on a cold night.

She inherited all he had in the world. £100 in used notes

tucked in his trouser pocket. Their origin was a mystery. The coroner muttered his usual banalities and recorded an open verdict. It would not make much of a story. Page ten, a paragraph at the bottom, maybe.

The police never did find out what had happened to Jennifer Morgan. The coroner recorded an open verdict there also. They were not able to say if her death had been an accident, misadventure or *Foul Play*.

You see, it turned out that she had been at Charlie's the night she disappeared with a man from the office she had been seeing off and on.

Predictably, Martin Parker, 31, was married. (The mysterious, M, or Mr M, had never been fully identified but he seemed the best contender.) When they separated following a tiff in the club Parker had not reported her missing. How could he explain that? After her death he had not wanted to come forward for the same mundane, obvious reasons.

The note, signed 'M', had revealed two fingerprints, as had the dusting of her flat. One set was unknown, but Parker had once been arrested for possession of ecstasy and amphetamines and was on the police system. He and Jenny had argued in Charlie's not long after arriving. He was jealous about another man. She had told him to piss off. A waiter's memory was jogged by his photograph. He remembered the argument taking place by the cloakrooms, him grabbing her arm, Jenny pulling away, throwing a drink at him.

They'd kept that out of the news.

I remember him in court. He looked about 35 with floppy brown hair. I imagined how he could be attractive, if not good-looking, were he not tense and tie-strangled in the dock. The attendant at the petrol station near the stadium remembered him that night, seemingly a little drunk, getting fuel and cigarettes.

Parker insisted he and Jenny had only been going out for a few months and that they'd had sex just three times. She was obsessed with another guy. After the altercation he'd gone over to her flat later that evening to make it up, make her promise not to tell his wife and colleagues as she'd threatened.

But there was no light on. No one had answered. He'd gone straight home, he said. They dropped the case in the end. There was no real evidence. It was all circumstantial. As it happened, the CCTV camera that points at the bridge near Jenny's flat was broken that night, and not for the first time. It was always going off-line.

Of course, Parker lost his wife, his kids and his job before it was all tied up. Before that night he had been a quiet manager, mildly approaching a rather early middle age. Later he became a drink-driving, adulterous murderer in all but conviction, without even realising it. And who's to say he wasn't?

I didn't write a story on it. I was working for TV by that time. You've probably seen me actually, not all that often but fairly regularly, reporting from here and there now and then. I'm the pretty, trendy one with the blonde hair in her late twenties.

Afterlife

I sit in our neat and minimalist living room, wine in hand, TV on. David potters around reassuringly in the background, neither cooking nor cleaning but rearranging, I think. There are dirty dishes piled neatly at the sink, their life there short and fitful, regular stays of a few hours a time. There is a mountain bike under the stairs. Photographs of us in sun and sand adorn the walls. St Mark's Square, the Pontevecchio, the Coliseum, Pompeii, Capri. We share a love of travel.

The sofa is impossibly comfortable, the wooden floor impossibly slippery, lethal really, lying in wait for one lapse of concentration, one foot out of place. Our neighbours are quiet and we are quiet in return. Model, ideal, unassuming.

David and I discuss politics, cinema, politics, music, world affairs, politics, holidays and the state of the nation. We know each other as well as can be expected, perhaps as well as we should.

He knows nothing about the girl that danced in silver bracelets, long and languid on the dancefloor, or of her other faces, which is just as well. She is writing a strange, dark, novel in which the names have been changed, in the quiet of her thoughts between essential fat fighting trips to the gym, to the supermarket – between the newsroom and the pubs and friends' homes. There are oceans of thoughts, adrift inside her, trying to anchor themselves to a page where they may finally make sense.

David works long shifts. A policeman needs to, of course. There's no such thing as nine-to-five crime, he says wryly, when the phone rings in the middle of the night and pulls him woolly-headed from our bed.

He asked me out about three weeks after Cora's attempted suicide, three weeks after he drove me home in my own car from her house after the ambulance had left with Cora and Mike in it. But it was much longer before he admitted that he had conveniently turned up on the door because he had followed me there.

He was off shift, technically. He just hadn't had the guts to ask me out at the court house, you see. All that, 'I shouldn't really be telling you this,' had been his only way of engaging me in conversation. Smalltalk, flirting, courtship.

He was demoralised that he'd made so little headway with Jenny's death. She was his first dead body. The first proper crime he'd worked on. They thought all along that there was something suspicious about her ending up in the river. He'd really wanted to shine, to get that promotion, to solve it with a flash of insight, revealing a kernel of clues that would cause the case to break open. But it had drawn a blank, a large watery void. The cause of death remained unconfirmed.

When David spotted me in the street as he was getting off his shift he had taken a chance, wanting to ask me for coffee. What else did he have to lose? He trailed me in his own car, intending to offer me dinner. But he lost his nerve near the house. I shudder when I think how it might have turned out if I had carried out my plan. It would have been difficult to talk my way out of that one with a police officer placing me at the scene at the time of Cora's supposed overdose!

Or if he had been a better policeman, he might have noticed a few things. With the earring and the clippings sitting a few feet away from the chair in which he comforted me, a man's worn leather jacket sat in the evidence room at the station ready to be disposed of. He shook hands with the man who owned it as the ambulance men taped up his wife's wrists. In the corner of the photo showing the tangerine dress, that man is even wearing it.

Now, as I stare around the always half-neat room, I wish I could tell him the truth of how we met. The man to whom I regularly say 'I love you'. But how can I? Because if he doesn't know about the beers and the cheap wine, the novels and poetry and cheap kisses, how could he know the rest? How could he live with a woman who was prepared to kill but too lazy to tell the truth? Too frightened to be alone, too desperate to say no. He is a policeman, after all, and I am very lucky he is not a very good one.

Did I get away with it then? Yes, I did. Everything that I did and failed to do.

Sometimes when David works the early shift he ends up in bed by four in the afternoon, exhausted by the pool of human scum he wades through while awake. So, after the hug and kiss and sleepy smile, I sit downstairs, aimlessly flicking through the channels, as the shadow-people within send their images across the walls of the sitting room, so I am not alone.

In winter it is already dark by the time I push a well-intentioned plate of vegetables away from me and reach for my third or fourth glass of wine. I will stay awake for as long as possible to avoid what I know is waiting in the bedroom, snoring slightly on its stomach. My disappointment, and my memories of a half-reluctant kiss in darkness.

We laundered our own sheets and pillow cases a long time ago. I make a point of washing any cups and glasses, marrying any lone shoes and stacking magazines and mail. Order is control and neatness is the illusion of both. Eventually, after I have flicked the locks and light switches, I know where I must go.

Sometimes I stand in the doorframe for minutes on end and watch his naked form clutched in the covers, a leg here, an arm there, escaping. In the light from the street I see a young, handsome man, face down in sleep. A human form I can call my own. Or as close to it as is possible.

Something I cannot describe reaches up and grabs me by the throat and I think I will choke on the white hot ball that tries to stop me breathing. Mercifully, he looks nothing like Mike. Eventually I will squeeze myself into my side of the king size, trying to avoid any limbs, perched on the edge of the world of oblivion, listening to the captive breathing of my willing bed mate. If he senses me he will slide a warm arm over my waist, sometimes nuzzling at my neck, he will mutter half-words from far away.

And only then, as I fight back the tears, am I glad of him.

But there are other times, like this Saturday when we are going to Cora's and Mike's for a barbecue, that things are good. They are in a new house now. Bigger. It is Mike's 30th birthday. Nothing fancy though, just a few glasses of a nice red or white and the usual burnt offerings, and Stevie.

Stevie will bring his new girlfriend, the one from the record shop. He's only seen her half a dozen times and we have met her once. But she seems nice, faintly Chinese looking, beautiful eyes, seven years younger than him. She's into drum and bass apparently.

We will play music from the old days, which she won't like much, and later in the evening we will probably dance on the carefully cut square of grass that is almost a lawn. And we won't try very hard not to annoy the neighbours.

No one will even think of, let alone mention, the scars on Cora's wrists, as she turns the burgers and the sausages just once more, as the wine flows in a never-ending stream from fridge to glass. She will make a big deal of virtuously abstaining because of the baby, the new life that will erase the one lost and complain about her feet and the fact she has to wear a flowery smock, without really minding a bit. Oddly, the smock suits her better than anything she ever used to wear.

She will cook. Mike may even sing, if coaxed ever-so-slightly and David will join in. He likes Mike – they get on. And we will all smile and laugh a lot. And remember. Stevie will take photos that will never be put into albums. If there is good weather it will be very pleasant.

Perhaps you can't choose your friends after all.

Sometimes I think that if I could, I would fly above this garden, rising high over the squat roofs of the city, roads rolling away to the rising hills. I would see hundreds of neat and not so neat gardens, dozens of barbecues just like this one. Who knows what stories hide there and what I might see?

And what if I was to try to tell David my story? How would I begin? Once, not so long ago, and nearer than you think, there were four friends – two girls and two boys who loved each other

280

very much – at least as well as they knew how. Some of them loved more than the others, more than anything, though not all of them realised it then. And some loved less. One was adored and two could only hope for it.

You see, that's where I must finally fall silent. That's why it would never work. Because, even after all this time, I'm still not sure which of us would be which.

Better to end it this way.

COMING SOON

Holiday Money

~

Beverley Jones

After ten years of being together, Jen is getting ready
to marry her partner Dan, a recently appointed Police
Inspector. Then a telephone call from a mysterious
woman changes everything.

Could the call be proof of an affair and the excuse
Jen needs to leave the stifling normality of her life
in Wales? Or will the video of an uncharacteristic
one night stand and the threat of a starring role on
the Surf Sluts' website leave her with no choice?

ISBN 978-1-908122-14-8

£7.99